BURNED UP

RYAN CHAISE BOOK 1

STUART G YATES

To Mike, who would have enjoyed this story,
and Nan who would have liked it even more.
And to Janice, of course, for making life better.

Lighting the embers…

You shouldn't pick up strangers on the road. Ever seen the film The Hitcher, the one staring Rutger Hauer? Hitchhiker, a real psychopath, deals out death like a gambler does cards. Dismissive. Advice given freely – don't risk picking up strangers. It's not worth it.

This is what happens when such advice is ignored…

ONE

The plan hadn't been fully worked out in his head and so, almost from the very start, it all went wrong. He'd met the girl in a bar, parking his Suzuki Samurai and strolling in, deciding to buy a beer and some tapas before moving on. Ten minutes later, she came in and he couldn't take his eyes off her. She dripped sex. She wore a tightfitting blue top that accentuated the curve of her breasts and the thin white skirt, split almost to the top of the thigh to reveal burnished limbs, left nothing to the imagination. He felt sure she wasn't wearing panties. Eventually, she noticed his gaze and liked what she saw. He knew that by the way she smiled, turned her head away and then looked again. When he returned her gaze, she ran her tongue along her bottom lip. That made him feel good.

She was with some friends and they laughed a lot. He liked that in a girl, hating how some of them were so serious, giving you the hard stare, trying to make you feel like you were not fit to walk the planet. But this one was different. Her name was Sarah. That's what one of her friends called her when she moved over to the bar to order a round of drinks. He didn't wait a moment before he sidled over to her.

"Sarah?"

Her eyes flashed. "How did you ...?" She caught his look and she smiled again.

They made love up in the hills surrounding the little village. It was a cool night and the mosquitoes didn't bite that much. She was gloriously slim, her bronzed body sliding through his fingers like cream. He thought that perhaps he could spend more time with her, get to know her properly. When they lay on the ground, spent, her breasts rising and falling with each breath, he studied her lines and realized that here was a girl who could give him everything he had ever wanted.

If only they had time.

They walked around for a while, and he held her to him, kissing her. Looking into his eyes, she moaned, "God, I'm so glad we met!" He liked that, liked the way she yielded to him.

From where they stood, the tiny village twinkled in the hollow of the surrounding hills, a perfect picture from a tourist guide. Simple rustic charm. She sighed, studied his outline in the dark and asked, "Why aren't you married?"

"Who said I'm not?"

She traced her fingers across his left hand, settling around the knuckle. "I thought that most men wore rings nowadays."

"Do they? I wouldn't know – not being married."

She laughed, more with relief it sounded to him, and they kissed again. The fire rekindled, they went back to where they had parked up their respective vehicles and they made love for a second time in the back seat of her Audi.

"Come home with me," she said, stroking his face.

"So, you're not married either?"

"He's away, in England. Business. He'll be gone for a few more days."

"And he's left you all alone, to fall for temptation? That was foolish."

"He trusts me."

"That makes him a real fool."

She pushed him away, not as angry as she tried to make out, but hurt, nonetheless. "No, he's not a fool. He's very successful, even now when things aren't so good. But ..." She shrugged, readjusted her clothing, "He doesn't satisfy me if you know what I mean."

He did and grinned. "I see. So that was what this was all about – you being satisfied?"

"Partly. Why, does that bother you?"

He thought about that for a moment, the idea of being used. A thrill ran through his loins. Much to his surprise, the idea excited him. "I'm curious as to what he would say when he finds out."

Without a moment's hesitation she said, "Oh, he knows. And he's perfectly okay with it. In fact, you could say he encourages me."

"What, to go out with other men?"

"To screw other men. It's the one thing he can't give me – so we made a deal. I wouldn't leave him, and he'd turn a blind eye. We may be married, but we have different surnames. Simple." She leaned forward and kissed him. "Don't say you didn't enjoy it, don't say it doesn't turn you on ... just a little?"

He tried to deny it, but how could he? Every word she had said was true. So, he laughed instead.

"You'll stay the night?"

He had to admit, the thought of not only sharing her bed but

3

also waking up afresh in a warm bed was an enticing one. The plan had been to drive through the night, make it to Benidorm by the morning. But what difference would a few hours make, he decided, and nobody would think of looking for him here. Grinning, he pulled her to him, kissed her and said, "That would be great."

They set off, up into the mountains, him following her in the little Suzuki, making easy progress up the winding path that led to her villa.

But it was dark. Pitch. He didn't see the turn and the Suzuki fell into a wide, gaping dip. Usually, it would be able to handle something like this, but the dip was wide and deep, and it hit the bottom hard, jolting him out of his seat. He cut the engine, fearful of it bursting into flame. However, the horrible, grinding crunch underneath caused him most concern.

The torchlight cut through the darkness. She came back for him, hands on hips. "Oh dear," she said.

He was bent down, groping around in the dark, trying to judge the extent of the damage. "By the sound of it, I think the axle might be broke."

"Don't worry – we'll call someone out in the morning. Try not to worry about it until then." Putting it to the back of his mind, he didn't worry at all.

Neither did he get much sleep.

It was already blisteringly hot as he scrambled under the ditched Suzuki the following morning to get a better look. It was as he'd feared. The axle was snapped. The hole in which the Suzuki rested was big and deep, cut out of the side of the road and strewn with jagged rocks. He was lucky he hadn't been seriously hurt. However, that wasn't his major concern – time was. It would be days, if not weeks before the car would be fixed, time he simply didn't have. He'd left Sarah sleeping and crept out of the villa before the sun had fully risen over the mountain tops, hoping against hope that his original prognosis was wrong. Now, as the enormity of the situation hit him, he felt the first stirrings of panic low in his stomach.

There was no choice. He'd have to take Sarah's car. Cursing, he went back up the hill, his shirt already sticking to his back as the heat made itself felt. He slipped back inside the sprawling villa and went straight to where she had dropped her bag and coat. He rifled through various pockets and found the keys. He picked up his own bags from the door and strode outside. As he crossed the drive, he opened the car doors with the key-remote. He slung his bags into the boot and went round to the driver's door, keeping the shoulder bag with him as always.

"What the hell are you doing?"

Her voice sounded more like a scream and he looked up to see her hanging over the balcony, face contorted into a sort of gargoyle mask. She went back into the bedroom, appearing a few moments later at the front door. She flew out across the forecourt like a tigress, mouth open, teeth bared. He leaned against the car and sighed. Great, just what he needed.

She was on him. "You bastard," she rasped, pulling him around to face her, "are you trying to steal my car?"

Her hands gripped the front of his shirt and she shook him, face close now.

"Give me my keys!"

He struck out wildly and hit her backhanded. The blow caught her under the left eye, and she fell, hip cracking against the hard ground. She screamed again, but quieter this time. A scream of pain.

"Sorry," he said, without emotion, knowing what he had to do. She was trying to drag herself away across the ground, blubbering a little, probably realizing what a mess she'd got herself involved in. He reached over, lifted her by the throat with his left hand and hit her again. At the last moment, she managed to twist her face away and he did it all wrong, caught his knuckle on her jaw. He cried out, dropping her like a stone, flapping his hand around like it was a flag caught in the wind. Sudden, surprisingly intense pain brought tears to his eyes and he cursed. He wanted to hit her again, but she was gone, out like a light, a large bruise already developing along her face. The eye too had exploded as it hit the hard gravel. No point in striking her again so he left her and clambered in behind the wheel. Ignoring the pain, he flexed his hand a few times and, to his relief, discovered nothing was broken. However, the knuckles were already swelling. Hurt like buggery too. He took a moment to regulate his breathing, calmed himself and calculated he probably had about thirty minutes to get away before she recovered and phoned the police. Another thirty minutes before the Guardia even bothered to call round to the villa. By that time, he would have made it to the next village, abandoned the Audi and hitched a lift. Not perfect, but possibly safer. No one would be able to trace him. He put the car into gear and moved away.

In the rear-view mirror, he could see her climbing to her feet, a trembling hand wiping the blood from her face. She was tough. He admired that. He noted how her long, slim legs shimmered in the morning sun and a little thrill ran through him. She was gorgeous, and he had made love to her until she was spent. Maybe, in a different life …

He raised his hand in farewell and took the Audi out of the driveway, along the path and past his Suzuki. He'd miss that car. He'd miss Sarah. But hey, they'll be many more like her, and cars a lot better than the jeep. His hand ached but he allowed himself a smile of self-satisfaction. Perhaps things were going to be all right after all.

All he needed was some luck.

TWO

As the morning progressed, the heat became intense enough to fry eggs on the pavement. No joke. Ryan Chaise had seen that done once, in Eilat. This was Spain, the Costa Del Sol. Inland, hotter than hell on party night with the furnaces newly stoked with the souls of the sinners. Thank God for the air-con, which he turned to full blast.

The office had made the appointment at this ridiculous time, but what could he do? Opportunities were few and far between nowadays, and any pickings were better than nothing at all. Chaise gratefully received the scraps thrown from the king's table, but if that was all there was, so be it. He had no intention of starving.

He saw them straight away. A couple, on the wrong side of sixty, lily-white legs exposed, both sporting wide-brimmed straw hats, outrageous multi-coloured shirts, and beige shorts with turn-ups. Sensible, but not the most attractive of accessories for the discerning Brit-abroad. Chaise chuckled to himself and pulled his car alongside the kerb, rolled down the window and called out to them, "Mr and Mrs Smithson?"

The man doffed his hat and leaned into the car. Up close, his meaty face oozed with sweat. "Is it always this hot?"

Chaise smiled knowingly. "Only on the cooler days. Get in, we haven't got far to go."

Riogordo screamed with the heat, the sunshine reflected off the white-faced walls of the houses clustered close together in the side streets.

"This is quaint," said Mrs Smithson as they all stood in the hallway of the house they had arranged to view.

Chaise smiled but remained silent. He could have told them about the lack of air-con, the roof that needed replacing, the damp in the garage and the bathroom. He said nothing. Sales were few and he didn't want to lose this one.

The house, nevertheless, was good value for what it was. Nothing special, but it stood next to a beautifully restored townhouse, a testament of what could be achieved with a little imagination and a lot of money. Chaise did his best to detail all the things the Smithsons could do to improve this, their own house if they chose to buy it. Which would be a bargain purchase, especially now when things weren't moving.

"It's not exactly ..." The wife's voice trailed away and when she stepped into the kitchen, she gave a little cry of despair and returned almost instantly, hand over mouth. "There's something dead in there!"

Chaise closed his eyes. Damn the office for not sending somcone out to check the property over first. He dipped into the kitchen, saw the dead cat, and came out again.

"Obviously, we'd clear it all for you before you moved in."

"It would need quite a lot of work to make it habitable," said Mr Smithson.

Now, he's the more realistic one. Got his feet on the ground. He knows he has to spend a little to make the dream into reality. But she, she would be a much tougher nut to crack.

"New kitchen," said Chaise, "and a bathroom upgrade. Maybe do the patio. Roof is good. So, maybe several thousand? Not a lot to be honest."

"No, not a lot." Smithson looked at his wife, who still appeared shocked by the discovery of the cat. "It's the best we've seen."

She nodded but wasn't speaking.

"How many bedrooms?"

"Three. It's the garage which is the best thing – you could convert it into a studio flat. Rental opportunities, or just leave it. Storage is at a premium here. People would kill for a garage."

Smithson nodded, then grinned. "I hear they like killing."

"Oh yes," Chaise said with meaning. "They certainly do."

They went onto the roof terrace. The view towards the surrounding mountains never failed to impress. The river, from where the village got its name, had dried up and probably wouldn't experience water again until the spring rains took hold. December was wet, but nothing like March. Well, that was the theory. Sometimes it didn't quite work like that. He remembered last year when the rain began in December and didn't stop until the end of March. The worst rains in living memory. Roofs collapsed, rivers burst their banks, cars floated away. And now, in July, the same rivers were dry. Global warming. Crazy.

"Those houses over there, they don't seem finished."

Frowning, Chaise stepped up next to Smithson and took in the buildings opposite. A lot of them had upper storeys which had not been completed. "Yeah, it's got something to do with tax, I think. You only pay tax on a finished property. Something like that."

"So, they're illegal?"

"No, not exactly. Just another loophole. Spain has got lots of them. And then there's the corruption. It's a way of life here, always has been. But they're cracking down on that, at last. Lots of mayors in prison."

"Mayors?" Mrs Smithson held onto her husband's arm. "Good God. I never knew."

Chaise shrugged. "It rarely gets into the Tui brochure. Doesn't serve the tourist trade well."

"But it's not dangerous is it?"

Chaise laughed. "Dangerous? Spain?" He shook his head. "Nah, Spain is fine. One of the safest places in Europe."

"Wasn't a gangster shot and killed here, not so very long ago?"

"That was further down the coast. Drugs, as usual. But no, the gangsters are on their way out. New agreements between governments, greater openness, more exchange of information. It'll all be like Disneyland down there soon. Fit only for families and kids."

That was why Chaise had come here, for his 'family' and left the old life behind. The old life that still came to keep him company at night, the memories he'd tried so hard to forget. He thought to start again might help and for a while, it had worked. He decided to go far, far away, South America or New Zealand. A place no one could find him. But his girlfriend was half-Spanish and already had offers of a job there. It seemed the obvious thing to do, the move, so they made the plunge. That was five years ago, and the years had slipped by. They settled into a sort of domestic bliss. Chaise loved Angelina. Whatever happened, they got through it together. Fortunately, nothing had happened, so everyone was happy.

Unfortunately, as Chaise knew only too well from experience, happiness didn't last for long.

THREE

After dropping the Smithsons at the office and introducing them to Leanne, who would take them through the paperwork, Chaise headed back to his home in the mountains. He hated the city and spent as little time there as possible. Certainly, at this time of year, the heat trapped amongst the oppressive, stuffy streets made the place simply unbearable to work in.

The motorway was quiet, and he made good time; soon he was taking the back road. As he passed through the various villages and took in the rolling hills, he once again gave a little sigh of contentment, as he always did when the stark loveliness of the place struck him. The Spain that few people rarely saw. Not just the beaches and the sea, Spain had so much more to offer. This landscape for one, as if sketched out of the pages of a Larry McMurtry novel; the high sierras ached with unspoiled, gut-wrenching beauty.

He took the car along the winding, twisting track leading to his villa set in the hills surrounding Vélez Málaga. As he slowed down for the speed-ramps just outside Benamargosa, he saw the man at the roadside, bags at his feet, shirt open to the midriff, drenched in sweat. No hat. Idiot! When he stuck out his thumb, Chaise at first ignored him, but soon the guilt played around the nape of his neck and he pulled over.

"Oh, man," the stranger gushed, enthusiastically pulling at the rear door handle. "Thank you so much."

"Where you headed?"

"Nerja."

"I'm not going that far."

"Okay … well, anywhere close. Vélez would be good. I could hitch another ride from there easy enough."

Vélez Málaga wasn't so far, but it would mean a detour. Tired, in need of a plunge in the pool followed by a nap, Chaise didn't fancy a thirty-minute detour, but the guy looked strung out, dehydrated, so he sighed and said, "All right, climb in, I'll drop you at Trebiche."

Grinning his thanks, the stranger threw his bag into the back and got into the passenger seat. Chaise noted how he clung onto a little, intricately patterned canvas shoulder bag, pressing it to his chest as if he were fearful of it being snatched away.

"I'm Ricky Treach," he said, thrusting out his hand.

Chaise looked at the proffered hand, wet with sweat, and kept his hands on the wheel. "Ryan Chaise. Treach? Wasn't he a pirate?"

"That's Teach, better known as Blackbeard. Treach is the name of a rap artist from the States."

"Oh."

Chaise mulled over that one as he negotiated the broken, rutted road. The guy appeared educated, knew a little history. How many people knew that Blackbeard's real name was Edward Teach? Perhaps a university student on a walking tour of La Axarquía, but whoever he was by the look of him he had recently fallen on hard times. From the corner of his eyes, he watched him unwrap his improvised bandage and massage the swollen knuckles. Caused by a punch? Chaise wondered who the victim was. Old stirrings jingled around in his brain, his radar for trouble, which had kept him alive for so long out in the Middle East. Feelings never needed here, he believed had gone. The quiet life. And now, this guy...Something wasn't right.

Sensing Chaise's questioning frown, Treach stopped massaging his hand and gripped the bag again. "Bashed it on the wall. Wasn't looking where I was going." He gave a short, awkward-sounding laugh.

Chaise shrugged, pushed aside his unease, and concentrated on the road. "Where are you heading after Vélez? Nerja, didn't you say?"

"Further down the coast, but not too far. My car broke down, you see. I have to get to a friend's house, then I'll come back and pick it up."

Broke down? Why didn't he just call the *grua*? That's what the system was for and it worked well. Everyone who took out car insurance received the services of a roadside pick-up if they ever broke down. So, leaving a car by the side of the road, that just wasn't supposed to happen.

"It's so hot," said Treach, cutting through Chaise's thoughts. "I honestly believed I was going to die out there."

"This is the worst time of day. You should have worn a hat. Or found some shade."

"I would have missed this lift if I had! And," he shook his head, the long hair flopping across his brow, "I think this will protect me."

"Yeah." Unconsciously, Chaise ran a hand over his short-cropped hair. The sign of the rapidly balding man, shorn hair. Better than a Bobby Charlton, that was for sure.

Well, that was his opinion, and he was sticking with it.

Around the next bend came the first sight of the village nestling beside the dried riverbed, which gave the village its name.

"What's this place called?"

"Benamargosa."

"You live here?"

"Close."

"Close enough to walk?"

Chaise frowned. Weird question. He snapped his head to the right. He saw it and cursed himself for not following his initial instincts. Stupid. Losing the edge. One of the penalties of choosing suburban life. That look in Treach's eyes, the look Chaise knew so well. He readied himself, his voice taking on a hard edge. "Maybe. What do you have in mind?"

There was a long pause. Chaise kept turning his head back to the road, all the while ready for what he knew was going to happen.

He thought it might be a fist, perhaps even a knife. But the Sig-Sauer P220 was something of a surprise. Best automatic pistol in the world, so the experts say. And Chaise was something of an expert himself. Right now, it was sitting in Ricky Treach's hand, pulled out of that beautiful embroidered shoulder bag, pointed straight at him.

"I'm going to have to ask you to stop the car and get out."

"Would you mind telling me why I would do that?"

"Well," Treach smiled, "there are several reasons. The most pressing is that I left something in the first car that picked me up. I didn't notice until he'd driven off. I have to get it back. I'll use this car to drive back and find him."

"I see. Must have something valuable inside it."

"You could say that."

"Any other reasons."

"Yeah. I'll kill you if you don't."

Chaise nodded. Most people would have run off the road in fear by now, hands unable to control the wheel. Fear was like that, played havoc with the nervous system. Chaise never suffered from such a reaction. Even in the very dark days, when he was painting the palace in Baghdad, he never showed any emotion at all, even when Saddam breezed in, grinning like the fat ape he was. Reggie Lawrence used to marvel about that, Chaise's unflappable exterior. "How come you never sweat, lad?" Reggie Lawrence, an out of work scouser, painting Saddam Hussein's palace with half a dozen others, including Ryan Chaise, Special Boat Service. Intel Officer. Killer. If Reggie only knew.

"Hey! I'm telling you to stop the fucking car, tough guy, or I'll blow your fucking head off."

"That's clean off, Ricky."

Treach gaped. "*What?*"

"The line Eastwood says in Dirty Harry. You fancy yourself as a bit of a Clint, do you not? 'I'll blow your head clean off'."

"Are you some sort of nutcase or something?"

"Yeah. Something like that."

Without any warning, Chaise rammed on the brakes, pulling down hard on the steering wheel at the same time. The car went into a wild skid, dust and debris flung up in a billowing cloud. Treach, who like most people in those parts, had not bothered to put on his seat belt, hit the dash with a jarring smack, full in the chest. He cried out, the gun almost falling from his fingers, but not quite.

As the car came to a grinding halt, tyres sluicing through the impacted ground, Chaise seized Treach's gun arm and twisted it viciously. Before Treach could react, Chaise rammed his elbow back into the man's face. Chaise heard the satisfying snap of shattered bone, the squelch of the blood as it gushed, and Treach's scream. His fingers, however, held on.

It was cramped in the front of the car, not enough space for Chaise to get a firm hold. He almost had it, but Treach was stronger than he looked. Probably brought on by desperation. They struggled and Treach somehow managed to get his free arm around to claw at Chaise's face. Another elbow strike put paid to that. Chaise wrenched the arm a little more, bending the wrist down and back. A sound like a piece of cardboard being ripped apart. Treach screamed again.

Then the gun went off.

The noise from the blast in that confined space was enormous, causing Chaise's ears to ring painfully. A terrible silence followed and Treach went limp.

"Shit."

The cordite smoke cleared, but Chaise already knew exactly what had happened. He didn't need to look too closely at the hole in the man's chest, or the wide-open eyes to realise poor Ricky Treach was dead.

FOUR

Alex Piers's wife was out. Nothing odd in that, she always was. Most mornings, virtually every night. Amy, their eight-year-old daughter, had gone to summer school. The house echoed to the sound of his shoes as he crossed the wide entrance hall and went straight into the kitchen. An empty, lonely house. He poured himself some ice-cold water from a bottle in the fridge, leaned back on the worktop and looked out through the large patio windows to the swimming pool.

He stared at the pool, his mind an empty shell. For too long he'd thought about where it had all gone wrong, how he could turn it all around, make her love him again. But he knew this would never happen. It was burned too deep. The deceit. The lies. Too much had been said to ever make it all right again.

Two weeks ago, as Amy started summer school, his wife came out with the news.

"We're going back."

Alex felt as if he'd been hit by a bus. All the strength left his legs. He collapsed into a chair. Numb, he listened to her. "It's not working, you know it's not. And it's not good for Amy, listening to us rowing all the time." We hardly ever row, you bitch – you're never here! He heard the words in his head but from his mouth only silence. "So, it will be best for everyone if we go back at the end of summer. I'll scc my solicitor, get all the paperwork done. All you'll need to do is sign."

Mind swirling, he managed to ask the question he already knew the answer to: "With him?"

"What?" Her voice, always so cutting, so sharp. Treating him like an imbecile. Perhaps he was.

He drew in a deep, quivering breath. "Are you moving back with him?"

"Yes. But that's not the reason."

Even though he knew this would be the answer, to hear it from her lips cut deep. Leaning forward, he put his face in his hands. "I can't allow that, Diane. You can't just walk out of my life with Amy – to live with him." He'd recovered a little now. Panic, mixed with anger, it all came to the fore. Uncontrolled, ill-thought, ill-judged.

"You can't allow it? What the hell are you going to do, Alex? Lock us away in the cellar?"

His hands dropped. "You fucking bitch! What gives you the right—"

"Stop right there – you have no place to talk to me about rights, you pompous old fart! You gave up any rights when you went off with her!"

She always used that one, the counterpunch to any accusation. She'd been with other men, he'd doubted he'd ever know how many, but there was one, a few years ago now, that she fell for. She kicked Alex out, took this new guy into her bed So, Alex strayed. Nothing looked for, nothing planned. He got talking to her in a bar and that was that. Being Alex, he had to tell Diane and she flipped her lid. How is that fair, even explainable? When he begged her to take him back, Diane relented, with one proviso – that he let her continue seeing the other man.

He'd lost some good friends when they found out about his decision.

It had worked at first, until the guy's wife somehow got their number, rang Diane in the middle of the night, threatened her with solicitors and a lot more besides. Diane backed off, stopped seeing the guy, but for weeks she stomped around the house like a petulant teenager. Alex dare not ask her anything. Eventually, she came round and found another lover. She seemed happy; the rows stopped. But family life? That never existed. They didn't do anything together and little Amy would sit on the couch, watching Tiny Pop and she'd say, "Come and watch this with me, Mummy and Daddy." Alex would smile but inside his heart broke, and he wished more than anything that he could turn the clock back, undo all the hurt, the blame. Anything so that Amy's life could be as perfect as possible.

Then, completely out of the blue, the other guy returned. He'd left his wife and wanted to make a go of it with Diane.

She jumped at the chance. Hell, she loved him. Alex didn't figure in anything anymore. All he was good for was providing.

Now, he was going to be alone. Diane was returning to the UK and Amy would be going with her. Alex would have to get used to looking out of this window, gazing at the swimming pool, listening to the silence. No more outbursts of giggling from his Amy, her little legs driving herself along like a piston, throwing herself at him, bowling him over, "My daddy!" This was the beginning of the rest of his life.

He could feel his eyes growing moist. He had to harden his heart, stiffen his resolve, follow all the shitty advice that the wise and all-knowing put out about break-ups, and how he could still see her, and that she will always be 'his Amy'. What the hell did they know? Had they ever once, in their oh-so-perfect lives experienced real pain? The thought made him angry, which was a whole lot more desirable than feeling depressed.

"Wonderful," he said out loud, drained his glass and pulled in a huge breath, trying to make himself forget before the tears came. He stomped upstairs to get changed. His shirt was stuck to his back and he couldn't wait to get into his swimming shorts and take a dip. The bedroom was perfect as always. Everything neatly folded, the duvet turned down, the pillows well plumped. Out of habit, he took a look inside Amy's room. It reflected her age, the posters of her favourite boy band on the walls, mixed in with a couple of Miley Cyrus. Pride of place was a photo of her with her dad, big grins, flanking Mickey Mouse. Disneyland Paris, taken last year. He always stopped and stared at it, especially at times like this. Memories. Good memories. For Amy too, he hoped. He went up and kissed her smiling face. The first tear came then, despite his best efforts.

He padded into the bathroom, splashed his face, and looked at his reflection. He could see the lines, cut deep into the teak coloured skin. He used to say they were laughter lines and he remembered how, when he was spotty teenager, he'd spend hours screwing up his eyes to make himself look tough and hard. Then, later, they became those 'laughter lines'. He doubted if anybody was fooled. Wrinkles. That's what they were. He was getting older and as he peered closer, he could see where the white lines ran across his temples, the area where his sunglasses had been. The lines made him look slightly ridiculous. Memory jolted, he patted his trouser pockets and cursed himself for leaving the glasses in the car. If he was going to spend a pleasant hour or two by the pool, he'd need to go and get them, otherwise, the glare from the water would be too bright. He pulled off his trousers, replacing them with swimming shorts, and went outside to the car barefooted.

The patio tiles were red hot and burned the soles of his feet. He hopped and skipped over to the car and pulled open the passenger door, leaned in to reach for the sunglasses tossed carelessly on the dash.

He stopped. Something caught his eye, jammed under the passenger seat. He caught the edge of it sticking out. A parcel, wrapped in brown paper and masses of black tape. He pulled it out. It was heavy, like a bag of sugar, but flatter and more giving, as if what was inside was sand or powder.

The penny dropped then. Not just a penny, more like the proverbial Monty Python ton weight. Straight through his skull.

Drugs.

For some reason he couldn't fathom, he quickly looked around. There was no one there, and no surveillance cameras were recording his actions. This was his driveway, his house, but hey, who knows, perhaps the drugs squad were already nearby, camped out, ready to spring the big bust. Stupid.

Nonetheless, he tucked the package down his shorts and ran back inside. In the hallway, he fell against the cool wall for a moment to gather his senses. Before he realised he'd forgotten his sunglasses. "Damn!"

He considered fetching them but thinking about it, they didn't matter anymore. Any idea of a relaxing swim in the pool had suddenly lost all of its attraction.

FIVE

The policeman didn't smile. He sat behind his desk in the air-conditioned office, leaning forward slightly, running through the report that the Guardia Civil had made after they'd arrived at the scene. Fairly soon, others arrived. Heavy-duty. National Police. Big guys, mean-looking. Even meaner than the Guardia.

After the killing, Chaise clambered out of the car and sat on the side of the road, punching out the number on his mobile. His Spanish was good and there was no misunderstanding. Within five minutes they arrived. In the pause, Chaise made another call to Angelina. Without any preamble, he put it plain and simple, "Hi. I've got a problem."

"Oh God, don't tell me it's the car."

"No. Worse. Much worse." He tried to keep his voice flat, void of emotion. It was becoming harder. The shock was kicking in now, and his hand shook. "I picked up a guy. He's dead."

A silence, whilst the words bit home. "Dead? What do you mean, like a heart attack or something?"

"No. I mean I killed him. Shot him. And he's dead. Stone cold."

"Oh my God."

That little tiny voice, cloaked in total terror, would stay with him for a long time.

The office door opened, jerking Chaise out of his reverie. A ferret of a man came in, eyes darting nervously, saw Chaise, grinned, and sat down. He thrust out a small, sticky hand. "Leonard Phelps. Consular official. Sorry, they asked me to come in. You are ..." He studied a page in a small, black notebook, "Mr Chaise?" Chaise nodded. "Good." He opened his attaché case and, as if noticing the waiting police officer behind the desk for the first time, acknowledged him with a curt, "Buenos Dias, Señor Domingo." Domingo grunted but didn't look up from his papers. Phelps sighed and looked at Chaise. "Not good, this." He pulled out a slip of paper and read through it. "They e-mailed me the details. Thought I'd drop everything, seeing as it's slightly – you know – difficult."

"I killed a man, Mr Phelps."

"Yes. Precisely." Phelps forced a smile again, but it looked more like he was in pain. "I'm here to give you advice, support, translate any technical jargon you may not understand, but I'm not here to represent you legally. You understand that?" Chaise nodded. "You have a lawyer, here in Spain?"

"I have the guy who did the work for our house purchase."

"Ah. Well, yes. I suppose ... you'll have to give me his number. I can ring him for you."

"I haven't been formally charged with anything, Mr Phelps. I haven't been arrested."

"No." He looked at his sheet again. "No, really? I see ... Well, in that case—"

With a sudden burst of movement, Domingo threw down his file and leaned back in his seat, eyes fixed on Chaise. "So, Mr Chaise. You say this man stops you, and he gets in your car. Then he pulls out a gun and you struggle. Then you shoot him."

Chaise went straight into the explanation, without a pause.

"It went off in the struggle. It could just as well have been me that got shot."

"Yes, I understand that. But why did he have a gun?"

"I have no idea."

"I think there is a problem with the gun."

Chaise frowned. "A problem? I don't understand."

Domingo's eyes swept across to Phelps briefly. "How do you say forensics in English?"

Phelps swallowed hard and gave Chaise the translation.

Chaise blinked. "It was his gun if that's what the problem is."

Domingo shook his head, the smile lingering. "No. That is not it. The problem is this gun, I think – I might be wrong, you understand, and forensics will tell me if I am – but this gun was used maybe seven or eight days ago in the shooting of another man, Daniel Leary. You know him?"

"No, can't say I do."

"You don't read the papers, the Sur in English perhaps?"

"Rarely."

"It was reported in the Friday issue. He was gunned down in front of a dozen witnesses. One of the witnesses was a policeman, on his holidays. From Bradford. Very observant. He told us about the gunman, what he was wearing, his face, even his shoes – and the gun. It is the same gun, I believe, Mr Chaise."

"I see. But they all look pretty much the same nowadays."

A raised eyebrow. "Yes. But they make different sounds. The policeman knew the sound. He was in firearms … er …" He looked at the file again, running a stubby finger across the words. "Yes, Armed-Response Unit." He rubbed his chin. "We have similar units, but perhaps we need one for Benamargosa."

Silence fell like a concrete slab over the room. Chaise didn't like the implication of the man's words, but he decided to remain quiet. It was Phelps who recovered first. "With respect, we seem to be wandering off the path, so to speak. Señor Domingo, do you wish to hold Mr Chaise?"

"No." Domingo stood up. A short man, with a large spare tyre around his midriff, his trousers sagged, and his jacket strained across the shoulders. He gestured to the door with his hand. "But we shall want to speak to you again, Mr Chaise. Please, leave your passport at the desk."

Wincing, Chaise wanted to protest but knew it would be useless. He walked out, leaving Phelps to mumble something to Domingo before he joined Chaise by the main desk as he signed a form and handed over his passport. They both strode out into the harsh sunlight. Phelps struggled to cram the papers into his case. "Well, that didn't go so badly, did it?"

"You think not? They have my passport, Mr Phelps."

"Procedure. I think the point is, to be perfectly frank, he believes your story."

"*Story*? It's not a story, Mr Phelps – it's the truth."

"Oh yes, I didn't mean …" Chaise walked off at a brisk pace, forcing Phelps to break into a run to catch up with him. "Mr Chaise, please, if you could just …" Chaise stopped, waited. Phelps was already out of breath, and he'd only covered less than twenty meters. "I'm not used to this heat. I've only been here for two months. Sorry."

Sighing, Chaise folded his arms. "Why exactly are you here, Mr Phelps? I didn't request you; the police made no mention of you being invited, and I certainly didn't need your translation. Who contacted you, Mr Phelps, and ordered you to go to the police station?"

"I beg your … well, obviously, it was Señor Domingo."

"No, he didn't." Chaise looked away, the anger brewing. "It was London. My name came down the wire and someone, somewhere panicked. That's it, isn't it?"

"I…" Phelps produced a handkerchief and mopped at his

sweating brow. "Oh dear, I haven't made a very good impression, have I?"

"Who contacted you?"

Phelps swallowed hard. "One of my colleagues. From Madrid."

"The embassy? That was quick."

"As you said, your name came down the wire. Who are you, Mr Chaise? I thought you were an estate agent."

"Have you got a car?"

"Of course, but—"

"Good, you can give me a lift home. They've impounded mine."

SIX

The small package lay on the kitchen worktop dominating everything as if it were the only thing in existence. All of Alex's attention was fixed upon it, every nerve sizzling, sweat running down his face. He rarely smoked, but this was one of those times when he had to. Diane would go ballistic when she came in. She hated smoking in the house. Even outside, near the pool, every flick of ash had to be cleared away. Some of their friends smoked, but that was different of course. They were her friends. Alex had given up three years ago, one heavy New Year's Eve. Today he started again.

He pulled out a stool from under the breakfast bar and sat staring at the package. What the hell was it? Cocaine, heroin, any one of a hundred derivatives? He had no idea. The closest he'd ever got to drugs was back in his college days when he'd tried a spliff. Is that what they called it? 'Draw' some blue-eyed blonde told him. Was that marijuana? He didn't know, he didn't care up until now with that packet in his kitchen. He stared, wondered, and he didn't have a clue what to do.

The obvious thing, he thought, was to ring the police. He'd tell them the story, which was innocent enough, as well as true.

How this sweaty guy with long hair, had flagged him down on the back road coming out of Riogordo, heading towards Vélez-Malaga. He wanted to get to Nerja or Motril, he said, if that were possible. Alex told him it wasn't, that he was only going as far as La Zubia. Close enough, the guy had said. His car had broken down, a friend's car. No petrol. Someone would pick it up, but he had to get going. He was in a rush.

It all went well until an idiot driving too fast on a scooter came scorching around the corner, forcing Alex to swerve. The guy flew forward, his bag spilling out of his grasp. Something heavy clunked on the floor, but Alex paid no attention to what it was – he had the window down and was mouthing off at the idiot on the bike. The idiot just grinned. Alex slammed the car back into gear, swearing under his breath, and drove on. The guy next to him meanwhile, obviously shaken by what had happened, was quickly stuffing things back in his bag, and then they were at the village and Alex pulled up. Grinned. The guy, confused, looking around with an expression of alarm on his face, got out, took his holdall from the back seat and Alex drove off without a word. He couldn't swear to it, but in the rear-view mirror, he was sure he saw a look of horror on the guy's face as he checked his shoulder bag.

Of course now, with hindsight, Alex realized full well why the guy had been checking his bag, and why he looked so horror-struck – he'd dropped his bloody drugs in the car!

What would he do, that longhaired guy? Panic, almost certainly. Had he taken Alex's registration number? Doubtful, but even if he had, he wasn't likely to go running to the police to tell them what had happened. Unless he had connections, how could he possibly trace the registration? By now, he would know for sure that Alex had discovered the packet. So, what are *you* going to do, Alex my lad? Run around like a headless chicken, empty your bowels behind the nearest bush. He propped his elbows onto the worktop and put his chin in his hands. A bloody nightmare, that's what it was.

So, he really should tell the police.

Alex reached over and picked the packet up. It was thick and sagging a little in the middle due to its weight. Heavier than his first estimate. At least a kilo, possibly more. With a sudden thought, he reached underneath the worktop and brought out a set of scales. He slapped the packet down in the tray and read off the weight.

Exactly one kilogramme and five hundred grams. He stepped back and sighed. But one and a half kilogrammes of what?

Around an hour later, time he'd spent wrestling with his conscience, Alex finally gave Shaun a call. His closest friend, Shaun had followed Alex out to Spain, the idea being they would set up a small business together, fitting kitchens. They diversified when business failed to materialise, went into distribution, cleaning swimming pools, doing odd-jobs here and there – none of it worked. Alex had managed to get himself a TEFL qualification and now he spent his afternoons and evenings teaching English to snotty Spanish kids in Malaga. Shaun, as broad a Geordie as they come, had no such pretensions. "They won't understand a word I say!" It was probably true, they both joked. So, whilst Alex managed to hold down a job and bring in some money, Shaun relied on his charm, networking, finding odd jobs he managed to survive. But only just.

This fly-by-night existence had brought Shaun into contact with some rather shady and distinctly undesirable characters. Alex had kept his distance. Given the current situation, those characters could hold the answer to the conundrum Alex was faced with.

It took him a while to track down Shaun. Siesta time for him usually stretched from when he went to bed in the early hours, until he rose at around four in the afternoon. "Adolf Hitler did it," he would say, "and look what he achieved."

"Yeah, the most universally hated man who has ever lived, and a really bad moustache."

"Good painter though."

"Yeah, whilst he slept."

He was in Colmenar, enjoying his first drink of the day when Alex walked into 'The Englishman's Bar' and sat down next to him on one of the well-worn but comfortable sofas in the lounge. The bar tried to recreate a homely atmosphere and it succeeded very well, partly due to the warm welcome you always received, but also due to the great, and simple food they served. As Alex sat, a plate of said fare was placed before Shaun, who looked up from his beer, smiled a 'thank you' to the waitress and looked at his friend keenly. "Trouble?"

"What makes you say that?"

"You only ever come looking for me when you want something." He sliced through the steak and took his first mouthful, closing his eyes in ecstasy.

Alex pointed to the half-finished beer. "Another?"

"God, it must be serious!" He winked. "Yeah. Grande, por favor."

With the beers bought, Alex gave the room a swift scan in case any big ears were listening and leaned forward. "You're right, I have … a puzzle. Not a problem as such. Something has happened, and I need your advice."

"Diane up to her old tricks?"

"Shaun, please."

"What? It usually is Diane that causes you stress." He shovelled a large piece of meat into his mouth and chewed it noisily. "Who's she screwed now?"

Alex ran a hand over his face. "It's nothing to do with her, okay. Not this time."

Gulping down beer, Shaun peered at him, intrigued. "So, what is it?"

"I picked up a hitch-hiker. Funny looking bloke, like someone out of the Seventies. Long hair, flares, the lot."

"Smoking hashish?"

Alex stopped. "Sort of."

Interest growing, Shaun played with his chips, dragging them around the plate, soaking up as much of the gravy as he could before plunging the forkful into his mouth. "So, a backpacker? Stranger, yeah?" He washed down his food with more beer.

"Right, both times. Never seen him before. He said he was going to Nerja, then on to Motril. I dropped him at La Zubia."

"That was kind of you."

"I nearly hit a kid on a moto. Scared the living daylights out of me."

"Bet he laughed."

"He did – but the hitch-hiker didn't. I had to brake hard and all his stuff went flying around the car. It was only after I dropped him off and went back home that I spotted it."

Finishing his last mouthful, Shaun pushed his plate away and sat back, a smile of satisfaction on his florid face. "Don't tell me, he dropped his wallet."

"Just about the biggest, fattest wallet you're ever likely to see." Alex delved inside the carrier bag he had with him and grunted as he dropped the heavy package on the table. "What do you make of that?"

Not usually one to be lost for words, Shaun sat in stunned silence for a few seconds, eyes bulging as he considered the package. He quickly scanned the bar before jumping to his feet. "I think we need to go and talk about this, Alex. Now." Scooping up the package he strode to the exit with Alex close behind.

. . .

The drive to Alex's home was taken in silence, Shaun nursing the package on his lap, gazing through the window at the passing countryside. Glancing across to him, Alex noticed the thin film of sweat on his friend's brow, the tightened jaw. He didn't think he'd ever seen Shaun so serious.

Arriving at the villa, Shaun sat in the lounge whilst Alex fixed them both cold drinks. Shaun had the packet on a coffee table, armchair pulled up close tapping the wrapping paper with his fingers. "You've not opened it?"

Alex set the drinks on the table and sat down opposite his friend. "No. Wasn't sure whether I should."

Shaun, deep in thought, nodded his head repeatedly. "Okay." He sat back, ramming a finger into his mouth to chew at a nail. "I guess you must have some thoughts?"

"Drugs. That's my *only* thought, Shaun."

"You don't need to be a genius to work that out. What type, do you think?"

"Let's open it and find out." Alex produced his Swiss-Army knife, the one he always carried everywhere with him, an echo from his Boy Scout days. He eased open the penknife and hovered the blade over the packet. "Shall I?"

"Jesus, Alex – how the hell should I know?"

"I thought you might have some experience with this sort of thing."

"I smoke weed now and again, Alex. I'm not exactly Tony Montana."

Alex studied him for a moment, drew in a large breath, and carefully began to slice through the outer wrapping. He pulled out a second layer, wrapped this time in black plastic. With meticulous care, he delicately cut through the adhesive tape, gradually opening up the plastic to reveal the white powder contents. He sat back without pulling the opening any further apart. "What do you think? Don't we taste it, or something?"

"They do that in the movies, Alex. This isn't a movie. How the hell should I know what any of it tastes like?"

"No, but you know some people, people who might know what this is?"

Shaun licked a finger and dabbed it into the powder. "Yes. Someone might know if it's cocaine, but I don't. I've never taken it because it's always scared me." He tasted it and pulled a face.

"Is it heroin?"

"Alex – I don't bloody know!"

"Yeah, but cocaine numbs your gums, I know that much."

Smacking his lips, Shaun shook his head. "It's bitter. Not sweet and there's no numbness."

"Then it might be heroin. There's a kilogramme and a half here. I know, I weighed it. How much do you think it's worth?"

"A bloody fortune, I shouldn't wonder. Let's look it up." He made as if to stand.

"Look it up? What do you mean?"

"I mean on the Internet, der-head!"

"What, you can actually find out its street value on the Net? You're joking me?"

Shaun didn't answer and crossed over to Alex's PC in the corner. Shaun agitated the mouse and brought it out of hibernation. Alex stood and peered over his shoulder. In a few, brief minutes, Shaun selected the page he needed. There, in front of them both, was an Excel sheet, current street values already entered.

There were columns for cocaine, crack cocaine and heroin. Shaun did the numbers, tapped the packet, and gave a little chuckle. "Shit, Alex, on average, given where we are, this little beauty has a street value of almost two-hundred and fifty to four-hundred thousand dollars per kilo."

Alex staggered back to his chair and flopped down. He felt drained, unable to fully comprehend what Shaun had just said. *Four hundred thousand dollars?* A cold sweat broke out across his forehead and it took him a few moments to find his voice, which sounded hoarse when he spoke. "This is insane. That would make that lot worth almost half a million. Dear God, Shaun, can this be real?"

"I think so, Alex. What we have here, my friend, is the gateway to a new life." He stabbed a finger against the flat screen of the monitor. "If we distribute this, in half-gram bags as it says here, we are going to be super-rich!"

"Hold on." Suddenly, none of this sounded right. Alex's stomach may well be in knots, but his brain still functioned. He stood up and paced the room, putting distance between himself and the computer as if he could also distance himself from the situation. He held up both his hands. "Stop, Shaun. This is madness. Distribution – are you nuts? This is the Costa del Crime, controlled by gangs – violent gangs! Didn't you read what happened to that Brit who came over here to sell marijuana? They shot him dead, Shaun, tied him up to a chair and left him outside the airport as a warning. We can't do this; we can't mess with gangsters. We're going to have to give it back."

"Give it back?" Shaun's swivelled around on the chair, and his face turned livid. "Who to? The guy you told me about?" He shook his head, growing more agitated by the second. "Okay, let's think about that one. Simple question – where is he? Did you get his name, his telephone number? Or maybe, you think he's still hanging around in La Zubia waiting for you to turn up again? Hey mate, you dropped something – thought I'd come down and give it right back!" Shaun stood up, his face set hard. "No fucking way, Alex. You don't know the guy; he doesn't know you. He dropped it, you found it. End-of!"

Alex ran his fingers around the inside of his shirt collar as dryness squeezed his throat. All of this was getting out of control, a runaway train with no means to apply the brakes. "Christ almighty, Shaun, are you listening to yourself? We can't do this; we can't keep it. We're not criminals, for God's sake. We are way out of our depth. We'll have to hand it all over to the police."

"The ..." Shaun ran a hand through his hair. "The police are the biggest gangsters of them all, Alex. If we hand it over to them, never mind all the questions they'll ask, never mind all the publicity – and just think about that for a minute, yeah. I can see the headline," he traced it out in the air, "Ex-pat discovers quarter-million haul under the front seat of his car. Local resident Alex Piers ..." Shaun shook his head. "As soon as that headline hits the front pages, every fucking gangster from here to Estepona is going to want a slice of you. As for the ones who owned the stuff – they'll blow your brains out, that's what they'll do."

Alex rocked backwards as the sense of Shaun's words hit home. Drugs, gangsters, murder. This was something out of the worst type of *film-noir*. It couldn't be happening. A kilo and a half of heroin. Clutching at the last vestiges of a life bereft of such experiences, he said in an uncertain, lost voice, "We don't actually know if this has anything to do with gangsters."

Shaun arched a cynical eyebrow. "Alex – think about it. How many shop-assistants or lifeguards do you know who walk around with a half a million in hard drugs stuck in their pockets?"

"That still doesn't mean—"

Shaun's face twisted with exasperation. "This *is* gangster business, Alex, all of it, and always has been. They don't take prisoners so if we're going to get through this alive, we have got to keep it secret." He crossed the room and laid his hand on Alex's arm. "Whatever we do, Alex, we can't tell another soul if we want to come through this with both our legs intact."

Alex's legs may have been intact at that moment, but they felt as if they were made of rubber. Unable to stand, he sat staring with wild, terrified eyes at the package on the coffee table. "Shit ..."

"This guy you picked up, he's no ordinary bloke out for a jolly jaunt around the mountains of the Axarquia. He must be a member of a gang, a what-do-you-call-it ..." He squeezed his fingers into his eyes for a second, then suddenly threw up one index finger, "That's it – courier! He'd have been told to deliver the stuff to some big noise down in Motril. You said he was going there, didn't you?" Alex nodded, feeling the world pressing in on him from all sides. "Well, that's it, that's what he was doing before he decided to take it for himself. When he doesn't show two things will happen – one, they'll find him and kill him for being a naughty boy, and two, they'll start looking for the drugs. With your kipper all over the TV screen, they'll know exactly where to look."

"This can't be happening."

"As for the police, Alex. The Guardia. What do you think they'll do, eh? Oh, they'll be all self-righteous and thank you for being so honourable, a stand-up citizen helping Spain overcome the menace of organized crime. Then what'll they do? I'll tell you. They'll have it for themselves, that's what they'll do." He sat down across from his friend. "I know it's wrong. Of course, I do, but just consider what this means *for us*. This is a once-in-a-lifetime opportunity, a chance for us to make something out of this shitty world. We'll never have this opportunity again. We're just ordinary blokes trying to get through. This," he pointed at the packet of drugs, "this is our passport to a better life."

"Better? How the hell can it be better?"

"Listen. I know some guys. Small-time dealers. I'll take a sample to them; they can get it analysed. Maybe do some sort of deal."

"You said we weren't to tell another soul – your words, Shaun."

"I won't tell them where I got it."

"A kilo-and-a-half of heroin just fell out of a tree, is that it?" Alex put his face in his hands, terror gripping him. He was pitching helplessly into the realms of hell, the whole episode spiralling out of control. "My life is going straight down the toilet."

"Your life is already there, Alex."

"Thanks!"

"You have a beautiful home, true enough and a daughter who is your world together with a wife that doesn't love you! Your share of the money will change everything for the better."

"But the idea of conspiring with criminals, heavyweight gangsters, that's something which should remain within the confines of the cinema or between the pages of a book. Not here, in my comfortable, mundane, and sad little existence. Everything about this is total madness."

"Then why the hell did you get in touch with me, Alex? You must have had some weird and wonderful plan zapping around in your head."

Before he could reply, the front door opened.

Both friends stared at each other, eyes bulging in panic. As Shaun opened his mouth to speak, Alex was on his feet, pulling off his T-shirt and throwing it over the package just as Dianne, his wife, came into the room.

Dianne was the sort of woman that most middle-aged men dream about, and young men appreciate and fantasize over but never tell their mates. The older woman. A MILF, they would call her. Tall, slim, shoulder-length Vandyke brown coloured hair, she wore a tight top and a skimpy white tennis skirt that showed off her legs to best effect.

Shaun whistled softly. Dianne gave him a look that would kill. "What's he doing here?"

"Nice to see you too, Di."

"Piss off, Shaun. Alex, what the hell is going on?"

Alex stood like a little boy caught doing something he

shouldn't. Aware of his naked torso, he made a pathetic attempt of crossing his arms to look nonchalant. He failed. "Where's Amy?"

"With Mum." Dianne's parents lived just down on the coast, past Torre del Mar. They'd moved there to be closer to their grandchild. Alex always wondered if they were aware of Dianne's plans to return to the UK. She never said. Then again, she never said anything much about anything.

Without giving as much as a glance towards the coffee table, Dianne glided past them and went into the kitchen. The villa was open-plan, so whilst Shaun made a strategic move to block her view, Alex swept up the packet, quickly pressed down the adhesive tape, and rolled it up in his shirt. Without a word, Shaun took the hastily arranged bundle and went to the door. As he opened it, he called out, "Bye Di! Lovely to see you again." He winked at Alex, mouthed 'See ya soon', and left.

Alex wondered if he could make a quick getaway before his wife started on the third-degree. But she was already back in the room, glass in hand, her eyes narrowing in that accusing look of hers, an expression that seemed a permanent feature nowadays. "So, where's your shirt gone?"

"Eh?"

She stepped closer, face a mask of sheer indifference as she sipped her drink. "I saw Shaun taking it outside. Is he your laundryman now?"

What to say, how to say it? Alex's felt the colour draining from his face as nausea welled up from within. All he could do was shrug.

"Alex," she said, voice hard, authoritative. "We need to talk."

SEVEN

The doorbell rang. Through the frosted glass, Chaise saw the colour of the uniform, the outline of the shape. Police. He groaned and took a breath to steady himself before opening the door.

Domingo stood short and squat, flanked by two uniformed officers. Years of training had equipped them with a look designed to intimidate.

"A word, Mr Chaise."

Chaise fumed inside. Now every neighbour within a thousand meters would know of this visitation. No doubt most of them would take great pleasure in telling Angelina. Then the questions would start. Chaise knew he would have to tell her, but he preferred to do it on his own terms. She wouldn't be home until late and God knows which of his neighbours would hijack her first.

There was no preamble to Domingo this time, none of the false niceties of the previous meeting. He pushed past Chaise and sauntered into the lounge, his colleagues close behind. Chaise stood leaning against the door jamb, arms folded, waiting.

"We have a problem," said Domingo, voice weary. He swatted at a fly that seemed to be particularly attracted to him. The action tended to deprive him of his aura of being in control.

Chaise did not flicker and gave his best bored expression. "What sort of a problem?" He met the uniformed officers' glares. Intimidation never worked on Ryan Chaise. He stared them down, something which, from their agitated expressions, they did not appreciate.

"Your fingerprints for one." Domingo gave that oily-smile he'd used so often during their previous meeting. "We took them off the gun. You remember the gun, Señor Chaise?"

"Just get to the point."

The detective wagged a finger. "There, that's another thing – your attitude."

Chaise sighed. Somewhere a clock chimed. Eight o'clock. Angelina would be home soon. That's when the real explaining would begin. "What attitude?"

"This," Domingo waved his hand around, "carefree, relaxed manner of yours. As if none of this means very much. You killed someone, Señor Chaise."

"By accident."

"Accident or not, most people would be devastated, full of remorse and guilt. But you, it is as if it is something you are used to."

Domingo watched him carefully. Chaise glanced away, refusing confrontation. How much to give away, how many secrets to tell? "What has that got to do with fingerprints?"

"Well, I started thinking. A man who kills someone, and is unresponsive, unaffected, I think that maybe this man has done it before." He smiled the fake smile again. "Killed someone, I mean."

He's fishing, thought Chaise. He doesn't know, he just thinks he does. The truth, if revealed, would probably send Domingo into apoplexy.

As it was, for the moment at least. Domingo was prepared to be patient. He moved into the dining room, which was dominated by a long glass-topped table surrounded by six chairs. Carefully laid out cutlery, silver candelabra, ready for a dinner party. "You are expecting company?"

"Guests are coming tomorrow evening."

Nodding, Domingo's eyes roamed around, noting the expensive decorations. "Nice house. Is it yours?"

"My girlfriend's."

"Ah, yes. She is a doctor, no?"

Domingo had done his homework. Almost. "A surgeon, yes."

"Yes. I believe she is based in Malaga?"

Chaise moved wearily to the table and sat down. Angelina did indeed work in a private Malaga hospital, but he wasn't about to give Domingo the satisfaction of an affirmation. "You already know all this, Domingo, so stop wasting time – the fingerprints?"

The detective clapped his hands together, "Yes, I forgot. The sight of your beautiful home has distracted me. May we sit?"

Chaise motioned to the archway behind Domingo's shoulder, which led back to the room beyond where the other officers remained standing.

Domingo took his time before settling down. He leaned back in the armchair, legs stretched out, crossed at the ankles, hands clasped together over his paunch. "Very nice." He sounded and looked content. His eyes drooped slightly.

Chaise thought that within a few moments the detective may well drift off to sleep. He cleared his throat and said, "I wish you'd get to the point – my girlfriend will be home soon."

"Oh?" Alert again, Domingo's eyes narrowed. "Why is that such a problem? Don't you want her to know about what has happened?"

Chaise felt his hackles rise. He'd dealt with men like Domingo before, better than him, trained professionals, well versed in the arts of interrogation and intimidation. Domingo's ploy was classic: to appear friendly – taken from the 'Columbo' school of detective work – before delivering the sucker punch. Designed to lure the victim in, establishing trust through familiarity, concern and understanding. Then, throw in the quick, cutting remark, try to catch the suspect out, make them disclose something. But Domingo's easy manner didn't fool Chaise. He calmed himself, went over to the small drinks cabinet in the corner and poured himself an orange juice. He felt Domingo shift but deliberately didn't offer the policeman anything. This was a game that two could play.

Chaise drained his glass and noted the look on Domingo's face – the mask beginning to slip? "Let me save you the trouble," Chaise said, setting the glass on top of the cabinet. "You took a few samples, sent them to the lab, and the report came back. There are no records of my fingerprints. But that shouldn't be a cause for concern – there are hundreds of thousands of people whose prints are not on record simply because they've never been in trouble with the law. What worries you, is that there are virtually no records about me at all. You delved further. You got in touch with the British Embassy and they passed you on to someone, possibly someone in London. A few polite rebuttals, no records, no files, but the fact that they knew me straight away, well that in itself is strange. And why would they give you the instant referral to London? Not the usual thing, is it? Then there's Phelps. Why did he suddenly just show up – you hadn't called him in. Perhaps your superiors told you of his arrival? But then, the big clincher, the one thing that has really raised your hackles – you get a call from one of your own people, National Police perhaps, or some shady, government department in Madrid. They tell you to back off, to turn away. You don't like that, you don't appreciate being told how to do your job, so you decide to come here anyway, delve a bit deeper. How am I doing, detective?"

Domingo's face remained unchanged as he listened. Now, with Chaise finished, he leaned forward, all humour gone. "The gun was used in that other killing, Mr Chaise, the one I told you about. To use the parlance, 'a gangland hit'. An argument gone bad, a debt unpaid, it doesn't matter. What does matter is that it was done in broad daylight, in a restaurant, on a normal, sunny afternoon in full view of tourists. Now that means two things – desperation, or a message. The other point is you, Mr Chaise. The examination of the body of the man you killed—"

"He said his name was Treach."

"Did he? Well, this *Treach* had some rather interesting injuries. Sprained wrist, torn ligaments, broken nose, and cheekbones. You didn't just struggle with this man, Mr Chaise, you expertly took him apart. And then you shot him."

Chaise ran his tongue across his bottom lip but didn't speak.

"Who are you, Mr Chaise?"

"An estate agent."

"One expert in karate?"

"I've never studied karate."

"Then how did you know what to do? The medical examiner said he had never seen such precise blows, delivered with such expertise."

"I'd like you to leave now, Señor Domingo."

Domingo's eyes narrowed, his breathing uneven, the anger and frustration rising. He stood up. "This isn't going to go away, Señor Chaise. I won't stop until I find out who you are and what your part in all of this is. When a murder has been committed, even 'shady government departments' won't be able to stop me getting to the truth. I don't like secrets, Mr Chaise, and you are full of secrets, I think. Living here, amongst the mountains, selling your houses ..." He shook his head. "I think there is a lot more to you than meets the eye."

A dog with a bone he may well be, but Chaise knew that this particular dog was the worst kind. Not simply stubborn –

obsessed. He thought he had something, a tiny inkling that Chaise might not be who he said he was, and that was enough. He'd pursue it until he proved himself right.

Chaise went through the archway to the hall and opened the door. The uniformed officers exchanged confused looks as they stepped outside. Domingo paused at the threshold. "I'll be back," he said.

Chaise controlled the urge to quip something about Arnold Schwarzenegger. He watched the policemen get to their patrol car just as a second vehicle rumbled into the driveway. A red MGB Roadster, top-down, a gorgeous woman behind the wheel. Chaise groaned.

Angelina was home.

EIGHT

The bar was situated some way from the beachfront on a forgotten side street. One of those drab, dark places that appear outwardly unfriendly, intimidating almost. The sort of place where as soon as you stop to consider entering, men sat at the bar turn and scowl, forcing you to move on. Shaun knew it well and he liked it.

Jose Luis sat in a corner, a glass of *sol y sombre* next to him, reading a free newspaper. He barely glanced up as Shaun sat down opposite. Pulling out a crumpled pack of Chesterfield cigarettes, Shaun knocked one out and passed it over. Jose Luis took it and placed it behind his ear. He still hadn't looked up.

"I need your help, Jose Luis."

The Spaniard turned a page, sniggered at something before slowly folding the newspaper closed. He raised his glass. "You always do." He drained his drink.

"This time it's serious." Shaun twisted around, to make sure no one was close. Satisfied, he pulled out a tiny plastic bag and palmed it to Jose Luis. "I want you to check that. See how good it is."

Without a word, Jose Luis placed the bag in his pocket and picked up his newspaper again.

Shaun leaned closer. "How long?"

Jose Luis shrugged, "Could be an hour, could be a whole day. It depends."

Shaun pushed over a thick envelope. "Let's make it within the hour, yeah?" He stood up. "You've got my mobile. If you're not back to me by," he checked his watch, "eleven-thirty, I'm coming back for you. Understand?"

"Must be serious!"

"I kid you not, Jose. If you don't contact me, I'll break your fucking legs. You understand that?"

"Hey, amigo," Jose Luis beamed, "Have I ever let you down."

"You're Spanish – no sense of urgency. It's a national disease."

He strode out.

At four minutes before the deadline, Shaun's mobile vibrated into life. He answered, listened, and put it back in his pocket. He was at a beachside *chiringuito*, enjoying a late breakfast of coffee and *pitufo sin aceite*. Shaun hated olive oil, an unfortunate trait in someone living in Spain, so he took his tostada with tomato only. Most waiters gave him a curious look, questioning his order. He was used to this now, always giving a tired, "Si, solo tomate." Still not convinced, the waiter would shuffle away, peering at his order pad, wondering if he had got it wrong.

Munching down a last mouthful, Shaun left the payment on the table and crossed the road. He made his way through the narrow side streets of this part of Malaga and found the bar. Jose Luis was in the same corner, but this time his air of indifference had been replaced by wide-eyed excitement.

"Shaun!" He waved Shaun to the seat, clicked his fingers to order drinks, and leaned across the table, his face as eager as a child's in Hamleys. "Shaun, this stuff is gold. Do you understand? Top-notch, unadulterated, pure crack-cocaine!"

"I thought it might be heroin as it had no taste."

"No, it is … how you say…unadulterated? Pure. Where the hell did you get it?"

"Hey," Shaun's turn to lean forward, "that's my concern, okay? All I want from you is a simple answer." He sat back as the barman appeared with two beers. When he drifted away, Shaun watched him, then returned to Jose Luis. "I want you to try and sell it for me."

The Spaniard-s eyes grew wide. "Sell it? Hombre that will not be easy. Not here."

"I don't care where you try, just sell it. Further down the coast perhaps. Estepona, Marbella. Wherever."

Jose Luis snorted, "Si, and have those Irish gangsters trussing me up like a turkey – I don't think so. Besides, it's hot down there now, the Guardia are everywhere. The glory days are gone now, Shaun. It's not as easy as it once was." He spread out his hands, palms upwards. "Even so, if any of those gangsters got wind of me trying to push this kind of stuff, they'll slit my throat. Worse still, maybe the Guardia would do it for them."

"Okay." Shaun sat thinking for a moment and decided to give Jose Luis just a taster of the truth. "I'll tell you this, Jose. I've got half a kilo of that stuff. Maybe more."

"Half a – that is serious money, Shaun."

"I'll give you ten per cent of its street value. That's a nice little earner for you, Jose. Well worth the aggravation."

Jose Luis sucked in his bottom lip, drank his beer, worked out the numbers and, from the evidence of his broad grin, came up with a figure well worth working for. "Okay, I might know someone. I did a job for these guys not so long ago. They know me, trust me, I guess. They are the real deal, Shaun, so if they buy, you had better deliver. But they are fair. Reasonable. Not vicious thugs, you get me?"

"Professional gangsters, yeah I get you, Jose. Tremendous guys. Gentlemen." He shook his head, feeling his face redden. He hated all this "honour amongst thieves" bullshit. They were criminals of the worst kind, striving so hard to be "respectable." It made him feel sick. And now he was about to enter into their world, become the very thing he detested most. The lure of easy money does that, as we all know. There was no point philosophising about it. Shaun had made his bed, so now he had to lie in it. He'd lied to Jose about the amount he had. If it all came good, he could move the rest. It would mean more deals, more swimming around in the sewer. "I don't give a toss who they are – in fact, I don't want to know. Just do me the deal."

"I'll need the stuff."

"I'll give you half now, the other half when the deal's done."

"They won't like that."

"Tough."

Jose Luis took his time over another sip of beer. "Okay. I'll talk to them, see what they say. I'll call you later."

"Not too late, Jose. I need this done quick."

Jose Luis frowned. "You in trouble, mi amigo?"

Shaun stood up, finished his beer, and slammed the glass down on the tabletop so hard Jose Luis jumped. "You will be if you cock this up!"

NINE

S arah sat at her kitchen table cradling a large mug of coffee between her hands as if it were the most precious thing in the world. Point of fact, it probably was at that moment. After the incident with Ricky – that is what he said his name was – her world was in danger of falling apart. The bastard repeatedly spread her legs, destroyed her face, and stole her car, leaving her life broken into scattered pieces for everyone to see. The police had been kind, patient, the woman especially. The man just stood there, sunglasses masking his features, but she knew what he was thinking. Spanish men were so judgemental, so indifferent to how women felt. Spain, a strange dichotomy of a western European state trying desperately to become part of the twenty-first century mixed with ancient traditions and beliefs that held it back, simply refusing to budge. How many generations would it take before the modern world took dominance? She sighed, hating the chauvinistic attitude of the people in the land in which she lived, but loving the land itself. And now this, turning everything on its head.

She put her face in her hands, trying not to cry again. She knew if she looked in the mirror, she would do just that. When her husband returned from his business trip, she would have to tell him something to explain her bruises, the missing car, but what words would convince him that the attack was anything other than what it really was? A quick romp in the hay with a dangerous stranger? My God, her world truly would end right there and then. He'd check, of course, go to the police ... No, she'd have to think of something, something that had to be convincing.

A knock at the door. Sarah sighed, finished her coffee, and padded through the kitchen into the wide, open entrance hall. Her feet were bare, and she liked the feel of the cool marble on her soles. Her short grey skirt showed off her slim, brown legs to good effect. She liked to stay cool in the house. Her cut-off top revealed a hard stomach, toned arms. She hoped that whoever her caller was would concentrate on those aspects of her wonderful body rather than the car wreck that was now her face. She pressed a tissue against her eye, which was weeping, and pulled open the door.

The man gave a little gasp. He hadn't homed in on her body, just her face. "Oh my," he said immediately, then realized his error and held up his hand. "I'm sorry! Please ... sorry."

Sarah shook her head. The man was British. Somewhere from the north. Liverpool perhaps. Although he had tried hard to change his accent, it was still there. She knew this, being from the Wirral herself.

"It's okay," she said, keeping the tissue pressed against her eye. The whole side of her face screamed out in pain, but the corner of her eye was by far the worse place. A needlepoint of excruciating agony, the bones around the orbit shattered. The doctor had not sounded convincing when he had told her, 'It will take time'. How much time he didn't say. She had another appointment tomorrow. Until then, she had to make do with the tissue, but now that the painkillers were wearing off she found she had to work hard to keep her expression to the minimum. "Can I help you?"

"Yes," he said, reaching inside his pocket to pull out a business card.

"Leroy Silks and Company," she read aloud. "Lawyers? Sounds more like a cheap American sit-com."

She handed back the card and the man laughed. "Very good. Very droll," he said.

"Don't tell me." She tapped her lip with her free hand and looked up at the ceiling. "You're that little weasel's lawyer and you've come to do a deal. Have they caught him, then?"

"I'm sorry …" The man in the suit shook his head, dumbfounded. "I'm not sure I know what you're—"

"The little shit that did this—" Angry now, she pointed at her face. "Are you his lawyer?"

The man, mouth open, aghast but no sound. She went to shut the door, but he put up his hand, palm outstretched, and said quickly, "Please, if you could just let me have a few words." Sarah glared at him, forcing him to turn his face away, sheepish. "I promise you; I am not that 'little weasel's' lawyer. I'm here to talk to you about your car, that's all. The police have impounded it, you see, and there could well be a case for a substantial claim. Even a replacement."

The relief flooded in. Of course, the car! The police had told her it had been towed away, for forensic tests. They didn't say why, nor revealed details of its present state. Ricky's little Suzuki jeep had also been taken away, but she didn't give a damn about that – she just wanted the Audi fixed up before her husband returned in three days. Perhaps this man, this lawyer's representative, offered a way forward. She pulled open the door. "You'd better come in."

All the security manuals tell you the same thing. Television programmes too. Never let strangers into your house, not without proper identification. Even then, it's best to be certain.

A doorstep conversation can often serve just as well. And a quick call to the police, just to check that the caller had informed the local constabulary of their impending visit, wouldn't do any harm. Not if they were genuine.

Sarah didn't do any of these things. She opened the door wider still and let the man step inside.

As soon as she closed the door, it happened.

TEN

Alex went into the kitchen, half-hoping that she would still be there, but she wasn't. The tiny piece of optimism that had greeted him as he awoke vanished as if it had never existed. Last night, the *coup de grâce*, delivered with Diane's usual deadpan face, that she and Amy were going at the end of the week. Back to the U.K. "Amy will be staying at my mum's," she said, packing an overnight bag. "She'll stay there until I can sort something out for us back home." She zipped up the bag, eyes hard as ice and just as cold. "I'll be back tomorrow at noon with a van to pick up the rest of my stuff. I'd appreciate it if you weren't here." She hefted the bag and went downstairs. He followed her, legs feeling like lead, a defeated man, no fight left in him. Standing at the bottom of the stairs, he held onto the bannister rail and watched her. At the door, she turned. "Oh," she said as if suddenly remembering, "I've put the house up for sale. Someone will be around to take all the details, take a few photos and that." She went out, slamming the door behind her.

Alex stood as if frozen, unable to move or think. As the sound of the car starting up, the realisation dawned, and he crumbled inside. His knees buckled and he collapsed onto the step. "Amy," he said aloud in a small voice, the memories of his little girl already looming large in his mind. What would he do without her, the sound of her voice, the little cheeky grin? How could he function without the one good thing in a life turned bad? Gut-wrenching pain caused him to fold into a foetal position, where he remained and sobbed until his eyes stung and his throat was dry, and he could cry no more.

Chaise replaced the receiver. His office, sounding brisk – a new client wanting photographs taken of their house, quickly, within the next hour. They'd paid extra for the service and paid well so get it done.

He groaned. Angelina still in bed, hit hard by the previous evening's revelations. This morning, she'd phoned in sick, something she never did, not in all the years they'd been together. Always so fastidious, dedicated to her profession, dragging herself out of bed every morning, or indeed every night, depending on her shift, without complaint. Last night, he'd seen something different. His words, his story, affecting her in a way he never expected. Her face draining of colour, shocked by Chaise's apparent indifference. Her voice, brittle, uncertain, like a little girl's, sounding close to breaking when she asked, "I know you've never talked about it, and I've never asked but is this coldness all to do with what you did in the army?"

"You could say that." He sat on the couch, leaning forward, hands clamped together. He avoided her eyes.

"But you're not going to tell me, are you?"

"I can't, Linny," his pet name for Angelina. "I'm not allowed to."

"Not allowed to? What does that mean?"

"It means …" he took in a deep breath, eyes closed. "I'm bound by the Official Secrets Act. If I disclose so much as a single word, I'll be put away for longer than the Great Train robbers." He looked at her. Her face turned white and, for the first time in an age, she went over to the drinks cabinet. Linny never drank. He watched her hand shaking as she poured herself a whisky and threw it down in one gulp. Gasping, she held onto the edge of the cabinet and screwed up her face with something like disgust.

He wished to God he could tell her something to reassure her, but he simply couldn't. Bound was the word he'd used, and bound he was, trussed up for life, the past dominating his present, shaping his future. He could never sever himself from what he was. And if Angelina ever knew so much as a hint of the truth, would she stay? Could she stay? Sitting back, he stared at the wall with nothing to say. He hated the way it had all caught up with him again, the nightmare recurring; fate was such a bastard – if only he hadn't been driving down that particular piece of road at that particular time, if only he hadn't stopped, if only ... His mind returned to how it had been the other time. Years back. The scorching wind, whipping the sand up into little eddies that spat into your face, stinging you like a thousand needles. He had the scarf up around his mouth and nose, the sand-goggles pressed into his eyes, but the top of the cheekbones, they still bore the brunt of that sand. Sam Walker was sitting on the ground, as if he were at the beach, just sitting there, shirt off, head tilted towards the sun. This was no beach, however. Sam had a hole the size of a grapefruit in his back, the exit wound from the shot that had taken him down. Next to him, shaking his head, biting back the anger, was Tiny Windsor. Chaise had never seen Tiny so worked up. He had a young Arab lad by the throat, squeezing the boy so hard it looked as if his eyes were going to pop out of his head. He couldn't have been more than thirteen or fourteen. He'd waved the jeep down, babbling on about an emergency. They'd stopped. Rule break number one. Sam had stepped out. Rule break number two. The boy looked so genuine. Besides, he was only a boy. Chaise should have known better, but this was his first patrol. He'd been through the training, but this heat, it sapped you, made judgment blurry. They weren't even wearing combats it was so hot, throwing the vests into the back. This was not a dangerous sector, so how the hell did any of them know that any of this would happen? The bullet took Sam high in the chest, knocked him off his feet. Tiny swung round and took a bead on the sniper. Chaise had no idea how he did that, how he had the instinct to seek out the assassin's hideaway with such speed. He watched, heard the shots, and saw the plume of blood. The boy ran, and Chaise outpaced him, knocked him down, dragged him back. Now Tiny had him and it didn't look good, not for the boy.

"I'm going to take it out on his fucking balls," Tiny spat, sweeping out the broad-bladed Bowie-knife that everyone told him he shouldn't have. "I'm gonna slice him up, peg him out, and let him bleed to death."

"You can't do that, Tiny. There'll be questions – shit, we should never have stopped! It's a fucking mess."

The boy whimpered, the Arabic spewing out like static on the radio. Tiny squeezed tighter. "We do him, then take the bodies back, bury them somewhere. No one will know."

"But Sam, Tiny. What do we do about that? We have to report it."

"We will, you idiot! We'll tell 'em the truth. That we were shot at. We'll just leave out the bit about us stopping."

"What about the part where you tortured this kid?"

Tiny gave him a look, the one he reserved for people he was about to smack in the mouth. "Well, what the fuck do you wanna do with him, you sanctimonious twat!"

Chaise blinked, the words like slaps. Without a breath, he brought out the Glock, pressed it against the boy's head and fired.

It was the first time he had killed.

It never left him.

The investigation was not as thorough as any of them had feared. Tiny didn't bury the boy, and no one asked why he had been shot at point-blank range. Two months later Tiny himself was killed by a roadside bomb. Chaise then received the call and went for an interview in London. Pakistan beckoned and the killing stacked up.

If Angelina knew any of this, would she stay? He'd worked hard to put it all away, in a file marked 'Top Secret'. Now, someone had gone rooting through the old memories, a hitchhiker with a gun. It had all turned full circle.

ELEVEN

B efore Sarah could blink, he had her by the throat, pinning her against the wall. It happened so quickly that, for a moment, she was at a loss as to what to do or even think. Then it hit her, the panic. She thrashed out with arms and legs, managed to get a grip on his hand, dug her nails like claws into his flesh. He grinned and as she kicked out, he simply turned to the side, her foot hitting his shins, not his more vulnerable parts. He jutted his face close to hers, increasing the pressure of his fingers. Her eyes bulged, desperation overwhelming her. She tried to scream, but nothing would work. The smell of his aftershave invaded her nostrils and then he spoke, a voice like gravel, and so low that it made her blood freeze. "Stop struggling, and don't scream. If you do, I'll kill yer."

Then, like someone would toss away a piece of rubbish, he thrust out a foot and threw her sideways over it. She lost her balance, fell on her knees, gasping for breath. Her eyes filled up as a pounding sensation came into her ears and for a moment, she almost fainted. She managed to hold on, hands pressing down on the tiled floor, mouth open, taking in great gulps of air through her burning throat. Gradually, the pounding became less, the blurry vision cleared, replaced by increasing terror.

The man took a step towards her and Sarah whimpered, pushing herself backwards, a single arm raised in defence.

"Stupid bloody tart," he sneered, adjusting his tie, dismissive of her now. "Get in that room and keep yer mouth shut. You need to listen to what I've got to say."

She stumbled and staggered into the lounge and fell into the sofa. Ignoring her, the attacker came out of the kitchen and placed a tumbler of ice-cold water in front of her before sitting down opposite. Sarah gazed at the glass, not sure what to do, her heart beating so hard she thought it would burst. Her face was hot and wet. When he leaned forward, she jumped, expecting another assault. He merely pushed the glass a little closer to her. "Drink it," he said, and she did, without hesitation, very slowly.

The man opposite her was small and wiry, immaculately groomed, looking more like a salesman than the monster he was. This is what had fooled her, and she kicked herself for being so stupid. She could see it now in those cold, unfeeling eyes, the slight smirk on his thin lips. Why hadn't she paid more attention when she'd opened the door to him? She'd done that with his voice. His accent betrayed him as someone from Liverpool. She'd noticed that straight away, but it was much more pronounced now, the act he put on when he first called having convinced her that he was genuine. The other reason she'd let him in. What an idiot she was.

That same voice now sent a chill through her body. "I want you to listen to me very carefully, all right? I'm going to ask you some questions, and I want you to give me honest answers."

"Who are you?" Her voice sounded detached, from somewhere outside of her – she could hear it, but it was if it came from another room. Was this what they called an 'out-of-body experience', or just plain, simple fear?

His eyes narrowed and he shifted his position, leaning closer, hands in an attitude of prayer. "Listen, this is how it works, yeah? I ask you the questions, not the other way round. You understand?" She nodded, still holding the glass to her lips, her eyes never leaving his. "Good. I want you to tell me about this fella that went off with your car. What did he look like?"

It took a moment to register his words. This wasn't good. She mumbled, "Fella...?"

"Yeah," he shifted again as if the sofa made him uncomfortable. "The bloke, the guy that stole your car. Remember him, do yer, Sarah?"

She saw how he tapped his foot incessantly. This was a man on a mission, impatient, and she knew she couldn't delay her answers. "Yes, yes of course."

"Good. So, what the fucking hell did he look like – describe him!"

She gasped at his change of tone, the anger, the obvious threat. "He had, er, long hair, very slim, tall. Er ... flares. I remember he wore flares."

"Like a nineteen seventies hippy?"

"Yes, yes that's it. Hippy."

He reached inside his jacket and brought out a small postcard-sized photograph which he slid across the table to her. "Is that him?"

She stared down at the photograph and felt her throat instantly tighten. Her jaw dropped and, hand shaking, she took a large gulp of water. "Yes," she said, setting the glass down next to the picture. "That's him."

"Good." He picked up the photograph and put it back inside his jacket. "Okay. What I need to know is this – did he have any bags."

"Bags?" She saw that look, that change in his features, those eyes telling her not to ask questions. She rushed on, "Yes! Yes, he had bags. Two, I think."

60

"Two bags. All right, a big one and a little one? One a ropey thing, with a weird design on it, like something from the Aztecs?"

She gaped. How the hell did he know that? She nodded in response. "South American. Yes."

"All right. Now, this bag, the ropey one. Did he bring it into the house?"

She struggled with that. Whether he had bags with him was not the uppermost thought in her mind at that point. "Er, I think so."

"You think so? You need to do better than that, Sarah."

She swallowed hard, glanced at the water. There was none left. "God, I … I don't know. He just, I mean, we just…"

"Yeah, I know. You picked him up, brought him back here, and fucked his brains out, yeah?"

Sarah's voice trembled, "Yes."

"Okay, now this bit is important, yeah. He stole your car. Are you sure he didn't take anything out of his bag before he left? No packages, or anything like that?" She shook her head. "I want you to think, really hard. Are you certain he didn't leave anything behind?"

"I'm certain."

"And you never looked inside his bag?"

"No, I didn't. I swear."

"Have you looked around the house, checked that there isn't anything out of the ordinary?"

She shook her head, swallowing another question down. Out of the ordinary? "No, Nothing."

"Okay." He sat back, looking at the ceiling. For a few moments, he seemed to be considering what next to say. He closed his eyes, settling his breathing. Sarah studied him again, looking beyond the suit and the carefully groomed hair, the tanned face, the designer stubble. All she could see was a hideous, loathsome slug of a man who had invaded her privacy, brought everything crashing down around her ears, bringing a whole new meaning to the word fear. Never had she felt such terror. When that shithead had hit her yesterday, she had had no time to even think about it. All she had felt was the rage as he opened her car door the morning he left, after screwing her throughout the night. Wild, insatiable. She'd never known anything like it. Then, for him to walk out like that, without a word, how dare he! Anger had blinded her to the danger. She'd rushed out, confronted him, and then he'd hit her. That was bad. Very bad. Now, in this room, with this weasel of a man, this was an altogether different level entirely. And the most terrifying, bone-numbingly awful thing about it, she had no control. None. This was his party and he could play it out to the end if he so wanted.

His eyes opened and he leaned forward again. The smile returned. "All right, Sarah. You see, the thing is, I believe you. I'll tell you why I believe you – because, if you have lied to me, I'll come back. I'll come back and I'll hurt yer. Like no one has ever hurt you before. You understand?" She nodded limply, stomach turning to water, sweat smearing her brow. "Not like before, not like that. This time, I'll come back, and I'll cut you, you understand?" He pointed at her swollen eye. "That looks nasty, but it'll heal. The doctors will do what they do and in a couple of months, no one will ever know. But what I'll do, it will stay with yer for life. You get me?"

Sarah nodded again, her whole body screaming to run, to get away. Maybe she could outpace him, maybe she could make it to the road. Then what? The nearest neighbour was over four hundred meters away down a rutted track. He'd overtake her, knock her down, do whatever he needed to do. She just had to wait it out, agree with everything he said. That was the way. No other, in all seriousness, no other way at all.

"They'll bring yer car back in a day or so. The police. They'll strip it down, rip up the seats, the carpets, even look inside the tires. If what you tell me is the truth, though, they won't find anything, and they'll put it back together and no one will ever know. But," the smile becoming a sneer, "if they do find anything, or if you tell a single soul about any of this," he waved his hand around, "tell anyone about our little chat, I'll come back and I'll set fire to your fucking house, cut you up like a fucking fish and ruin your fucking life forever! You understand that Sarah, eh? Do yer?" He shot forward before she could react and seized her throat again, ramming her back in the sofa. She clawed at him, just like before, and just like before it was useless. The aftershave again, his smell as he leaned forward, pressing his face close to hers. Her stomach heaved. Then he did something beyond nightmares. Deliberately, he took his thumb and pressed it against her eye, right in the centre of the bruising. She felt the pain like a knife, penetrating her very brain. She wailed like a baby, squirmed beneath him, but his other hand had her by the throat, pinning her, and there was nothing she could do but hope that the pressure would lessen, and the pain go away. "You say one fucking word, to any living soul, and it all ends, Sarah. You got a husband, yeah?" She attempted to nod. Please God, stop him from pressing his thumb, stop the pain, please. "Well, I'll break both his fucking legs. Don't think I won't, because I will, Sarah. You open your fat gob and there'll be a fucking army coming after you, understand." He gave her one last shove with the thumb before releasing her and she spluttered, rolling over, holding her throat, gagging, squeezing her eyes shut, trying to make the pain disappear. Her whole head throbbed as if it had been used as a football.

She felt him move away and chanced a look. It was difficult to focus but she watched him adjust his tie, tuck his shirt into his trousers. He even had time to pose in front of the wall mirror, smooth down a lock of hair. The perfect salesman once again. "Okay, I'll be going now." He turned to her, smiled. "Don't forget what I said, will yer?"

Still, with her hands around her throat, she shook her head.

The smile widened. "Good girl." He began to move away, "I'll see meself out." At the door, he turned and winked. "Nice to have met yer." He was gone.

Sarah didn't want to move, believing that if she did, he would return, put that thumb in her eye again. Her throat burned, but the eye … The first tear rolled down her cheek, but she made no sound and sat there, in silence, for hours.

TWELVE

It gnawed away at him. Ever since the incident, the same nagging question. Despite his outward calm, Chaise wondered about his attacker's motives. For anyone to threaten another with a gun was beyond seriousness. If someone possessed a gun, they would use it at some point. Fundamental truth. This guy, if Domingo was to be believed, had used it before, with devastating effect. So, was that it? He was on the run, escaping from who? His erstwhile friends, paymasters, enemies? To shoot someone in broad daylight, to not have any concerns about being recognized or identified, that took either nerve or desperation. Which was it?

He'd said that his other car had broken down. Had that been in Benamargosa, Chaise wondered. Maybe a little outside the village. If so, it shouldn't be that difficult to find. He hadn't said what type of car, but the locals might know. They probably *would* know; they were so damned nosey. He had to go to that house and take the photographs, but a quick visit to a couple of bars wouldn't put him too far behind schedule. With some trepidation, he went to Angelina and found her sleeping. Smiling, he quietly went over, stroked a stray lock of hair from her face, and kissed her lightly on the forehead. She murmured and turned over, dragging away the single bedsheet with her. She was naked and Chaise rolled his eyes over the mound of her buttocks and felt the stirring in his loins. After four years, she still turned him on like nobody else. In a mad moment, he bent down and pressed his lips against one soft, curvaceous orb of her behind, then stood up straight, making a face as his erection strained against his shorts. He turned and quickly ran downstairs before the overwhelming desire to ravish her body became too much.

Leaving a note explaining where he had gone, Chaise stepped out into the sweltering day and jumped into his car. The aircon kicked in, blasting him in the face. He turned the CD player on full blast and let the soothing, enigmatic music of Sigur Ros transport him to a slightly less frantic place.

A visit to only two bars was all it took. The description was not of a broken-down car, but one of a large red, four-by-four that had off-loaded said 'long-haired skinny kid' in the village square. This made for a very interesting development. So, the dead guy had hitched another lift before thumbing down Chaise? Why lie about that, and where had he originally come from? Those were the questions now. A red four-by-four might mean any one of many cars, but it might mean just one. It would take time, but Chaise was determined. After all, the outlying villages were small, and the Spaniards loved to gossip. The task should not prove too difficult.

Sitting at the breakfast bar, sipping a cup of coffee, Alex flicked through the pages of an old newspaper, then got up and switched on the television. He never had been a great watcher of daytime TV, but it was almost midday and the news usually held some items of interest. He tilted the cafetière and topped up his cup. He was about to take a drink when his hand froze in mid-air.

The face on the television held all of his attention, almost stopping his heart. It was a photograph of a man with long, shoulder-length hair, high cheekbones, long nose, thin, cruel-looking mouth. The picture of the man Alex had given a lift to. He listened to the report, letting the words sink in, their enormity causing him to break out in a cold sweat. Apparently, the man had attacked a woman, a woman who lived not that far away. Alex blinked as her photograph came up on the screen. Sarah Banbury. He knew her, he felt sure. Or, at the very least, he recognized her. Riogordo was not such a big place, and the number of ex-pats who lived either in the village or in the surrounding hills wasn't large. Sarah Banbury. She had the kind of face that took your breath away. More than lovely, she exuded an almost base, animal sexuality. Diane was beautiful, but this girl was sheer pulsating sex. Rubbing his face, he tried hard to get his brain into gear and remember where exactly she lived.

"In a further incident involving the same man, local estate agent Ryan Chaise is alleged to have shot and killed the suspect, whose name is thought to be Richard Treach." A photograph of Chaise came on screen. A holiday snap, he was bending forward, smiling, bare torso. Behind him, a crowded beach. It looked local, Torrox possibly, or Torre del Mar. The newscaster's voice droned on, "Police were not available for comment at this time but have appealed for anyone with any information regarding any of these incidents to contact them immediately."

The news went onto another item, but Alex wasn't listening anymore. As if in a daze, he reached for the remote and switched the TV off. He drifted into the lounge and stared out the window for a long time, struggling to find a way through the mass of cotton wool that had invaded his head.

It was clear and simple what had happened. Ryan Chaise, whoever he was, had shot this guy because of the drugs. It was some sort of gangster-related 'hit', and now these same gangsters would be looking for the drugs. The police wanted witnesses and Alex knew he was the main one. However, if he revealed himself, the gangsters would be here within the blink of an eye, asking about the missing drugs. Everyone knew what their response would be when Alex revealed every sordid detail. He couldn't say a word – not to anyone.

Gazing out of the window, his eyes settled on his massive four-by-four sitting there like some beast from pre-history. A bigger advert he couldn't imagine. On impulse, he rushed out of the house, clambered behind the wheel, and took the car to the large double garage at the side of the villa. The sensors did their work and the garage doors slid open. He rolled the car into the semi-darkness, stepped out and took a moment to enjoy the cool of the interior, wishing he could stay there all day. Unfortunately, other pressures were making themselves felt and he needed to contact Shaun straight away to inform him of the latest developments. Exhaling loudly, he went back outside, pulled the garage door shut, locked it, then turned and took his mobile out of his pocket. In the act of punching in Shaun's number, another car rolled into the driveway, tires crunching across the gravel. Alex stared in disbelief. The shock, like a pile-driver in his chest, was greater than the one he'd received from the TV just a few moments ago.

The man behind the wheel was the same as the guy on the television news report. Ryan Chaise.

Chaise drove up to the impressive, sprawling villa and saw the man, who he assumed to be the owner, standing there, mouth open like a fish. Shock. Chaise could see it written in every line of the man's face and recognised it instantly. Sergeant Batters had been amongst the first to notice this somewhat unnerving sense Chaise possessed. "You know what I'm thinking, don't you, Chaise?" It may have been instinct, it may have been pure reaction, but when Batters threw a three-finger spear at Chaise's midriff, Chaise moved, parried, counter-attacked with elbow strikes, driving Batters back, the blows hitting him with such devastating precision that they had to hospitalise Batters afterwards. He retired in less than a month, a broken man. Chaise heard through the grapevine that Batters had hanged himself in his garage. A sad end to a somewhat distinguished career. Chaise hadn't felt any remorse, never had. Why should he? If the idiot hadn't tried that three-finger strike he might even be alive today.

Now, stepping out of his car, Chaise sensed it again. It had resurfaced with Ricky Treach and now it was right up inside every nerve-ending, his body alive with it. The man's fear and confusion. And something more. Chaise sensed guilt.

"Mr Piers?" Chaise thrust out his hand, forcing a smile. "My name is Ryan Chaise. I'm here to take the sales details of your beautiful home."

Chaise didn't think he had ever seen such a look of relief cross another human being's face.

THIRTEEN

Arthur Morgan took two calls that morning. The first was simple, requiring little in the way of response, except, "That's good, Jimmy. Come in now, will you."

The second came almost as soon as he put the phone down on its cradle. It proved a lot trickier.

Not a man to be trifled with, Morgan had made a fortune in property investments, coupled with an extensive prostitution business. He owned the three biggest brothels on the coast, but times were hard. The Lithuanians were one thing, but he could deal with them. What he had no control over was firstly the economic downturn and secondly, political uncertainty. Both of these developments – if they could be called that – had resulted in hordes of Brits returning home. Morgan relied on the steady flow of regular, loyal customers to keep his business flourishing. As more and more British left, so the cash registers rang out a lot less. Eventually, after some careful consideration, he turned to drugs, not in a big way, not at first. Drugs had always featured in his other business ventures, which was inevitable – they were a fairly foolproof way of keeping the girls under control. Lately, the distribution of hard drugs, slipped in from

North Africa, was becoming a mainstay. He'd fought hard to cement his position, had killed and would have no qualms about killing again. The Lithuanians understood that. A few had tried to muscle in, using the usual intimidation techniques. He'd suspended the leader of one gang over a barrel of boiling water and slowly submerged his head, leaving it there until it was completely cooked. He'd fed the results to his dogs. The remaining members of the gang soon disappeared after that, never to be heard of again.

Morgan had to appear strong and unforgiving. There was no choice if he were to maintain his position. And now, there was this nonsense with Ricky and what he'd done. Stupid. It wasn't the amount of drugs he'd stolen or their street value – it was the principle. Morgan had to get them back and be seen to do so with the utmost effectiveness and brutality, otherwise, every snivelling, cheap little villain from here to Almuñécar would fancy their chances. Besides anything else, the customer wanted his purchase.

The second call was from no snivelling cheap little villain. When he heard the all too familiar voice, Arthur Morgan's blood ran cold. The hand with which he held the receiver trembled. It was the customer and he was not happy.

"There was nothing in the car."

"I see," said Arthur, trying to keep his voice flat calm. "Thank you for letting me know."

"That can only mean one thing – the Englishman has it."

"Almost certainly."

"Then get your goons to pay him a visit and get this thing sorted, straight away."

"I will. Don't worry."

"And Arthur ... do it right. I paid you good money, I expect delivery. No strings, you understand, nothing to tie me to any of this."

"Of course. You can rely on me."

"I hope so. For your sake."

The phone went dead. Arthur Morgan reached for his handkerchief and dabbed at his brow, the relief washing over him. He threw the phone down, feeling angry and ashamed at how the conversation had left him shaking like a pathetic little schoolboy. He wondered, not for the first time, how he could free himself of that man's clutches. He'd have to speak to Jimmy, sort it out. It would be difficult, but not impossible. Morgan opened up the cigar box on his desk, chose a firm-looking Havana and sliced off the end with the cigar-cutter. He noted with a smile how his hand had stopped shaking. That was good. Now all he had to do was work out how to bring all this crap to a satisfactory conclusion.

FOURTEEN

"Nice house," said Chaise, dropping his digital camera back into its case.

"Thanks," Alex, at the bar, poured himself a glass of orange juice. "Would you like some?"

Smiling, Chaise said he would and, accepting the drink, downed it with relish. Pure, freshly squeezed, it tasted delicious.

Alex gestured towards the camera. "I've always believed that photographs of Spanish houses never do them justice."

Smacking his lips, Chaise carefully placed the empty glass on the worktop. Both men stood in the enormous kitchen, with its clean lines and bespoke units. Very modern, classy, and expensive. "In what way?"

"Interiors always look cramped, lived in. I've seen photographs of unmade beds, kitchens with pots and pans in the sink, tables still covered with the remnants of meals." He shook his head. "It's almost as if they don't care."

"I think it's more a case that they want to show it as a family home. Lived in sums it up. That's important to the Spanish."

"Yeah, but most of these properties will go to Brits, won't they?"

"Well, nowadays it'll be Dutch, Belgians, or possibly Germans. Lots of Scandinavians too," Chaise said. "I doubt if glossy photographs will help. Everyone is finding it hard now, Mr Piers. Selling property is becoming difficult. There just isn't the call for properties as there was a year or so ago, not even for properties as luxurious as this."

"So, what are you saying, exactly? That I won't be able to sell it?"

"Oh, I think you will, but the market is always difficult to judge. At the price you're asking, however, I think enough people will be suitably interested to secure a sale."

Alex seemed happy with that. He drained his glass and scooped up Chaise's. At the double sink, he rinsed them through under the tap. "You been here long, Mr Chaise? In Spain, I mean."

"Not that long. A couple of years. My girlfriend is half Spanish, so it seemed the logical thing to do when we thought about moving away."

"I see." Alex turned around. "And you've always been an estate agent?"

"Not by profession. You tend to fall into things over here, Mr Piers. Accidentally."

"That's happened with you, has it – you accidentally became an estate agent?"

"Often, the thing most unlooked-for happens."

"What's that, a quote or something?"

Chaise shrugged. A tiny tingling began to irritate the back of his neck. These weren't just off-the-cuff remarks, this was more like questioning with a purpose. The man appeared slightly on edge, the way he'd followed Chaise so closely into every room, almost as if he were checking nothing inappropriate happened. Of course, this could be entirely natural, having a stranger in the house, but there was more to it than that. The tension was palpable, the man's anxiety apparent and difficult to disguise. Almost as if he were afraid that Ryan might stumble upon something. "Just the way it is. And you, Mr Piers, what do you do?"

"Retired."

Chaise raised an eyebrow but didn't pursue the subject. This man was nothing more than another customer. Chaise had no interest in him beyond that, regardless of his somewhat curious manner. "I see," he said with a smile, rubbing his hands together, and turning to go. "Well, we'll be in touch, Mr Piers. It shouldn't be long. I'll get the office to email you the sales details this afternoon and, if they're okay, we'll start marketing it."

Alex walked with him to the door. "That your car is it, Mr Chaise?"

Chaise frowned. "No. I've had to hire it. My car is ..." He pulled in a breath. "Okay, Mr Piers, you've seen the news reports, yes?"

Alex Piers stopped dead, his tongue pressed against his bottom lip, tiny beads of sweat breaking out across his brows.

Chaise smiled. "Don't worry, Mr Piers, I'm not in the habit of shooting everyone I meet." He cocked his head, holding Alex's eyes. "Only those who try to shoot me first." Then he turned and went, glad that he had cleared the air. At least, that was what he hoped.

Alex watched him drive away and allowed himself to relax a little. But then, as he went to move inside, it came. A sudden, piercing pain. Suddenly weak, he reached out a hand, pressing it against the door to stop himself from falling. The tightness increased in his chest and he battled to overcome the panic, control his breathing, and give himself time until it eased. He moved back to the kitchen, rummaged in the drawer to find the packet of tiny aspirin, crammed one into his mouth, and swallowed it down with water from the tap. Holding onto the edge of the sink, he waited and focused his thoughts on what had happened.

The man, Chaise, was cool, bloody cool. But perhaps that's what his profession demanded. Estate agents had to appear professional, smart, in-the-know. One thing wasn't right in all of this, however, and the thought brought the tension back to Alex's chest. How the hell could Chaise appear so normal so quickly? He'd just shot a man, killed him. Right up close, in-your-face close. Alex couldn't work it out, shook his head, dragged his hand over his face to wipe away the sweat, pulled out his mobile, and called Shaun. He'd know the answers, help clear away the panic. Alex pressed the phone against his ear, muttering, "Come on, come on."

"Hello?"

"Shaun? Thank God. Listen, I think we might have a problem."

A long silence followed by Shaun's voice, low but thick with tension. "I agree with you, Alex, I think we have."

A pause during which Alex's confusion increased. "What the hell do you mean?"

"I think you need to get around here, as quick as you can. And for God's sake, don't bring your half of the stuff."

The phone went dead, and Alex stood, his heartbeat racing, the tightness in his chest growing worse. He needed to sit down, take things easy. Too much had happened too quickly. Diane taking Amy, the drugs and now Chaise. The previous night the pains had come, but he'd put it all down to nervous indigestion. Now, he wasn't so sure, and all sorts of nightmare scenarios raced around in his head. He went into his bedroom and stood in front of the mirror. He took off his shirt and studied his torso. A bit of excess weight under the armpits, the phenomena that was now called 'man breasts', the spare tire which he kept promising himself he would work off, but nothing out of the ordinary, nothing that would lead him to conclude that there was a problem. He checked his armpits. No swelling, no lumps. Nevertheless, he decided there and then that as soon as he had finished meeting Shaun, he would have to seriously consider visiting his doctor.

FIFTEEN

Some hours previously, Jose Luis had met with two men in grey suits, men he knew and had had dealings with before. They were young men, smart, seemingly intelligent. The first, Nigel, who had been educated at public schools, made the most of this fact by always wearing his old school tie. The other man, Michael, was bigger, much more strongly built. He'd served in the Coldstream Guards, had played rugby professionally for a while. Both men oozed charm and both men were ruthless when it came to doing business. Both men were killers.

"This is high-quality stuff you have here, Jose Luis. I think we can do a nice little deal." Nigel sat back, reaching inside his pocket for his cigarettes, which he kept in a silver case. Delicate fingers extracted a cigarette and he looked at it for a long time, rolling it between his fingers. "But ..." He smiled, then nodded towards Michael.

Michael Brannigan sat forward. They were in a nightclub, the lights dimmed. Empty. Quiet and oppressive. A sharp contrast to how it would be later that evening when swarms of invading customers danced to the thumping music until the small hours. Right now, its eerie atmosphere teemed with the ghosts of past revellers lurking in shadowy corners, the only sound the quiet hum of a vacuum cleaner from somewhere in the distance. "Where did you get this stuff, Jose?"

Jose Luis spread his hands, "You know I can't tell you that."

"Still," Michael smiled, "you must have got it from somewhere. This is not the usual sort of stuff you hawk around. This is high grade, top-quality shit, Jose. I'm curious."

"If I told you," Jose made a dramatic gesture of dragging his index finger across his throat. "I'm sorry, Señor Brannigan. You understand."

Michael and Nigel exchanged looks. "Okay. How much have you got?"

"Half a kilo."

"Half a kilo ..." Nigel lit his cigarette, replacing the silver case with a small pocket calculator. "All righty," he stabbed at the little keypad. "Is half a kilo all you can get hold of, Jose Luis?"

"I think so, yes."

Nigel nodded, pulled on the cigarette loudly, and blew out a long stream of smoke. "In that case, we'll say twenty-five grand."

Jose nearly fell off his chair, "Twenty-five?" He rapidly shook his head, "No. No, that's not enough. This stuff is worth five times that, and you know it."

Nigel shrugged and slipped the calculator back into his pocket. "That's the offer, Jose Luis. Take it or leave it. At the end of the day, this is a piddling amount, something we would probably buy for our own, personal use. It's not something we can put out on the street – there's not enough of it. Unless, of course, there is more ..."

Jose shrugged and reached out to take the little polythene bag of white powder that lay on the table. As he did so, Michael's hand struck out as fast as a snake and clamped Jose's hand to the tabletop. The little Spaniard squealed, and Michael leaned forward, snarling. "You take it, Jose. It's the best offer you'll get this side of hell."

"Don't be so dramatic, Michael" laughed Nigel, studying the end of his cigarette. "You see, Jose. You must have got this stuff from someone pretty big. Dangerous even. Who are they, Lithuanians, Moroccans? Whoever they are, we'd like to do some business with them, ensure a regular supply." He leaned back, crossing one arm across his chest. An oily smile spread across his face. "So, let's try again. Who are they?"

Jose tried to pull away, but Michael's grip was too strong. The Spaniard looked around, his eyes wide with terror.

"I can't tell you that."

"Just a name, Jose. That's all. Then we can by-pass the middleman, deal direct." Nigel smiled and nudged Michael with his knee.

Jose looked on with growing disbelief as Michael produced an evil looking flick knife. He pressed the catch and the blade appeared with a loud snap, and he waved it slowly in front of Jose Luis's face. He echoed his friend's words, "Just a name, Jose. That's all."

"You bastards," Jose said through gritted teeth. "I've always been fair with you, always brought you good stuff. What the hell is this?"

"Times are hard, Luis," said Nigel, drawing on the last of his cigarette. "We're all feeling the pinch, so we have to …" He spread out his arms, "broaden our horizons. Diversify. If we can get a regular supply of this stuff, we'd be very interested. Very interested indeed. But," his smile broadened, "we'd like to deal direct."

"So," said Michael, the knife coming closer until the blade rested against Jose's cheek. "The name, Jose, or even your dear old mama won't recognize you."

Less than ten seconds later, Jose told them everything they wanted to know.

. . .

Alex stood in Shaun's tiny apartment, watching his old friend pace up and down, sweating profusely, hands gesticulating this way and that as he ranted, "Thank God he got in touch with me to warn me. The bugger told them, told them everything, told them who I was, where I live – everything! They'll be coming here, Alex. Today, tonight, early hours of the morning, I don't know when, but they'll come. They'll want the stuff, Alex. They'll want the stuff."

"All right, Shaun! Christ, just calm down."

"Calm down! How the fuck am I supposed to calm down? Do you know who these guys are, Alex? Have you any fucking idea at all?" Alex shook his head. "I knew I shouldn't have trusted that little shit. He's dropped me right in it – twenty-five fucking thousand they offered!"

"Well, that's just a joke."

"Yeah, big bloody ha-ha! Do you know what," he stopped pacing and swung around, his face livid, eyes brimming up, "it's all right for you, they don't know who you are! Me, they've got me. You can't use diplomacy with these people, can't plead or bargain. They want the stuff – they want to know where we got it and they won't stop exerting the pressure until we tell them." He crumpled into a chair and rocked forward, face in hands, fingers clawing at his skull as if he were trying to rip through the scalp. "You know what they'll do when they come here, eh? Do you? They'll force me to sell the stuff for even less! And if I don't sell, they'll fucking stripe me, Alex! They'll probably do that anyway."

"Look, let's just think about this." Alex struggled to keep himself detached from Shaun's panic, but inside he was crumbling. The pain in his chest wasn't going away, despite him taking two Alka-Seltzers. "Okay, I don't think they're going to do anything –" He held up his hand before Shaun could speak.

"Just hold on, for a minute. If they try to hurt you, they'll be cutting off their own noses. All we have to do is string them along a bit. They obviously want all the stuff, yeah? Well, we'll come to some sort of deal with them, but we'll do it slowly. We have to be careful not to tell them how we came by it and convince them that we might be able to get some more. That way, they'll ease off, hoping that we can give them a constant supply."

"And when we can't, Alex? What about that, eh?" Shaun wrung his hands, "When they realize we've strung them a line, they'll fucking find us, Alex, and slice us up!"

"No, they won't." Alex turned excited eyes towards his old friend. The idea had come to Alex in a flash. "Because we won't be here. We're going to take the money and the dope and run."

Shaun pressed himself back into his chair, completely deflated. "Jesus ... Alex." His voice sounded confused, shaken as if he couldn't comprehend what his friend had just said. "Run. Run where? How?"

Alex got down on his haunches, "This is the perfect time, Shaun. We take the money and get as much as we can for the stuff we offer them. Look, if it's worth well over three hundred thousand, we can accept, two-fifty, maybe even two hundred thousand. That's a hundred and twenty-five thousand each maybe. Enough for us to go somewhere else. Italy maybe, one of the Greek islands. Buy a bar, disappear."

Shaun was shaking his head, none of this sinking in. "But ... but what about Di? Amy?"

The words, the questions Alex had been preparing himself forever since Diane had walked out, having delivered her earth-shattering news. None of this had anything to do with the drugs. He knew his life was going to change no matter what happened. This, this was going to make everything so much easier. Not completely, of course. Nothing could do that. The impact of not having Amy in his life anymore would hit him hard, perhaps harder than anything he had ever had to deal with. Even now, little things reminded him of her, little tugs at his heartstrings, the sound of the river conjuring memories of when they went fishing, a motorbike roaring by bringing back the day when he hired a tiny scooter down on the coast and they went all the way along the promenade to Nerja. So many things, so many images. Would he ever be able to function again? "It's all right, Shaun. I can deal with that."

"Are you sure?"

Pressing his lips together, Alex felt the pinch of pain gripping him, tiny stabs in his arm, repeating themselves again and again. He held on, biting through it. "No," he managed, "no I'm not sure ... I don't have much choice anymore. Diane, she ... she's going back to the UK, taking Amy. It's all over. Everything. I've put the house on the market."

"My God, I never believed that would happen." Shaun looked towards the one window in the room, the one that looked out across the town of Torre del Mar. A comfortable apartment, nothing fancy. Simple but desirable, that's what the estate agents had said. It still was. "I could sell this place too, make a little on it." He grinned, turning to his friend. "More to put into our bar."

Alex pressed his hands down on Shaun's knees and stood up. He groaned a little, stomach yawning empty. A quite disturbing sensation, a need to be sick. He wiped the back of his hand across his forehead. The sweat was pouring out of him. He needed to sit, slow down. "Can I have some water, Shaun. An aspirin if you have one."

Without a word, Shaun went over to the tiny galley kitchen and opened the fridge. He poured out a tumbler of ice-cold water and handed it over, together with a paracetamol tablet. Alex waved it away and drank the water down in one go. He gasped, gave the glass back. "That's better. Look, I'm going. You need to get out of here, take what you need, then go and visit the estate agents. We'll meet up later, at The English Bar, then you can come back to mine and we'll try and work something out with your friend, Jose. He can act as our go-between until we reach a suitable selling price."

"You've got this all worked out, Alex. I'm impressed." Shaun picked up his mobile. "I'm going to call them now – the estate agents. See what they can do. No time like the present, eh?" He grinned, then turned away as his call was answered.

Alex rubbed his arm hard, trying to bring back the feeling. He knew what was happening, of course. He didn't need to be a hypochondriac to understand that this was the start of a heart attack. He'd been here before. All he had to do was try and remain calm, ease himself through the next half hour or so, get to the doctor's, have it checked out. He looked up sharply as Shaun snapped his mobile phone shut and said, "I'm anxious to get this sorted – quickly."

Shaun nodded, a frown creasing his face. "Are you feeling okay, you look like shit."

"Thanks!" Alex ran a hand through his hair. "I'm going to see my doctor. I had a scare, about a year ago now. It was like this."

"Scare? What sort of scare?"

"Heart. Nothing major, just a little twinge, you know. Nothing since. But you can't be too careful." He tried to laugh it off, but he knew he wasn't convincing anyone, least of all himself. "What did the agents say?"

"They're going to send someone round, but they still have most of the details on their computer, so they'll put it on today."

Alex breathed a sigh of relief. "Okay." He clapped Shaun on the shoulder. "Eight o'clock, don't be late."

Shaun gave him a smile and was already crossing into his bedroom. Alex let himself out.

Alex took the lift down to the main entrance, leaning against the lift wall, eyes closed, trying to breathe through the stabs of pain. This was more than "a little twinge" and he knew it. Maybe the doctor could give him something, or book him into hospital. That would be okay. Shaun could stay at his house in the meantime, oversee any problems that might arise with the sale. Whoever these people were who had spoken to Jose Luis, they couldn't link Shaun to Alex. Everything was going to be okay, all he had to do for now was take it easy, no need to rush. He closed his eyes, breathed lightly through his mouth, calming himself, listening to his palpating heart. Just a few more minutes, then he would be fine.

The door swished open and Alex moved out, having to step aside for a large man in a grey suit. He didn't look at him, keeping his head down, concentrating on his heartbeat, keeping it controlled, even. By the time he got outside, the pains had receded, and he slowly began to feel a little better.

When he got into his car and drove away, it was as if all of it had been nothing more than a very bad dream.

Sometimes, however, bad dreams can come true.

SIXTEEN

After serving a prison term for aggravated assault and robbery, on his release, Jimmy McNulty used the contacts he had made inside to find himself a nice little position working for Arthur Morgan. One of the great benefits of the British prison system is the opportunities it affords habitual criminals to develop their careers.

He got to know people, unscrupulous types who pointed him in the right direction. During his quiet moments, he'd pump iron, did a bit of boxing. He grew tougher, stronger. After his first stint inside ended, he managed to find a job on a building site, as a hod-carrier. He was only short but powerful. The men were impressed, liked him, would buy joints from him.

Dealing supplemented his income and provided him with new opportunities to explore. One of his co-workers was a part-time bouncer at a local nightclub. He took Jimmy along one night, and Jimmy proved extremely capable. Local toughs always underestimated him because of his size, but word soon got around. Jimmy McNulty became a byword for the term 'hard'. He gained respect, people he didn't know would nod in his direction, greet him like a friend. No one wanted to upset or disrespect Jimmy McNulty.

Now he was in Spain, the old life far away, the damp dark streets of Liverpool no more than a blurred image. Standing on Arthur's roof terrace, mind full of the past, he looked across the expanse of Lake Vinuela, deep blue in colour, surface barely rippling. The mountains formed a beautiful backdrop, lending an almost Alpine feel to the vista. It was as far away from Merseyside as you could imagine.

"Jimmy?"

He jumped at the sound of the voice and turned to find Morgan standing with drinks in hands, a curious twisted smile on his pale lips. Jimmy laughed, feeling a little self-conscious. "Sorry, Mr Morgan. I drifted off there."

Morgan nodded, handed over a drink, then shuffled over to one of the many sun-loungers surrounding the pool and lay down with a sigh.

Jimmy noted how Morgan's ample belly wobbled as he stretched himself out. He wished he had the time, the inclination to strip off and relax. The late afternoon sun was too intense for Jimmy, and he tugged at his collar to circulate some air around his sweating body.

"Go and sit down under the shade, Jimmy." Morgan pointed to where a brightly coloured parasol cast a large shadow over a cluster of tables and chairs. Grateful for the opportunity to be out of the sun's glare, Jimmy went over and sat down.

Morgan sipped a mouthful of his drink through an orange straw, taking his time, sighing with satisfaction.

From where he sat, Jimmy couldn't help but tap his foot. Impatient, he needed to get on with things, move it all along. Like before with the woman, Sarah What's-her-face. That was just the sort of thing he needed, to make him feel alive. Job satisfaction. He thought about it now as he waited, at what she was like before he beat her. Slim, smooth, those legs as brown as nutmeg. In another life, he could make a go of things with a woman like that, settle down, build a future. He closed his eyes and allowed himself to be consumed with the image of her, his erection growing as he dreamed of sliding between her thighs, to caress her young breasts, feel the heat of her skin on his lips as he gently—

"Jimmy! Are you listening to a single word I'm saying?"

Jimmy sat up, rubbing his face, forcing an embarrassed laugh, "Sorry, I-er-drifted off again."

"What the bloody hell is the matter with you?"

"Me? Oh, I'm just – you know, tired. Sorry."

Arthur Morgan frowned deeply, took another sip of his drink, swung his legs over the side of the lounger and sat up. He peered at Jimmy under heavy brows. "You're sure she wasn't lying?"

"Mr Morgan," Jimmy shook his head, a little hurt that his boss didn't fully accept his words, "I told you – she wasn't lying. I can guarantee it."

"All right. Listen, Jimmy. I've been given some information, about the car. Her car. It's clean. One hundred per cent. Not even any residue. That means, the stuff is somewhere else."

"The guy that shot Ricky, you think he might have it?"

Morgan nodded. "That seems to be the conclusion of everyone concerned. His car is being looked over as we speak."

"But he'll be our best bet, yeah? I mean, there's no one else, so it has to be him."

"Exactly." Morgan finished his drink and very carefully laid the glass back down on the small table. "You'll have to pay him a visit, Jimmy." He held up his hand. "But don't go on your own this time. This guy, I don't know ... one of our contacts in the Guardia thinks he's a little bit out of the ordinary."

Jimmy titled his head, frowning. "What does that mean?"

"The way he was after killing Ricky. There was nothing from him apparently. No reaction, no sweats, just like stone."

"So? Why should that be a cause for concern, Mr Morgan?"

"Isn't it obvious?" Jimmy shook his head. "A man like that, stone-cold, it means he's used to it, Jimmy. He's done it before."

Sitting back, Jimmy crossed his arms and thought about what Morgan said. It made sense if indeed the man was stone-cold. Jimmy had met men like that before. No conscience, no sense of consequence for anything they did. Jimmy sometimes had that sense, like with Sarah. He looked up, a sudden thought. "Mr Morgan, do you think I might be able to take her car back?"

"Whose car?"

"That Sarah What's-it. Do you think I could take the car back to her? I think I need to have another little chat, you know, just to see if she knows anything about this bloke. The stone-cold killer." He grinned, holding his breath, hoping that Morgan wouldn't work out his real motives.

Morgan shrugged. "If you think it will help." He stood and stretched, looking across Puente Don Manuel baking under the relentless sun. "I want this dope back, Jimmy. It's an intrusion into my life. Aggravation that I don't need. Get it back for me Jimmy and it's yours." He turned, his face a perfect mask of contained fury. "You hear what I said? The whole lot – over a quarter of a mil – it's yours if you do this cleanly and quickly."

"All of it, Mr Morgan? I thought it belonged to a customer?"

"It does, but I can get it replaced. It's the shame of it, Jimmy. Being shat on like that, it's not good for business."

Jimmy nodded. "Yeah, I understand that Mr Morgan. You can't be thought of as being soft."

"Exactly. I don't want anyone taking any liberties. Just get it back, whatever it takes."

"Whatever it takes, Mr Morgan?" Jimmy stood up, smoothing out the creases in his trousers. "Are you sure about that?"

Morgan nodded. "Yes, I am, Jim. Whatever it takes."

An intense thrill raced through Jimmy McNulty's loins and he smiled. "Then have no fear, Mr Morgan. It's as good as sorted."

SEVENTEEN

Alex pulled on his shirt, one eye on the doctor punching the keys of his computer. "I'm sending you for a check-up at the hospital, Alex. Run some tests, all that."

"That'll take days, weeks even."

"Not with your level of insurance. I doubt if it will be any longer than a day or two."

"Really?" The news made him feel much better. "I'm not in any imminent danger, then?"

Doctor Reece Nialls took off his spectacles and played with the arm whilst he measured Alex with a serious look. "Anything to do with the heart is dangerous, Alex. I want you to go home and rest. Do you understand? Wait for the call from the hospital and let's just hope that this is nothing more than ..." He shrugged. "Let's just wait and see." He stood up. "You did the right thing, coming in so quickly. Most men would have ignored it, struggled on. Taken a couple of aspirin."

"I'm going to do that anyway."

Nialls smiled. "Just rest, eh? You're obviously under a lot of strain." He stopped, waiting for something from Alex, an explanation, anything. But Alex merely returned the smile and adjusted his trouser belt. Nialls shook his head slightly and came around the desk, taking Alex gently by the arm. "Just try, yes?"

Alex opened the door. "I'll do my best," and he went out, knowing no matter how hard he tried, the stress and strain would refuse to go away.

Outside, in the private car park, he got in behind the wheel of his big Nissan and started up the engine. He sat there for a moment, mulling over the idea that had been formulating in his brain. Something that Shaun had said. The idea that they could perhaps find some more of the stuff, gather together a little more cash. Make that proposed move to Poros or Kos that little bit more comfortable. It was an idea worth pursuing, and Alex knew where he might find some answers.

Sarah Banbury.

There was a message on his mobile when he checked. It was from Diane. 'Pick up Lotty from the Reiners.' Alex exhaled loudly as he took the red Nissan out into the traffic and headed back towards his home. Lotty was their three-year-old fox-terrier who had gone to be trimmed by their neighbour, Jessica Reiner.

Lotty looked like a shorn sheep when he picked her up. Back inside their home, he, gave her some food before he took a quick shower. Afterwards, wrapped in a towelling robe, he settled down on the sofa, Lotty snuggled up beside him looking distinctly sorry for herself, and he trawled through the telephone directory.

He found the number without much difficulty. Dressing quickly in shorts and T-shirt, he left Lotty in the garden, where there was plenty of shade and lots of water and got back into the Nissan. He didn't know how to broach the subject of the drugs, but the first thing was to establish a rapport of some kind. He wasn't sure how easy any of that was going to be.

. . .

The policeman behind the desk scowled down at the release form, unwilling or unable to put pen to paper and sign it. Jimmy rapped his fingers on the desk with growing impatience. All the policeman did was stare at the fingers, waiting for them to stop. They stopped. Jimmy smiled. The policeman scowled.

"You are not relative?"

"No. I'm not a relative."

Shaking his head, the policeman straightened his back. "You have to be relative. Or have permission."

"I have permission."

The policeman cocked an eyebrow. Jimmy, smiling again, slid the notes across the desk and nodded. "Permission."

His feet crunched across the gravel as he slowly walked towards the porch doorway. Alex sighed, relishing the coolness afforded by the shade. He looked around. A beautiful house, far more luxurious than his own. This was serious money, not so much a villa as a mansion. He knocked on the door and waited.

The seconds ticked by and he tried again. After another wait, there was still nothing, not a hint that there might be someone at home. Reluctantly, he backed out into the driveway and stared towards the upper level, shielding his eyes from the glare with his hand.

A slight movement, a shadow, flitted across one of the windows. Was there someone, or a trick of the light perhaps? Cupping both hands around his mouth he shouted, "Sarah? Sarah, I need to speak to you for a moment."

Again, no response. Allowing his shoulders to slump, he turned to go but as he did so, he heard the unmistakable sound of a sliding door. He swung round and there, on the balcony, stood Sarah Banbury.

"What do you want?"

He held up his hand but from this distance, he couldn't make out her features

"I asked you what you want. You can either tell me or bugger off. Or maybe I'll just ring the police."

"No, please don't do that." He tried not to sound too desperate, hadn't quite managed it. "I'm sorry for calling round like this, but I just need a few words. It won't take long."

"Who are you?"

"My name is Alex. Alex Piers."

"Alex ..." She leaned against the balcony railing. "You're Diane's husband, aren't you?"

The relief hit him like a wave. "Yes! Yes, I am. Sorry, I didn't realize you knew my wife."

She shrugged, "I know her a little. We've met a few times." She ran a hand through her hair, "What are you doing here?"

He shrugged, shook his head, grinned like an idiot. Felt like an idiot. Was an idiot. "I was just, er, passing. Heard about your ... you know. Just came to see if you were okay."

She gazed at him, her mouth open. Then slowly the smile crept across her face. Not a wide smile, but a warm, genuine smile. Even from this distance, Alex felt something buzz through him. That same sensation he'd had when her photograph had come up on the television screen. Sensual, raw. Exciting.

"God, Alex that is so nice of you! Hang on." She disappeared back into her room.

After a few moments, the front door opened and there she stood, gesturing for him to step inside. But then saw her face, the swelling, the ugliness of the eyes, the purple, red and black wound, laced with streaks of yellow. "Bloody hell," he breathed, barely able to form the words.

He instantly regretted it, as her face blushed bright red and her hand flew up to the left side of her face to mask the damage. "I'm a bit of a sight, I know," she mumbled. "Listen, the last guy who called scared the hell out of me so I'm a bit … You are Alex Piers, are you?"

He rummaged inside his pockets and pulled out his passport, which he always had with him. She squinted at the photograph and smiled. "Sorry to be so cautious," she said.

"No, no, please, I understand." He took back the passport and for the briefest of moments their fingers touched. Impulsively, he reached out to her. She flinched and pulled away, startled. This was all a mistake to impose upon her like this, he thought, and he should simply turn around and go. "I just wanted to make sure … I'll go."

He turned to go, but she stopped him with a single, "No," and he turned to see her stepping aside, beckoning for him to enter. Then suddenly she was crying. Deep, powerful sobs, juddering through her tiny body and she fell against his chest. He hesitated, not sure what to do before he slowly wrapped his arms around her and held her, chin resting on the top of her head, waiting for the tidal wave of despair to subside.

He had to wait quite a long time.

Sometime later, as she sat on the couch, legs drawn up beneath her, he made her a gin and tonic, which she drank down almost in one. Alex smiled, fixed another one, and poured himself just a tonic. She took her time with this one. "Sorry, Alex, for being so emotional. I've had a shock. You won't tell Diane?"

He laughed at that. Tell Diane? What the bloody hell has any of this to do with Diane? He sat back, sipping at his drink, struggling to keep his eyes from her legs. He didn't think he'd seen legs so brown. The way the muscles strained against the flesh, that sheen, brimming with health, fitness.

"… it's not only that, it's the, you know …" She smiled, took a sip, then put her head back. "You do understand, don't you?"

Did he? He didn't have a clue about anything she'd said so far. He grinned, nevertheless. "Yes. Yes, of course."

"Thanks." She closed her eyes.

With her head back like this, the undamaged part of her face in profile towards him, he could see how lovely she was. Elfin, childlike features. Small boned, short stubby nose, lovely full lips, cheekbones that could cut through plate steel. Then he saw her neck, the bruising. "What a bastard he was," he said quietly.

"Who?" She looked at him, frowning and jabbed a finger towards the bruising. The rawness of her damaged left side made him wince. "The guy that did this – he's dead. Who gives a fuck?"

"Yeah, well …"

"And this …" She drew her fingertip along her throat, skimming the surface of the painful-looking swelling. "The other guy did this."

Her face went white and she stood up, all at once flustered, unsure, her head turning this way and that. Alex watched the transformation as she became like a tiny animal caught in the headlights. Terrified. "Sarah?"

She stopped, gaping down at him. "I'm fine," she blurted, a little too loudly. "Honestly, I'm fine. He's gone, that's all that matters."

But there was something, Alex knew it. That mention of "the other guy", the way she'd reacted, almost as if the mere memory of him was enough to send her into apoplexy. But what did she mean? Had there been two attackers, had this Ricky Treach character an accomplice? Alex felt his gut twist at the thought. "Sarah, I, er, just need to—"

She came forward, touching his arm. "Alex. I'm really tired, you know. Thanks for dropping by, it was kind. And for, you know …" She shrugged, her cheeks colouring again.

Alex reached out to touch her bar arm. The flesh was warm, smooth as satin. The T-shirt was skimpy, cut off at the midriff. Her stomach was flat, bronzed.

"Perhaps I could call again?" He looked up and gazed into her one undamaged eye.

"I must look a mess."

Before he knew it, it just came out, "You look gorgeous."

A mutual gasp, an awkward silence. Both of them, standing there, each touching the other's arm. She broke off first, more colour in her cheeks. Alex coughed, turned, and went towards the front door. She followed, bare feet padding across the cold terracotta tiles. "Thanks again," she said, pulling the door open. A blast of heat hit them. Thick, muggy. It was going to be an uncomfortable night. Another slight touch of his arm. "Alex, you won't say anything to anyone, will you?" Alex frowned. "To Frank, I mean." Alex shook his head.

"My husband. He doesn't know anything about, you know, what happened. He will in time, of course." She brushed the back of her hand against her damaged cheek. "But he doesn't know the details – nothing about the night that guy and I had together."

"Of course not. Besides, I don't know your husband very well. I think I've only met him once."

"No, but Diane does and if she knew …" She let her voice float away, no need to embroider any further.

"Don't worry, I won't say a word." He crossed to his car and turned to wave to her, but she had already closed the door. A little disappointed, he swung the big four-by-four out of the driveway.

A few meters down the track, he pulled over and put his face in his hands. Christ, what a bloody shambles that was. He hadn't achieved anything that he had wanted to and was no closer to discovering if there was any more dope lying around. One thing he had learned, however, one thing that made everything a lot more complicated, and potentially a whole lot more dangerous. There was "another guy." He'd have to tell Shaun as soon as he got back.

Putting the Nissan into gear, he set off down the twisting track, doing his utmost to keep his concerns well battened down.

The Audi purred as it effortlessly ate up the kilometres towards Sarah Banbury's hill-top villa. It was one of those cars that you looked forward to driving, to experience the sheer joy of being ensconced in its soft embrace, to feel the latent power of the engine, to let the ambience seep into every pore. This was not driving; it was seduction and Jimmy felt a little pang of regret as he swung the car into Sarah's driveway. That big Nissan he'd passed. Now that was not a car to love. It was a machine, a big practical machine, built to do its job. This Audi, this was luxury. Pure and simple.

When he stepped out, he could see that the front door stood slightly ajar. Suddenly all feelings about cars, seductive or otherwise, were swept away, and he pulled out the automatic pistol from its holster and crept forward, careful not to make any noise on the crunchy gravel.

EIGHTEEN

I t was good that Alex Piers had woken her. She'd never been able to get into the habit of siestas and always felt a twinge of guilt if she did manage an hour or two in the afternoon. Now, fully awake and with Alex gone, she took out the bag of rubbish that had been lying around the kitchen for days, dropped it in the big bin next to the entrance to the drive and strolled round to the swimming pool at the back of the house.

Sighing deeply, she pulled off her T-shirt, wincing a little as the material glanced over her cheek, and threw it down. She titled her head backwards and luxuriated in the warmth of the sun on her naked body. Two days, two days and Frank would be back and then she'd have to tell him something. He'd find out, of course. Everyone would tell him. There might even be some form of delegation waiting for him at the airport as he flew in. Eager beavers delighting in revealing yet another piece of juicy gossip.

The sticking point was the pick-up in the bar. Why had she allowed herself to be drawn in like that? Because he was so good-looking, because he looked so sexy in that open shirt, and his long hair hanging down around his shoulders, like a girl?

Was that what it was because he was like a girl? She'd had girls before now, enjoyed it, longed for it to happen again. The touch of their skin, the smell of their sex as she ran her tongue over their swollen flesh…

No, that wasn't it. She just wanted a good screw, and man could he screw! But now he was dead. How to explain all of that and still keep Frank sweet? She'd have to conjure up some fairly erotic lines to feed him, get him all hard and excited. That way he'd accept anything, pay for the finest plastic surgeons on the coast to fix her cheek, get her back to how she was. Bastard, to have hit her like that.

The hand came and closed itself around her mouth, so slowly that she didn't even notice before it was too late.

Then the press of his body against her back as she tried to wriggle free, the mouth close against her ear, "Don't scream." So softly. Like a lover. The solid thrust of hard metal in the small of her back made her go limp. Gently he pulled the hand away and turned her around to face him.

She saw him. The hard features. The smile. Then the gun. Suddenly she was pitching into blackness, a yawning chasm swallowing her up, no cares now, no worries. No resistance. Just blackness.

Coming out of the office, Chaise readjusted his sunglasses and sauntered over to a nearby bar, ordered some iced water, and slowly drank it down.

He knew the man across the street was watching. When he first noticed the Seat Leon in the rear-view mirror, he paid it no heed. Why should he, that sort of car was ten-a-penny all across Spain? But that old, nagging feeling, an itch nibbling away at the nape of his neck, simply wouldn't go away. When he pulled in and waited, the car rolled up about a hundred meters behind, and when he drove off again, it was there. No doubting now. He was being followed.

The big question, of course, was who the man was. The various options ran through his mind: police, the gangsters who owned the drugs, TV or newspaper reporter ... or someone far, far worse.

The man didn't appear to be Spanish, not from this distance. He stood leaning against his car, arms folded, pale-faced, slightly uncomfortable looking in the heat as if he had only just got off the plane from Stanstead. Chaise stared straight back at the stranger, who didn't flinch. Definitely not Spanish. Reaching inside his trouser pocket, Chaise pulled out his wallet, found the card and pressed the number into his mobile. It rang three times before the little voice answered, "Hello, Leonard Phelps."

"Hello, Mr Phelps. How are you?"

Chaise could feel the man's expression turn to total anguish. "Mr Chaise, is that you?"

"The very same. Mr Phelps, I need your advice."

"Ah," the sound of shuffling papers, a short cough. Giving himself time to recover from the shock. "I, er, can't really give legal advice, Mr Chaise. I thought I, er, made that clear when we—"

"No, it's not that sort of advice. Mr Phelps, you haven't put a tail on me by any chance?"

A moment of total silence during which Chaise imagined Phelps sitting there, the sweat breaking out, chewing his lip, wondering what the hell to say. "Goodness me, Mr Chaise, why on earth would I—"

"Well, maybe not you exactly. Our good friends in London, perhaps."

"Our good friends ...? Mr Chaise, I really haven't got a single idea what you're talking about."

"No? Then it would be perfectly all right for me to just go

over there, talk to him? He's standing across the street, Mr Phelps."

"I don't …"

"No, of course you don't. But listen, Mr Phelps, if things get nasty, you'll let London know, won't you? That I did try and ask you to help … but you refused."

Suddenly, Phelps's voice changed. It was serious now and sounded more tense. Chaise had hit the right nerve, just as he thought he would. "Mr Chaise, please. All right, listen. Yes, yes, the man is working for us. But, please, don't do anything hasty. Just … just let me talk to him, would you?"

Smiling, Chaise kept the mobile to his ear whilst he beckoned the man with his other hand. The man, putting on a passable display of feigning ignorance, shrugged his shoulders dramatically and looked away. "He hasn't reacted, Mr Phelps. Just a minute whilst I grab his attention." Before Phelps could say anything, Chaise crossed the road and strode towards the man with exaggerated confidence.

At first, it looked as though the man would remain standing there and allow Chaise to confront him. However, just as Chaise reached the curb, the man spun around and moved away at a brisk pace.

Chaise accelerated, studying his quarry as he closed in. Dressed in a thin blue short-sleeved shirt and beige chinos, the man could blend perfectly into any crowd. If it wasn't for the well-muscled shoulders, the tapered waist, and the way he moved cat-like along the pavement, he could pass for anyone. Which was how it always was. Nondescript, Mr Average.

Catching up to him, Chaise tapped him on the shoulder.

It happened fast. Faster than Chaise expected. A thrust of a hand, palm outwards. Chaise could feel the air driven forward by the force of the blow, which he expertly slipped and struck back. A flicker of surprise crossed the man's face just before Chaise's elbow cracked across the jaw. More from shock than anything else, he fell against a shop window, hitting it with a low thud. Fortunately, it didn't give way. It had not been a powerful blow but even so, the man appeared a little dazed. He gathered himself to launch another assault before Chaise raised the mobile and waggled it. "Hold on, champ, he wants to talk to you."

A few passers-by gave them a wide berth, one or two shop assistants and bar holders peered out from dark doorways. No one did anything, no one dared. Besides, it had lasted, what, five seconds. Bang, bang, just like that. Blink and you would have missed it.

A moment now of inner debate followed by a sigh. The man's eyes never left Chaise's as he took the mobile and breathed, "Yes?"

Chaise watched. The man listened. Less than a minute later he returned the phone to Chaise who spoke into it. "Well, Mr Phelps?"

"He'll talk to you."

"Thank you, Mr Phelps." Smiling, he dropped the phone into his pocket, raised an eyebrow, and pointed to the nearest bar.

The other man didn't smile but followed Chaise inside.

Without asking, Chaise ordered coffee and they both sat in silence until the drinks arrived. The man stared at the little cup for a long time before he finally reached over and took a tentative sip. All the while Chaise studied him, gauging him. Wiry, tough-looking, the man appeared to be in his mid-thirties, possibly ex-forces, more than likely SAS. There was a blackened smudge near to his right eye, which Ryan guessed might have been a gunshot wound, a near miss. Close quarter struggle. The rest of him, in his casual wear, seemed unscathed. Apart, that is, from the slight reddening across his jaw. He hadn't touched it, no doubt embarrassed at having been so easily duped.

"Not many people can do that," he said unexpectedly, unblinking. As if to accentuate the point, he ran the back of his hand across the slight bruise.

"Not many people try and hit me."

The man's smile was thin, not a hint of humour.

"I'd like to know," said Chaise, turning his cup around between his hands, "who sent you."

"Phelps said I was to tell you everything, so I will. You don't need to question me."

"Very well," Chaise drained his coffee. "So, tell me."

"London. They don't like the fact that you've got yourself mixed up in something. You were supposed to lie low, become invisible. Instead, you kill someone. They're angry."

"Angry?" Chaise scoffed. "So, they send you to do what, check up on me? Make sure I'm not breaking the rules…or slap my wrist for being a naughty boy?"

"I said I'd tell you, so do me a favour. Shut up and listen."

Chaise spread out his hands, palms up. "I'm all ears."

"They want this sorted out, quickly and cleanly. They don't want to see your face on the TV screens or in the newspapers. They sent me to check that this was going to be the case, to impress upon you their concerns. What exactly were you doing with that character in your car?"

"Nothing sinister. I picked him up. He was a hitch-hiker."

"And then he pulls a gun on you … to do what, exactly?"

Chaise let out a long, patient sigh. "To hijack the car, of course."

"So, you shot him. Just like that?"

"No, not *just like that*. We struggled, the gun went off, he died."

"And the police believe you, do they?"

"Don't you?"

The man looked down at his coffee to give himself time to consider his response. "Nice coffee," he said and finished it.

104

Folding his arms, Chaise sat back and waited.

"London told me to convey upon you their anxiety concerning this. Some don't believe your story and, quite frankly, I can't blame them."

"Do you think I give a flying fuck what any of you believe?" Chaise leaned forward. "If they have any anxieties they can bloody well come and talk to me about it themselves, not send their messenger boy to do their dirty for them."

The man raised an eyebrow. "Hey, just because you caught me once doesn't mean you can do it again."

Chaise shook his head, "Jesus, what are you, a boy scout?"

"No." The man pushed away his coffee cup and placed his hands, palm down on the tabletop as if bracing himself. His eyes bored straight into Chaise like steel nails. "I'm Major Howard Embleton, Special Air Service, seconded to M.I.6 for the prime purpose of making sure you're not shitting in your own nest, Commander. Our nest. Anything you do that will bring you to the attention of Her Majesty's enemies is something we would prefer not to happen. Putting it simply, you've been fucking stupid. You should have let him take the car."

Yes, he should. Chaise could see the sense of that. However, thinking logically is not always easy when you have a 9-millimetre automatic pointed straight at you.

"So," continued Major Embleton, "this is how it works. I'll be shadowing you, every step of the way until this whole sorry business is put to bed. If you do anything untoward, or even slightly out of the ordinary, my orders are simple."

Chaise tensed as he waited, every nerve jangling, every ounce of his self-control focused in on not reaching over and ripping the smarmy bastard's head right off. "I'm all ears, Major."

"As I said, you won't be able to do it again."

"No, maybe not. Not in the same way, but I'll still bounce you down the fucking street if I have to."

The Major shook his head, "No you won't, Commander Chaise. Because if you so much as spit in my direction, I will kill you." He stood up and looked around the little cafe. "Nice place, nice country. You've got a nice life here. Nice ... girlfriend."

That was it, the final straw. Ryan had had enough, and he pushed back his chair with a violent shove. It went hurtling backwards and some of the old men in the corner looked up from their newspapers and their games of dominoes. Chaise stood still, eyes blazing, his breathing coming in sharp gasps. "I don't take kindly to threats, Major, even the veiled kind. Certainly not the kick-in-the-balls kind. Tell London I don't need a nursemaid, and I don't need to be spoken to like this."

"Then get it sorted as I said. You cooperate with the police and get the investigation closed. Quickly and cleanly, without fuss."

"That's what I've been trying to do,"

"Then try harder."

Chaise watched Embleton stroll out of the cafe, pause at the doorway to prepare himself for the heat, and then he was gone.

He'd won the round. He'd touched the nerve and Chaise had reacted, just as the Major knew he would. Just as London had told him he would. Throwing the chair back, jumping to his feet, ready to go the full twelve rounds. Stupid, *bloody stupid* to walk straight into it like that, eyes wide open and brain completely out of control. What he had to do was ensure that nothing else went wrong. That would mean getting himself in gear, returning to a world he had hoped was long dead.

Ignoring the curious gazes of the customers, he put his eyes straight ahead and walked outside to his car.

NINETEEN

The rain had finally stopped when Mr and Mrs Owen stepped down from the aeroplane at Malaga International. Jim Owen breathed in the air and liked it. It smelled fresh and clean. Susan, however, merely grimaced. She'd left rain in Norwich and had hoped for two weeks of uninterrupted sun. Now, she wasn't so sure.

After they picked up the luggage and made their way out of the terminal, they took the voucher to the appropriate car hire firm and started their journey. The owner of the little house where they were staying had very kindly provided them with idiot-proof directions on how to get to their holiday let.

Just after ten o'clock, they drove into the village of Riogordo. The local band was practising, the wail of the trumpets drifting down from somewhere way up on the other side of the village. It made Owen imagine they were in New Mexico again, where they'd honey-mooned all those years before. Susan held onto his arm as they went up to the front door. The neighbour, who sat outside his house on a fragile-looking wicker chair, nodded to them. Owen gave a brief wave, put the key in the door and stepped inside their rented holiday home.

"This is going to be lovely," Susan said, casting an appreciative eye over the decor.

Owen smiled, thankful that his wife's mood had brightened since their arrival. He had to agree with her sentiments – it really was going to be lovely.

A similar mood could not be felt by Alex Piers at that moment as he sat in the Englishman's Bar, tapping his foot nervously on the rail, leaning forward across the counter, turning his half-empty beer-glass around and around. For the umpteenth time, he checked his wristwatch. The hands had barely moved at all. Shaun was almost two hours late and his mobile was showing unavailable. He dared not leave a voice message to avoid unwanted interest from someone undesirable. So, here he was waiting, twirling his glass, breathing hard. He knew he couldn't do it for much longer. Another check of his watch made up his mind for him. He said his farewells to the barman and went out into the close, muggy night.

Despite it being warm enough for shirt-sleeve order, a cold chill ran through his veins. This was so unlike Shaun, not to even phone. Alex didn't want to dwell on any of the possibilities but obviously, something had happened. Something bad. Worried, dejected, he crossed to his car and got in.

The drive home was uneventful. He pulled his car into the drive, hoping against hope that Shaun might already be there. When the security lights didn't go on, his anxiety set in, stomach tightening. If Shaun was there, waiting for him, why switch off the lights? Of course, it could be a power cut. There were plenty of those, often accompanied by the water being turned off. His was one of the few houses in the country that had mains water. Through the window, he scanned the mountainside. A myriad amount of lights twinkled across the blackened backdrop, like stars in the sky. This was no power cut.

The knot in his gut tightened as he got out. No lights and Lotty wasn't barking either. She was a good guard dog, despite being as daft as a brush, but her bark made her sound ferocious. She could, of course, still be in shock after her trim, or Shaun could be sitting there, tickling her tummy.

Always looking for reasons.

Instead of slamming the door shut, Alex pressed his back against it until it clicked into place. Taking his time, careful not to crunch the gravel, he moved over to the front door.

What he saw turned him ice-cold with fear.

The front door was open, every light in the house off.

He stood listening. The house, as silent as a tomb, the interior cold, the atmosphere changed, the homeliness that always greeted him despite the deteriorating relationship with his wife absent. If Shaun was inside, how come he was sitting in the dark? And why wasn't Lotty bounding down the hallway towards him?

Holding his breath, Alex knew something was wrong, very wrong.

He groped for the light switch on the inside wall next to the door and pressed it on. The lights blazed. No power cut thought Alex.

From the door, he peered through the inner porch and the open room beyond. Everything was as he had left it. He scanned furniture, ornaments, bookshelves, hi-fi system, television, none of them touched. If someone had broken in, surely there would be some sign, some hint of them walking through his home? Had he, perhaps, left the door open himself? He hadn't been in the best of spirits when he had gone out earlier to visit Sarah. Possibly, with his thoughts in disarray over Shaun, the drugs, his wife, Amy, he had simply left without closing the door?

Relaxing a little, he walked into the kitchen, trying to remember the moment he'd left the house. His head was so full of stress and worry, he simply hadn't been concentrating. Spain did that to you sometimes. Crime was rare, even big houses like his were hardly ever 'visited' by thieves of any kind. Much to the despair of the insurance companies, he'd known people leave their front doors wide open for weeks and not suffer a burglary.

Then he saw it and everything he had ever believed in, ever wished and hoped for, was blown out of the water within that single blink of an eye.

Lotty, his dog, or what was left of her, lay pegged out upon the central worktop isle. Her stomach had been sliced open, from the breastbone down to her tail, the ribs pulled apart and the entrails draped over her sides to hang down over the table-top edges. Her eyes stared sightlessly to the ceiling, but he could see the terror that still burned there. His legs gave way as the pain shot through his chest, clamping his lungs tight shut, and he fell, the darkness engulfing him.

TWENTY

Someone was smoking at the bar, so Chaise went outside. Fortunately, it was very warm, and he found himself a quiet table and sat down with his beer. He'd sent a text to Linny. She had decided to go back into work, taking a night shift to make up for lost time. Chaise knew that his revelations had hit her hard and, in many ways, she was running away, trying to escape from it all. He couldn't blame her; knowing your partner was a hardened killer was a difficult pill to swallow.

He stretched out his legs and let himself relax, the tension slipping out of his muscles. He suddenly realized how tired he was. An early night was called for. He glanced at his watch. Just gone ten. He lifted his glass and was about to finish his drink when Alvaro came over and sat down opposite him.

Alvaro rarely spoke. No one seemed to know very much about him, what he did, how he spent his days, but he was always smiling. A buoyant and lively individual, with an eye for the girls. He was well into his sixties.

He leaned his gnarled, deeply etched face towards Chaise and breathed beer fumes over him. "That car you asked about, Señor Ryan. You have found it?"

Chaise shook his head. "Not yet. You know who owns it?"
Alvaro shrugged, jutting out his bottom lip. "I may do. Then, I
may not."

Chaise sighed and reached inside his pocket. He slid a ten
euro note across the table. Alvaro and smiled and gave a little
giggle, "Señor Ryan…this is important?"

"It might be."

"I know what happened." He looked around. "Everyone
knows what happened, Señor Ryan. You think this car will help
you?"

"Help me do what?"

"With the police – their investigations. They are
investigating you, no?"

"That's right." Chaise drained his glass and stood up.
"They're not investigating me." He reached out and took back
the banknote.

Alvaro's face suddenly drained of colour and he made a grab
for the money. "Please, Señor Ryan! I'll tell you."

Chaise continued to hold on to the note, between both his
hands, holding it up as if it were a banner. "I'm listening."

"There is only one man who drives such a red car as the one
you have described. His name is Alex Piers and he lives—"

Chaise held up his hand, his throat suddenly tight and he
would need another drink. He took Alvaro's glass and drank it
down. The Spaniard watched him, frowning deeply. Chaise
shook his head. "Alex Piers? Are you sure?"

"Certain. Er … Señor Ryan, my drink?"

Chaise looked at the glass as if for the first time and gave a
little laugh. He placed it gently on the tabletop with the
banknote inside it. Shaking his head, he turned to go.

"Señor Ryan – you will need his address, no?"

"Right once again, Alvaro." He pulled out his car keys,
deciding there and then that he would call on Alex without any
delay. "No. I won't need his address."

. . .

Chaise got out of the car and stepped into the darkened forecourt, peering towards the huge four-by-four standing in the gloom like some prehistoric beast. He moved to it and ran his hand over the bonnet. Still warm. The house beyond was mostly in darkness, except for a single light burning at the back. Chaise went to the front door and rang the bell. He stepped back, waiting, and checked his watch. Twenty-five minutes past ten. Not so late. He sighed, rang the bell again.

Nothing but silence came back at him.

Stepping across to the nearest window, Chaise cupped his hands around his face to block the reflection and looked inside. It was too dark to make out anything other than a soft glow in the back. Perhaps Alex was in the kitchen, preparing something to eat. Chaise banged on the window with the flat of his hand, shouting, "Alex!"

With no answer forthcoming, Chaise decided to go around the rear of the villa. The side gate was locked. The walled enclosure was high. Swearing, he retreated a few steps, then launched himself forwards, pulling himself up onto the top with the momentum of his charge. He paused to glance around before he dropped over the other side. He waited, straining to listen, body coiled, ready to react. If Alex came out of the door now, Chaise would have some explaining to do. But then, so would Alex. The biggest question being, why hadn't he come forward and told the police he had given Ricky Treach a lift?

With still no sign of life, he moved on. The light from the kitchen illuminated a large portion of the rear garden, making it easy for Chaise to continue without stumbling over the assorted tools, bits of hose and other paraphernalia that were strewn everywhere. Reaching the back door, he rattled the handle and cursed. It was locked. He looked through the window.

It took him a moment for his eyes to adjust. When they had, he almost cried out with shock.

Sarah blinked open her eyes and found herself on her back, staring up at the ceiling. For a few seconds, she struggled to remember what had happened. She'd been in the garden, taking in the air. Someone had come up behind her, someone very quiet. They'd put a gun into her back. She knew it was a gun. Her husband owned a gun. She'd held it, touched it. Dull, heavy, beautiful in a perverse sort of way. Fascinating how something so small could end a life with such ease. When it pressed against her skin, the coldness so sharp it took her breath away, she knew in that instant that death had come.

So, was this death? Or the aftermath?

The more she stared at the ceiling, everything came into focus and she realised what had happened. The gun had jammed into her back and she'd fainted. And now she was lying on her back, in her lounge, looking at the ceiling, but alive.

She rolled over and her heart jumped into her throat. Death would be more preferable to what was crouched beside her.

"Hello, Sarah," he said.

She couldn't scream. Nothing more than a whimper trickled out of her mouth. If she hadn't been lying down, she would have collapsed again. It was him, the monster, back in her life and for what this time? She didn't know, and she didn't care, fear the only emotion she felt now. The hurt he'd inflicted, not merely the pressing of his thumb into her eye, but his words. They'd touched her in a way nothing else had ever done, like poison. Their memory brought a renewed surge of terror and she drew her knees to her chest, making herself small, she rolled over onto her side and wept.

"I'm not here to hurt you," he said. Softer. More gentle.

His hand caressed her hair. The overwhelming sense of dread

and loathing proved too great and, wailing loudly, she kicked out in a pitiful attempt to defend herself from a man who, quite obviously, could do anything he wished. What was he doing here, what did he want? She'd told him everything, hadn't lied, she hadn't dared lie. She believed him when he had said he would break her legs, slice her up. All of that and more. What did he want with her now? She wanted to ask him, to put into words her fears, but her voice refused to respond. It was as if an unseen hand was squeezing her, squeezing as tight as possible, cutting off the words even as they formed within her throat.

"Stop it," he snapped.

Stop what? Stop fighting, stop trying to escape. She lashed out blindly and then as if physical exertion broke free her senses, she screamed. His hands folded like steel clamps around her throat. She struggled uselessly, the grip too strong. Two of them. Two hands. Both of them squeezing relentlessly.

Oh, sweet Jesus, this was it, the final act, and there was nothing she could do to prevent the inevitable. Her next scream filled the house.

"Shut the fuck up, will yer!"

The voice of the man, the monster. In her deranged mind, she knew she must do something to save herself. She kicked, and she fought, and she prepared herself to force out one, final scream.

Except she didn't scream. She couldn't.

Jimmy McNulty was strangling her to death.

TWENTY-ONE

Hospitals made him uneasy. They always had, ever since he'd been hit by a car when he was seven years old. On that day, they'd brought him in semi-conscious and, as he slipped in and out, the only thing he could ever remember was the smell. The same smell now that invaded his nostrils, so overpowering he almost baulked at stepping further inside. What was it, antiseptic? Shaking his head, ridding his mind of the memories, he paced the ward, and when Linny came round the corner he felt such relief he almost fainted.

Her face creased with concern and she held him, kissing him lightly on the cheek. "Are you all right?"

"I'm fine," said Chaise, sitting down on a nearby bench seat. "Is he?"

She nodded, "He's had a heart attack. Not big, but serious enough. What the hell happened?"

"I don't know. I found him on the floor after I'd broken into his house. After I checked his pulse, I put him in the recovery position, phoned the ambulance and waited. The dog ..." Chaise shook his head, the picture of the poor, eviscerated animal, brought bile to his throat. He'd seen things, things that no ordinary person would ever want to see, but never had he witnessed such a deliberate act of sadism in all his life. To be able to do that to a domestic dog, a pet, was beyond reason. Only the sickest of individuals could perpetrate something so horrible.

Linny put her hand on his shoulder. "Maybe you should go home, try and get some rest. As soon as I finish here, I'll do the same."

Nodding mechanically, Chaise climbed to his feet, suddenly feeling tired, limbs heavy. He forced a smile, leaned forward, and kissed her again. "Let me know if there's any change."

He made his way through the hospital, which pulsated with activity, as if in a dream. It was difficult to believe it was gone midnight. Outside, in the car park, he leaned against his car and took in a few deep breaths. The air was thick and muggy, not at all comfortable, and his shirt stuck to his back.

It promised to be another beautiful day tomorrow, but at that moment Chaise wasn't looking forward to anything. He'd already decided to take the day off, to try and switch off and consider how to bring a vestige of normality back to his life. But, as he clambered in behind the wheel, the dreadful images reared up in front of his eyes once more. Who would do that to a dog, and for what reason? What had Alex Piers got himself embroiled in and how was it all linked to the death of Ricky Treach? Chaise had a hunch it involved Costa gangsters squabbling over their turf and who controls what in the whole, ghastly drugs industry, but whatever the link he was determined to find out.

For a long time, Jimmy McNulty sat in the armchair opposite the sofa, one hand pressed around his mouth as he stared unblinking at the lifeless form of Sarah Banbury. Stupid bloody bitch, why the hell did she make so much noise, put up such a struggle? Didn't she know that he only wanted to talk with her, spend some time, try and make amends for what had happened earlier? Stupid bloody bitch!

Her eyes were wide open, like a doll's. Cloudy black, no light of life. In death she was still lovely, her long limbs draped over the edge of the sofa. He could have loved her, looked after her, shared the laughter. Instead, it had come to this. A mess. Total and complete. He'd made a monumental mistake bringing the Audi back. He'd been blinded by lust, that's what it was. Not his fault at all. If she hadn't been so bloody gorgeous, with her short skirt and her crop-top, none of this would have happened.

Throwing himself backwards in the chair, he stared at the ceiling and chided himself. Who was he trying to kid? None of it was her fault, he alone was to blame, letting his feelings get in the way of common sense. He should have left the police to return the car and he should have stayed away. Now, she was dead, his fingerprints all over the place and that car, the big red four-by-four, they would know. As soon as all this hit the news, the owner of that car would come forward. It wouldn't take long to put it all together. He'd have to hide his tracks, make good his mistake, expunge any clues that might lead the police to his door.

Whoever the owner of the car was, that was outside of his control right now but the rest he could deal with and would do within the next hour. The car, however, that would require more time. Perhaps a local person owned it; he would have to make some inquiries.

Over the next forty minutes or so, Jimmy McNulty did what he could. He found a can of petrol in the garage and drenched the lounge. Then he drove the Audi into the garage, laid a rope of old rags and whatever else he could find from the open fuel tank cap to the garage door. He went back into the house, lit the first patch of petrol and when everything was truly ablaze, he returned to the makeshift rope and set fire to that as well. The flames soon licked their way along, until they reached the car. By this time Jimmy was running, getting as much distance as he could between himself and the house. He'd made about a hundred meters when the car exploded. He threw himself to the ground, pressed his hands over his head and waited for the succession of terrific blasts to subside.

An acrid, oily smell wafted over him. He stood up and looked back to see the sky lit with a deep orange glow, intermingled with plumes of thick black smoke. It wouldn't be that long before the police arrived. Without waiting, he scrambled from the path and wove through the olive groves towards the little village of Riogordo, nestling in the valley below.

Crossing the small bridge at the entrance to the village, Jimmy called in a few favours. Simon Winters had bought and sold some barely legal motorcars for Arthur Morgan over the years. A small, overweight man, in semi-retirement due to bad health, he occasionally provided false number plates and other dubious documentation for vehicles in Morgan's organization. He picked Jimmy up without question and took him to his home where Jimmy showered and changed clothes. Simon gave him a comfortable bed for the night and woke him the following morning with a cup of coffee and two slices of buttered toast.

No words were exchanged until Jimmy prepared to leave. He asked Simon who the owner of a large four-by-four might be. "There's plenty of them," said Simon without enthusiasm. "Tearing up the roads, no thought for anyone else. Why do you ask?"

Jimmy shrugged. "I need to speak to the owner, that's all."

"Best try the village. The locals know everyone, and if it's an Englishman, they'll let you know exactly who it is."

Simon duly dropped him off in the plaza. "Try there," he said, pointing to one of the bars on the corner. "You can usually find Alvaro taking his breakfast at this time. If anyone knows anything, it's him."

Jimmy got out without a word and strode into the bar. A gnarled man sat hunched over a table in the far corner, busily munching on a large bread roll, soaked in olive oil. He raised a quizzical eyebrow as Jimmy sat down opposite. "People tell me you know a lot about other people's business around here."

Alvaro made no answer and continued to chew on his bread. He finished one particularly large mouthful, then washed it down with a slurp of coffee. Patting at his mouth with a serviette, he made as if to leave. Jimmy's hand shot forward and gripped Alvaro's. arm "Sit down," he said quietly.

Frowning, Alvaro returned to his seat. He stared at Jimmy's hand. "You have a problem, Señor?"

"One that you might be able to solve for me." Jimmy pulled back his hand and reached inside his jacket. From his wallet, he extracted two, twenty-euro notes and laid them out on the table. "So, what do you say?"

"I say I will do the best I can, for twenty more."

Jimmy grinned, "If you give me the answer I want."

"Then ask it, Señor."

"The owner of a red four-by-four. Nissan. I need to know where he lives."

Alvaro titled his head. "English?" Jimmy nodded.

"Then I know exactly who it is you need. You are friends with Señor Ryan?"

Jimmy didn't even flinch. "Of course."

"Then he can tell you. I gave him the same information only yesterday."

"You see," Jimmy said, glancing around the quiet bar, "that's the problem. I haven't seen Señor Ryan recently, and I won't until later on. I need to get to this other guy's house as quickly as possible – muy rapido."

"You have another twenty?"

Without a pause, Jimmy placed a third crisp note on top of the others.

Alvaro grinned. "Then I will tell you."

Jimmy shook his head. "You can take me – I haven't got a car."

Alvaro sucked in his cheeks. "That will cost more, Señor."

"What makes you think I'm not surprised?"

Alvaro smiled as Jimmy added another note to the growing pile. Alvaro swept them up. Together they went out into the sunshine and clambered into Alvaro's beaten-up jeep.

Jimmy sat in silence as the jeep bucked and jumped over the dirt track towards a cluster of impressive-looking villas on the hillside outside of the village. He considered his next move.

Jimmy had no qualms about killing people. He'd done it often enough, no what he hated was the tidying up afterwards. The authorities would investigate the burning down of Sarah's home, and they would discover exactly what had happened, find his fingerprints over everything. His sloppy, amateurish work would result in him having to leave the country, go out east for a while. And now, there was Alvaro. He knew this Señor Ryan. It wouldn't be long before news of Jimmy tracking down the four-by-four owner became common knowledge, which would mean even more tidying up. He sighed. Sometimes he wished he had a more 'normal' type of profession. Plumber, or electrician. Good, stable work. That's what he would have preferred. Not this.

Alvaro brought the jeep to a halt and, with the engine still running, pointed up a track towards where a villa sat perched on the top of a large, flat outcrop. "That is it, Señor. The owner of the vehicle you seek is Alex Piers. He has lived here for many years, with his wife and daughter, although I have not seen them for some days. I think maybe they have gone on holiday."

"You don't miss much."

"No Señor." Alvaro smiled. "I will drop you here, it is only a short walk to the villa. You will be able to get back on your own?"

"I think so," said Jimmy. He leaned over and switched the engine off. Alvaro gasped as Jimmy took the keys and dropped them into his pocket. "You can get out now," he said, his voice flat. He measured Alvaro with his stare and waited. The Spaniard seemed perplexed, so Jimmy helped him decide by bringing out his automatic and pointing it straight at him. "Out."

Alvaro didn't wait. Groping for the handle, he wriggled outside. When he turned, his face fell.

Jimmy had fitted a silencer. Smiling, he shot Alvaro through the head. The Spaniard pitched backwards and slid down the slope. There was nobody about, Jimmy had made sure of that on the journey up to the villa. It would be some hours before anyone suspected that there might be something wrong. Time enough for Jimmy to tidy up those remaining loose ends. He slithered across into the driver's seat, started up the car, and drove it to Alex's house.

TWENTY-TWO

Arthur came out of his villa and stood by the pool. Sighing with contentment, he took in the sweeping hills, glimpses of the distant, azure Mediterranean peeking through the gaps. This was a long way from Wem in Shropshire where, as a boy, he'd first begun to dabble in slightly dubious practices. An expert at shoplifting, he'd soon branched out into burglary and made his biggest deal when one particular break-in had resulted in the discovery of a large collection of stamps. The lot had brought him nearly a thousand pounds, a small fortune for a fifteen-year-old boy back in nineteen sixty-five. If anyone had told him then that over half a century later, he'd be soaking up the sun in Marbella, living in a luxury village worth almost five million pounds, he'd have laughed in their faces. Truth was, none of this had featured in his plan. He'd never really had a plan, to be fair. Only a vague dream that one day he would not have to work, that money would never be a problem, and that others would respect him. The fact that he had decided to achieve all of these things dishonestly never concerned him. It was all a means to an end. Arthur Morgan had virtually everything he had ever wanted. Except love.

Someone came out onto the terrace. Arthur heard their breathing. It was fast, full of anxiety, even dread. He closed his eyes for a moment. Bad news, it had to be. Ever since that little shit Ricky had decided to do the dirty, there had been nothing but aggravation. The neat folds of life had suddenly become creased and Arthur hated that. Disorder. It caused him palpitations and Doctor Moreno had warned him against those. 'Avoid stress,' he'd said, his oil slick of a voice going well with his greasy hair, 'You have to learn to relax, Arthur. You're of that uncertain age now. Take things easy.'

Yeah, well that's all right for you mate, sitting there in your two hundred euro an hour consultation room, all cosy and calm, you haven't got a criminal empire to run, with little shits trying to undermine everything you've built up. A lifetime of graft, sweat, and blood, all of it rocked by one, stupid, insensitive act. And such a trifling amount. Three-hundred thousand. That's it. Now people were beginning to think that Arthur Morgan was soft, that he'd lost the plot. Already others were becoming more courageous, taking risks. How he longed to get hold of that bloody stupid Ricky's body and string it up in the middle of Malaga city and warn every single, sodding lot of them that anyone who crossed Arthur Morgan would receive the same.

Not that he'd done that to Ricky, of course.

That bloody Englishman had done that. The Englishman who'd shot Treach dead and seemed to know too much.

"Mr Morgan?"

He'd forgotten his visitor. Arthur turned to see Stevie standing there, one of Jimmy's more obvious recruits. Well over six foot six, Stevie Swinton looked what he was, an all-in wrestler with arms like tree trunks and a head bolted on to shoulders which were wider than Arthur was tall. "Yes, Stevie?"

Stevie shifted, looking uneasy. "Sorry about this, Mr Morgan. But I think you need to know."

Arthur sighed again. The day had barely begun, and already

bad news was stacking up. "What is it now?" he asked, his voice tired, all of him *tired*. He wanted it all swept away so he could get on with business. Business as usual.

"The woman, Mr Morgan. It's on the news."

"Woman?"

The big man pulled a face, eyes dropping to the ground.

"Stevie, just get to the fucking point will you."

Stevie's face paled. "Yeah, sorry Mr Morgan. The woman who Ricky went to see, the one who was with Ricky..."

"Sarah Bradbury? What about her?" Something in Stevie's voice made the hairs on Arthur's neck stand up. "She's been found dead, Mr Morgan. In her house. The whole lot, everything, burned down."

"Burned down? What, as in a fire?"

Stevie nodded. "They said on the news that they're treating it as suspicious."

Arthur's stomach clamped up as if iron fingers had seized him from the inside. He stared into the distance. This was as bad as it gets, he thought to himself. Slowly, he brought his face up to meet Stevie's. He did his best to keep his voice steely hard. "Get Jimmy on the fucking phone and tell him to get around here."

"No need, Mr Morgan." Arthur frowned. Stevie forced a not very convincing smile. "He's in the kitchen getting himself a piece of toast."

Stay calm, Moreno had said. The doctor's orders. Thrown out of the window without a single second of consideration as Arthur screamed, "Get him the fuck out here, now!"

Less than a minute later, Jimmy stood in front of his boss, hands behind his back, head down. "It's not what you think, Mr Morgan."

Arthur shook with rage, "You haven't got a fucking clue

what I'm thinking, Jimmy! What the hell were you doing going round there and setting fire to the place?"

Jimmy would have to be blind not to recognise the danger he was in. Arthur's head had taken on the shape and size, as well as the colour, of an overinflated leather football. The veins on his reddened cheeks protruded as if they were about to burst. His eyes boiled, mouth trembled. Jimmy didn't think he'd ever seen him looking so furious.

Jimmy spread out his hands, "It just got a bit ... you know ... awkward."

"*Awkward*? What the hell does that mean?" Arthur took a step closer, his face inches from Jimmy's. "Have you any idea what this means? If the police can place you at the scene, I won't be able to protect you! If you've murdered her ..." He turned away, blowing out his breath sharply.

"I never ... Mr Morgan, please, it wasn't supposed to happen the way it did. She started screaming and shouting, so I tried to shut her up. But ... well, you know how these things can get out of hand."

Arthur's breathing sounded erratic and laboured. Jimmy didn't like what this could mean. "Please, Mr Morgan, it's going to be okay. No one can link me to her, no one. And, even if they could, it'll be weeks, maybe even months before they come checking up." He held his breath as he came up close to Arthur's shoulder. "I went to see the other guy, the other one who gave Ricky a lift."

Arthur's face went slack. "What? You found him? How the hell did you do that?"

"Don't worry about that, Mr Morgan. He wasn't in as it happens. I took a good look round his house. Clean as a whisper, apart from the kitchen."

"The kitchen? Jimmy, please, just tell me everything without all the embellishments, yeah."

Jimmy smiled. "There was blood in the kitchen. On the

table. Old blood. So, obviously, someone had been there, and something had happened. But not now. He's gone."

"Where is he?"

"Dunno. But I'll find him."

Arthur held up an outstretched palm. "No, Jim. No. I want you to hide low for a while. This is getting out of hand, the whole bloody lot. This was supposed to be a nice, easy job. Just get the stuff back, no complications. I wouldn't mind, but it's not exactly a fucking fortune we're talking about here."

"It's the principle, Mr Morgan."

"Exactly. And right now, I'm being made out to be a right bloody Muppet! I want you to get some of your boys on the job, Jimmy. Spread the word. I want this sorted and sorted fast. You understand?" Jimmy nodded. "In the meantime, I think you should go away. The Canaries. You can go and look after business there for a while until things quiet down."

"I'd rather stay here, Mr Morgan. See it through."

Arthur squeezed his fingers into the bridge of his nose, eyes screwed up. "I'm not sure, Jimmy."

"Please. It's almost done. I'll find this other guy, this Alex bloke. Then the other one, Ryan Chaise. They're in this together, I know it. I'll find 'em, talk to 'em, and make everything right. You can trust me, Mr Morgan. I won't let you down."

Without opening his eyes or moving his hand from his face, Arthur nodded. "All right. But just do it quickly and do it quietly. Okay."

Jimmy released a long, low sigh. "Thank you, Mr Morgan," and he walked away. Arthur's breathing still sounded like sandpaper rubbing against a piece of wood. Imagine how much worse it would be, mused Jimmy if he knew about Alvaro.

. . .

He'd only taken one sip of coffee before Stevie came out onto the terrace again. Arthur groaned inside. He glared at the heavyweight. "For fuck's sake, can't I ever get a few moments to relax?"

Stevie thrust forward a mobile phone. "It's for you," he said softly. "And he sounds pissed."

Arthur groaned audibly now and took the phone, coffee suddenly forgotten. He winced as the familiar voice barked, "Arthur. You've heard about the fire."

"Yes. I'm sorry, I—"

"I don't want or need your apologies, Arthur. I won't be able to stop the investigation. I know it was you, or that stupid arse McNulty. Once the National Police become involved, there will be nothing I can do. And they will become involved, Arthur. Trust me. You end this quickly, Arthur because if you don't, the whole deck of cards is going to come crashing down. You understand me."

Arthur dragged his hand across his brow, wiping away the sweat. "It's already being sorted."

"It had better be, Arthur. For both our sakes."

The phone went dead, and Arthur handed it back to Stevie whose face looked grim. "I want you to follow Jimmy. Make sure he doesn't do anything else too … dramatic."

"And if he does?"

Arthur fell back on the sun-lounger and closed his eyes. "That is something I just don't want to think about."

TWENTY-THREE

When Linny came through the door, Chaise felt the weight slide from his shoulders and he fell into her, holding her, no words needed.

They stayed like that for a long time, Chaise enjoying the moment, the heat from her body giving him the comfort he yearned.

"Are you feeling okay?"

Catching the shock in her voice, he pulled away from the embrace. She wasn't used to this show of affection. He forced a smile. "I just needed a hug." A couple of days ago, that sort of admission wouldn't have entered into his head. Now, with the world gone haywire, he realized how much she meant to him. If he'd known it before, he had never confessed it to himself, but life had suddenly become a lot more precious.

Nodding, she turned and glided into the kitchen. He followed her and watched her heap a small mountain of coffee into the pot. She flicked the switch of the kettle. Chaise moved up behind her, slipping his arms around her waist. "I just need you to know I love you," he breathed into her neck. She'd just come off a twelve-hour shift, would she be able to handle the news of what had been going on. She turned in his arms, kissed him on the lips, and held him. "I could never find the words," he continued. "With everything that's happened, it's brought it all into sharp focus. What you mean to me."

"I don't need to know it all, Ryan. Just tell me that this business with Alex hasn't anything to do with your past life."

He flinched, looked at her, every nerve and fibre wanting to shout out that all of that was gone, nothing but a memory, that the man he used to be was dead and buried. But he couldn't, because a tiny part of him knew that he would always be that person. The stone-cold killer. How do you lock that away in a cupboard and throw away the key? You can't. It's there, eating away at you, tightening up your guts every time someone raised their voice in anger in a bar, every time some idiot cuts you up on the road, every time someone takes exception to you for wanting to breathe ... a constant battle to keep calm, not allow the blood to boil. "My past life has gone," he lied. "This business with Alex has nothing to do with any of that."

"Okay." She hugged him again. "I guess I should try and be more understanding, but it's hard, Ryan. There's so much of you which is a closed book."

"It has to be."

"I know. You said. Official Secrets Act and all that. I won't ask you, just ... just be careful."

He kissed the top of her head and started to go back into the lounge. A sudden thought held him back and as he turned and watched her pouring the water into the cafetiere, "I might go and see Alex this morning. What do you think?"

She had her back to him, so he couldn't see her expression, but her voice said it all. "What has he got himself involved in, Ryan? Something he'll need your help with?" She turned, holding the coffee cup in both her hands as if she were cold. "Something happened didn't it, at his house? Something so awful that he suffered a heart attack. And you know what it was, don't you?"

He swallowed hard. "I don't know all the details, not yet."

"Just the important ones?" She took a sip of the coffee, gazed down at the cup, lost in thought for a moment. "Is this another of those you don't need to know incidents? What's that other phrase, 'for your eyes only'? I always wondered what that meant when they brought out that James Bond film with the same title. Anyway, I looked it up and now I know. Is that what this is? Ultra top-secret?"

"Don't be daft! I've just said—"

"I know what you've just said, Ryan. Trouble is, I don't know whether to believe you or not."

"I simply want to check that he's okay, that's all. No secrets."

"As I said, I won't ask you. I don't want to know the details; I just need to know that it's nothing dangerous."

"I'll talk to him, get it all sorted. If there is anything dangerous, I'll take a step back."

"But not walk away completely."

He pressed his lips together. "Linny ... let's just wait and see."

She turned and filled her cup. Without looking back at him, she said quietly, "Take care, Ryan. Promise me that. I don't want to come into work during my next shift and find you laid out in A and E."

He laid his hands on her shoulders and gently turned her round to face him. Her face was streaked with a single tear that had rolled down her cheek. He wiped it away with a forefinger and kissed her. "I'll get it sorted. I promise."

Images of her face, like a little girl's, staring up at him with those doleful eyes remained with him as he drove into the hospital car park. Not even the blare of music from the radio could lighten his spirits. Linny was crumbling inside, he knew that. None of this was in her sphere of experience. Despite her being a doctor, dealing with car accidents, shootings, amputations, the whole gambit, to have it all thrust into her face, up close and personal, put it all on a much different level. She never allowed the horrors she witnessed at work to blight her everyday life, having the enviable ability to detach herself. This, however, was something else and the fear had seized control of her.

Chaise's responsibility was simple – get it sorted. He'd promised her, but that wasn't the only thing that had charged up his batteries. Someone was out there, capable of extreme violence, intimidation, threat. Chaise had the tools to fix the problem. If he used them, however, his promise to Linny would be broken. Choices. They gnawed away at him.

The receptionist barely looked up from her desk when he leaned over and asked about Alex Piers. She glanced at the computer screen, pushed a few keys, then shook her head. "The doctor says he still cannot receive visitors. Not for at least another ..." She craned forward, eyes moving across the screen, "Six hours maybe. Call back at lunchtime."

Sighing, Chaise pushed himself out from the desk. "Is it possible to speak to the doctor? I only want to know how Alex is, the prognosis."

Sending him a withering glance, she blew out a loud sigh, picked up a phone, and punched the numbers. "I have paged him. A few minutes." She nodded towards some seats set against the far wall. Chaise smiled his thanks and went to sit down.

Some moments later, the doctor came round the far corner at a rush. Chaise knew it was him in the purposeful way he came striding forward, hand already thrust out. Chaise shook it, looked into his clear blue eyes, and noted no hint of concern there. He relaxed a little.

"You are a close friend?" the doctor asked.

"Yes," Chaise lied. "Almost a brother."

"I can tell you he is better, more stable and I believe the danger has passed. You can see him this afternoon."

"Thank you." Chaise smiled. "I was concerned it might be life-threatening."

Chaise waited, knowing this was irregular. Family members alone had the right to know the full details. "It still might be," the doctor continued. "His wife, she is no longer..."

"No. They've ..." He shrugged. "He'll be staying with me."

"Good. He will need to be watched closely when we discharge him. I have informed his doctor. The other friend, you will let him know?"

A frozen moment, a thin trail of ice instantly trickling down his spine. "The other ..." He went through the possibilities of who this 'other friend' could be. Finding none, he hastily said, "Yes, yes I'll tell him. When did he call?"

The doctor shook his head. "Some time ago. Listen, I must go. Always something to do. Your partner, she works here, yes? A surgeon. This is why I told you about this patient. You understand. I shouldn't really ... you *do* understand?"

"Yes, of course. I appreciate your help. Thank you." Chaise waited until the doctor moved out of sight before crossing over to the receptionist again. "Thank you," he said. She looked up, without speaking. "Er ... the doctor mentioned something about another friend? Asking about Alex?"

"Si. A big man. Very ..." Her cheeks coloured a little and she swept away a lock of hair. "Handsome. He came earlier this morning, to bring Señor Piers something."

"Something? A present you mean?"

"Perhaps. I don't know." She reached beneath the desk and brought out a small brown package. She squeezed it with her fingers. "He said to make sure Mr Piers got it as soon as he woke up." She appeared to struggle with something of monumental importance for a few moments. "Perhaps you could give it to him?"

"Absolutely," Chaise said, taking the package from her. He ran his fingers over the brown paper. The object inside the package was small and circular. He weighed it in his hand and frowned. He caught her eyes, boring into him. Her curiosity was as strong as his own and he smiled, ripped through the seal with little difficulty and paused. His frown deepened as he pulled out the object from within.

The receptionist gave a little laugh. "That is a nice thought. Unusual present to give someone so ill, but..."

Chaise nodded despite not agreeing with her sentiments. Not in even a small way. There was nothing 'nice' or thoughtful about this particular present and the anger percolated deep inside him. "If this friend comes back at any time, could you please phone me? I don't know his address or anything and it's quite important that I speak to him, about Alex's condition."

She produced a card and scribbled down the number Chaise gave her. "No problem," she said.

With measured care, Chaise returned the dog collar inside the package and made his way back out to his car.

TWENTY-FOUR

Chaise drove into the village of Benamargosa and parked near the entrance to the swimming pool. He preferred the village pool to his own as here he could swim full lengths. On this day, it was quieter than usual. He strolled through the small park, paused to buy himself some water, paid the entrance money and found himself a spot on the grass. A few elderly people mingled in the far corner, their soft Scottish brogue a welcome change from the sharp, slightly raucous twang of the Spanish.

He settled himself under the shade of a straw parasol, laid out his towel and stripped off his shirt and jogging bottoms. He padded over to the pool and plunged in without hesitation.

The ice-cold water snatched his breath away, but he recovered quickly and struck out to complete several lengths of front-crawl before settling into a more leisurely breaststroke. The worries of the last couple of days receded and when he got out, he felt exhilarated and refreshed. He smiled at the Scottish people in the corner, rubbed a towel through his hair, and laid himself out on his back, eyes closed, soaking up the sunshine.

Their footfall came a few moments later.

He lay still and waited, every part of him coiled like a spring, heartbeat settled, alert.

Chaise rolled over and eyed the stranger who sat propped up against the nearby tree chewing on a strand of grass. His posture was at ease, one knee pulled up with the elbow of his right arm draped over it.

The man was trying hard to look like a holidaymaker, except he wasn't. Chaise took in the light grey, Armani suit, the Rotary wristwatch, sunglasses probably Police. Most telling was the slight bulge under his armpit.

If the stranger had followed Chaise from the hospital, this was a concern. It meant he was good. Very good because Chaise had missed him. Arrogant too. Chaise got that from the stranger's easy smile, the nonchalant air, the way he kept moving his knee from side to side, allowing the gun to be visible. The added bonus of two others close by, big, burly men, sitting under the shade of the tall, boundary hedge separating the pool complex from the village, served to charge the atmosphere.

Sitting up, Chaise pressed his towel against his face, a face wet with perspiration. It gave him a moment to ponder what to do. A man with a gun would only need reinforcements to intimidate. And these men were intimidating indeed. Chaise studied one of them approach the Scottish people. A short, sharp exchange followed. The big man smiled as the Scots gathered together their things and moved away.

A few simple equations ran through Chaise's mind. All three strangers were armed. You didn't need to be an expert to calculate how bad this was. And now the witnesses were gone. Chaise sighed, turned again to the stranger who continued to sit with his leg moving from side to side. "Do you actually want something, or is this all part of the same Vaudeville act?"

The stranger tilted his head, pushed his sunglasses back on his head and said, "Vaudeville? What's that?"

His accent was northern England. Merseyside. Funny that. The painters and decorators at Saddam's palace had been from Liverpool. Saddam used to laugh at their accent, finding it difficult to understand. Good workers though. Fast. No one suspected several were Special Forces. More importantly, neither did Saddam.

"Not a quiz-goer then?"

The stranger measured Chaise from head to toe and smiled pleasantly. "You keep yerself fit. Is that a personal thing? You know, to impress the ladies, or a professional calling? You're too old to be a boxer, maybe you're an ex-army man. I was an army man."

"Really? How fascinating." Chaise put the towel down, took a drink from his water bottle and reached for his shirt. The stranger moved, with surprising speed, his foot deliberately coming down on the shirt to prevent Chaise from taking it. At the same time, the two heavyweights moved from out of the shade and strode across the grass.

"We need to talk," the stranger said, words hissing through clenched teeth

Chaise did not take his eyes off the foot. It would take a few moments and now that the Scottish people weren't anywhere close, he had no qualms in doing what he had to do.

TWENTY-FIVE

L inny went to bed after her shower, the sound of a car, probably Ryan's, easing itself into the forecourt the last thing she heard before her head hit the pillow and sleep enveloped her. Two seconds later her eyes sprang open. The insistent thump of somebody pounding on the front door, a finger pressed against the bell. No let up. She swung herself out of bed, anger already replacing fatigue. If this was Ryan, forgetting his key, disturbing her like this, he'd bloody well feel the full weight of her wrath.

It wasn't her boyfriend. A small Spanish man mopping his brow with a handkerchief, sweating in his suit. His eyes grew rounder as he took in Linny. Very appreciative.

"Good morning, Señorita. I am Captain Domingo and I wish to speak to your husband."

Linny stifled a yawn, folded her arms and leaned against the door well. She wore grey shorts and a tight, white vest and nothing else. She noted the two uniformed policemen a little way off, both of them scanning her. She should have been angry at that, but this was Spain. A woman was an object to be admired. No point getting upset about it. Linny was half-Spanish, had spent most of her life in England, and quaint customs still took a little time to get used to. "If you mean Ryan, he's not in. He's gone to the hospital."

Domingo shook his head. "No. He has already left. It is important; I need to speak to him."

"Village pool."

Domingo frowned, puzzled.

"Benamargosa pool," Linny explained. "He often goes for a dip there, likes the solitude, the chance to swim without being disturbed."

"I see." The Captain of police turned and growled at the two men. As they returned to their patrol car, Domingo gave her a thin smile. "I will wait."

Linny let out her breath very slowly. "I've just come off my shift, Captain ... what did you say your name was?"

"Domingo."

"Well, I've just got home after twelve very long hours, Captain Domingo. I'm tired."

"I will not disturb you."

"You already have."

Domingo spread out his hands. "Apologies, but this is rather serious. You know Señor Chaise shot someone."

Linny stiffened. She knew very well what had happened but to hear it from someone else made her uneasy. "Yes," she said, cautiously.

"It seems that is not all he has done."

The world crashed in on her, all her fears and suspicions hitting her in one, massive blow. She failed to prevent the tremble from her voice. "What does that mean?"

Domingo tried his smile again. "If I could wait for Señor Chaise to return, I am sure we can sort everything out without much difficulty."

Yes. She most definitely would want that. Ryan hadn't been exactly open with her, despite his reassurances, promises, persuasive words. Not lies, exactly, but close enough for the edges to be blurred. She nodded, stepped aside and beckoned Domingo into the house.

TWENTY-SIX

Jimmy McNulty had been in quite a few fights. He knew what to do, and how to do it well. He'd trained with the best, the Red Triangle club in Liverpool had been his shrine. Famous people went there, legends. Andy Sherry, Terry O'Neill, the very best there was. Jimmy McNulty had never become famous, hadn't entered many competitions, but he had been right up there, at the very top. Mixed martial arts. He could cope with most opponents, on the cobbles or the mat. He'd learned a good deal, knew things that the trained fighters didn't know. A dirty fighter, some might say, but what the hell did that matter when you were struggling against someone who wanted to beat the hell out of you. He had no limits, no qualms, no conscience. Not many could stand against him, underestimating him because of his size. That had often been their undoing. But Jimmy McNulty had never met anyone like Ryan Chaise before, a man who had fought and killed. He was an opponent like no other.

Chaise moved fast. Jimmy did his best, tried to block, swerve, and counter, but already he knew this was bad. He'd made a critical error and assumed Chaise was a normal, average sort of bloke. Nothing special, nothing to be concerned about. Sure, he was fit, good body, strong-looking arms. But not what you'd call big, or dangerous. Mistake. Bad mistake.

The pace was frenetic, and Jimmy couldn't keep up. A blow erupted into his nether regions, the palm crushing testicles, pain burning through his lower abdomen, vomit coming up into his throat, overwhelming him. For a moment, a desperate struggle to ward off incapacity, but muscles refused to respond, brain not working. Even as his legs buckled and he began to fold, the second blow landed against his carotid artery and the blackness came over him so very quickly.

———

Chaise caught the man as he fell and rolled with him, taking the automatic from the holster. On one knee, he aimed the gun at the two heavyweights as they came bounding across the grass. They ground to a halt and Chaise stood up. They looked scared, clearly unsettled by the ease in which their boss had been despatched.

Chaise motioned with the gun. "With your left hands, bring out your guns and throw them down." There was a moment's hesitation. Chaise snarled, "Do it now or I'll kill you."

They did as ordered and flung two large automatics onto the grass. "Trousers," said Chaise. The men exchanged looks. "Take your trousers off, gentlemen."

Without complaint, they did so. Chaise, his gun trained unerringly them, stooped, and picked up his few belongings. "Fancy a dip?"

"You're a dead man," said one of them, red-faced, close to losing control.

"I don't think so. Perhaps you'd like to tell me who you work for."

"Perhaps you'd like to fuck off."

Chaise grinned. "Nice. I enjoy banter." With those few words, Chaise now knew the man came from somewhere down south. Essex maybe. A strange, eclectic mix of thugs. Essex and Liverpool. Not the usual pairing, knowing the animosity between the two. Must be a powerful boss keeping this tinder box from blowing up. "Listen. We can make this easy, or hard." Chaise glanced towards the unconscious Liverpudlian lying face down in the grass. There was blood coming out of his ear. Not a good sign. "He chose the hard route. What would you like to do?"

"I think you're full of shit."

Chaise crossed the six feet between them in two strides. He struck the guy across the face with the gun, more of a slap than a blow, but enough to drop him to his knees. Crying out, he clutched at his temple, a nasty welt already developing there. As the second man tried to respond, the barrel of the gun jammed against his Adam's apple and he gagged, eyes boiling over with fear.

Chaise said, "Your boss, tell me who he is."

"I'm dead if I do."

"You're dead if you don't."

From the ground, the other man groaned. "I'm going to fucking kill you."

Shaking his head, Chaise stepped back and pressed the gun against the groaning man's head. "I haven't got time for this, so I'll ask you one more time…"

"Arthur Morgan," said the other one quickly.

"Idiot," spat the one kneeling.

Nodding, Chaise backed away, never taking his eyes off the two men. "Okay, tough guys." He motioned with the automatic. "Help him up, then get into the pool."

The man standing took his companion by the arm and pulled him to his feet. Together they slinked off, Chaise watching them from a distance as they jumped into the shallow end. As they hit the water, the pool-attendant appeared from nowhere shouting and waving his arms. Ignoring him, Chaise put the gun in his waistband, pulled on his shirt and jogged towards the park entrance, the shouting behind him not letting up.

He came out of the entrance with the car keys already in his hand just as the police patrol car came down the path. Chaise stopped and waited, hands-on-hips, calculating the possibility of getting away without having to explain everything.

The young policeman stepped out from the car. "Señor Chaise?"

Chaise groaned. They knew who he was!

The heavyweights appeared, both soaked through, neither wearing their trousers. It might have been comical if it wasn't so deadly serious.

The young policeman raised his eyebrows and laughed. He seemed to be the only one who found the scene in any way amusing.

TWENTY-SEVEN

The coffee tasted good, and Chaise allowed himself to relax a little. The police had brought him back to the house in silence, leaving the two brutes in the entrance to the swimming pool looking frustrated and angry. Chaise knew it wouldn't be long before he came across them again, including the diminutive Liverpudlian he'd dumped so unceremoniously onto the ground.

Linny lingered whilst a smiling Domingo sampled the coffee. Chaise didn't care for the man's attitude and wondered what he'd told Linny. Chaise had no doubts that Domino liked to rock the boat if only to see what happened in the wake.

"I'll get straight to it, Mr Chaise," said Domingo. "You know Sarah Banbury?"

"Only from the news."

"That's not exactly true."

Both men looked up at Linny, who stood with her back against the breakfast bar, arms across her chest. She scowled. "I know Sarah. Not well, but well enough. I've met her a few times over at the tennis club. Her husband is something big in the City."

Domingo nodded, stuck out his bottom lip, and turned to Chaise. "You know her also?"

"Linny might. I don't."

"Very well." Domingo pulled in a large breath. "She is dead."

The words hung heavy in the air. For a moment, all Chaise could hear was his heartbeat pounding in his ears. Sarah Banbury, the girl assaulted, the girl who had given Ricky a lift. Dead?

"Oh my God." It was Linny, sounding genuinely shocked. She dropped onto the sofa. "But that's awful. Did she die from the complications?"

"Que? The what?"

Linny looked from Domingo to Chaise and back again. "The attack. The beating she took from that man."

"Oh … I see." Domingo gently laid down his finished coffee. "No. Not that. Someone broke into her home. We suspect she was murdered."

"Oh, God…"

Domingo nodded. "They, whoever "they" were, then set fire to her home. There is not much left. House, car, body. It is not …" He left the sentence unfinished.

"What has this to do with me?" said Chaise.

Domingo held Chaise's stare. "Well, Señor, quite a lot, I think. Quite a lot." His fingers toyed with the empty coffee cup. "You may think of us as slow, Señor Chaise. Slow at our job. After all, the Axarquia, it is very slow itself, is it not? Nice, quiet villages. Lots of heat. People don't rush, they take their time. Life, for the most part, passes us by. You may think it is the same with the police. We are not sophisticated detectives, like those working in London or New York, surrounded by technology, high-speed communication systems, all of that. But what we lack in modern machinery, we make up for with diligence, hard work, determination. Policing is a very patient job, Señor Chaise. One has to take things calmly and quietly so that nothing is missed." He sat back. "So, please, always remember that no matter what you or others might think, we are good at what we do."

"I never said you weren't."

"No, you didn't, but maybe," he tapped his forehead, "maybe you think it? Just a little?"

"What I think is immaterial. You came here to ask specific questions and I'll make it all very easy for you by telling you that I had nothing to do with Sarah Banbury's death."

"Not directly perhaps but you have connections to the case. She was assaulted by the man you killed, Señor Chaise. Ricky Treach. Ricky was a low-life criminal working out of Mijas Costa. He'd earn scraps running errands for the big boys down in Marbella. Then, one day, he is asked to do a simple job. He had to deliver a package. Nothing difficult in that, except that this particular package contained high-quality crack-cocaine. Pure. The best. One and a half kilos worth. On the streets," he shrugged, made a face, "maybe three hundred thousand English *pounds*. A lot of money for one man. Tempting. It would mean a new start for Ricky, a chance to get away, live a better life. So, he takes it for himself. He has contacts in Benidorm. He can get a good price for it there. But on the way, he meets Sarah Banbury. They spend time together, he leaves. Not in his car, however. Hers. His is broken. We know this, it is in our pound. Broken roll bar, I think it is called. Anyway, he takes her car, and she tries to stop him." He rubbed his forefinger across his eye. "Sarah is not a big girl … sorry, *was* not a big girl. And Ricky was not a nice man. He hits her, drives down into Riogordo and this car, this Audi that he has taken, it runs out of petrol. Silly, he should have checked but he didn't and now he is panicking because time has moved on and his employers know that he has not delivered. So, he hitches a lift."

"And I pick him up."

Domingo shook his head. "Not before someone else did. You

see, this is where it becomes interesting." He glanced over to Linny, who sat bolt upright, listening intensely to every word. Domingo leaned forward. "I believe Ricky left the drugs in Señor Piers's car after he had picked up Ricky."

That answers everything, thought Chaise, but kept his face neutral.

"Just a minute." Linny ran her tongue over her bottom lip. "You mean Alex? *Alex* Piers?"

"This gets better," Domingo beamed. "Like one, big, happy family. You know Alex?"

"I know most of the ex-pats around here, Señor Domingo. Not personally, not as a friend. Purely in passing. But I know his wife, Diane and his daughter Amy."

This seemed to please Domingo no end. Rubbing his hands, he sat forward. "Well, with Ricky dead, the owners of the drugs now have only one place to go, to get their merchandise back. Alex Piers."

"You seem to know an awful lot, Captain Domingo."

Domingo turned his beaming smile to Chaise. "It's like I said, we are patient people. We do our job, quietly and efficiently. Whilst you have been running around, trying to disentangle yourself from the mess you are in, Señor Chaise, I have been investigating. It's all quite simple."

"If that's true what do you need me for?"

"That too is very simple. I want you to get the drugs back for me."

TWENTY-EIGHT

They both stood in the doorway, the uniformed officers waiting in the patrol car. Domingo stared towards the sky. "Another beautiful day in paradise," he said, sounding bored. When he turned, his face had the patina of gunmetal. "Those men you encountered at the swimming pool, Señor Chaise, what you did. My colleagues told me …" He shook his head. "We will talk again, Señor Chaise. Until then, try and keep yourself alive."

Chaise watched the police captain get into the car and, as it slowly disappeared, Linny moved up next to him and he knew what was going to happen next. Her body was taut, her jaw set firm. Domingo's revelations had shocked him, God knows what they had done to Linny.

He took a breath. "I'm sorry," he said, in a very quiet voice. "This has all got out of control. I had no idea that Alex was in so deep, not at first. He must have let this crazy idea he had of keeping the drugs for himself take control of him. Madness."

She held his gaze, the tears welling up along the bottom lid of her eyes. "You said you didn't know Alex."

"I don't – I mean, I didn't. I went up to his house, to value it.

He wants to sell. He must have recognized me from the news report on the television."

"But now you've become involved. With drugs and gangsters."

"Gangsters? Linny, I—"

"I heard what Domingo said. About those men at the swimming pool? Who were they? What happened?"

"It was a misunderstanding, nothing more."

You're still not telling me everything." He reached out to her, but she pulled away, arm coming up to fend him off. "No. Don't touch me, you bastard! You've lied to me once too often, Ryan. About your past, about this drugs business. Christ, you killed a man, Ryan! And does it even bother you?" She pulled out a tissue and dabbed at her eyes. "I need time to think about all of this."

"What does that mean?"

"It means I'm going away for a few days, try and get my head clear."

"But you can't, Linny. Not now, not when all of this is coming to a head! You heard what Domingo said. Things are becoming dangerous."

"All the more reason why I shouldn't be here."

They stood like two pillars, neither moving. Chaise closed his eyes trying to steady his breathing. Everything was falling apart. In the old days, he had no one to worry about except himself but now his world had changed and become more complicated. But not in a bad way. Linny came into his life and made it better. How could he let her go? "Where will you go?"

"My mum's."

"Alicante? But that's miles away, Linny!" He wanted to say more, to plead, to beg, but something prevented him from doing so. The vestiges of the man he used to be perhaps. He fell against the doorframe, defeat looming. He looked into her eyes, but they were blank, void of expression. She shook her head and turned to go. As he reached out to her the telephone rang.

She got there first, listened, forehead creased in puzzlement, then held out the receiver towards Chaise. "It's the hospital. They need to talk to you. Something about a visitor wanting to see Alex?"

He blasted through the doors and sprinted along the corridor to the reception desk. The receptionist spotted him and held up her hand before he could speak. "He has been and gone."

Chaise let his head drop, frustration and disappointment overcoming him in equal measure. The drive over had been worthy of anything to be seen on the racetrack, but all of it for nothing.

"Mr Chaise?"

The surgeon who had spoken to him the last time approached. He still wore the same distant expression, a blank canvas, a man seldom troubled by concerns or worries. Chaise took his proffered hand. "Is there any improvement?"

"I'm positive, Mr Chaise. You can visit him if you wish."

"Just a moment." Chaise turned to the receptionist. "The man, did he say anything to you, give you anything?"

"No. But he asked me about the package. He wanted to know if you had received it."

"And you told him … ?"

The receptionist smiled in a coy, school-girlish way. "I told him nothing. Was I correct?"

"More than correct." Chaise touched her forearm. "Thanks." He saw her blush.

"Shall we go," said the surgeon.

Without another word, Chaise followed the surgeon along the corridor towards Alex's room.

A bank of machinery arranged at one side of Alex's bed

hummed softly, lights blinking, measuring every facet of his physiology.

"Try and not excite him," the surgeon said before he breezed out of the room.

Chaise pulled up a chair and sat down. Alex, his breathing shallow, skin a healthy colour, appeared peaceful enough. Chaise squinted at the chart hooked over the headrest. The various squiggles and numbers meant nothing to him.

"Hello."

Chaise gave a little jump at the sound of Alex's voice. He smiled. "Sorry, I didn't mean to wake you."

"I was only resting." His voice sounded weak.

"They said I could have a few minutes."

"They told me Diane was coming. Amy too."

"That's good. Cheer you up a bit."

"Yes. Maybe. Listen," Alex looked past Chaise as if he were half-expecting someone else to be there, "I know this is a lot to ask but I need you to find Shaun for me. I haven't heard from him and—"

"I don't know him. Who is he, a friend?"

"Best friend. We ..." His head fell back into the pillow and he released a long, shuddering sigh. "Oh Christ, you may as well know. Shaun was trying to sell some of the stuff. Said he had some contacts."

"Contacts?" Now it was Chaise's turn to give the room a quick scan. "Alex, things have developed. This whole thing has got out of control. There are others involved now, the sort of people nobody wants to know."

Alex closed his eyes. "Jeez, I knew all of this would happen. I told Shaun not to do anything, to give it back." His eyes sprung open again. They were wild eyes, frightened. Chaise placed his hand on Alex's arm in an attempt to calm him, but Alex shrugged it off, agitated. "I told him we should hand it over to the police, but he said that would be worse than giving it to the gangsters"

"Well, I think he could have been right about that."

"What do you mean?"

"I've had some interesting visits, let's put it that way."

"Oh my God. You have to find him for me, tell him to hand everything over then we can get all of this finished. I'm sorry you've become involved."

"I became involved as soon as that low-life got into my car."

"You weren't to know about the drugs though, Ryan. That was mine and Shaun's fault. We've dragged you into this, and God knows how many others."

"You don't have to worry about any of it, Alex. Not for a while. You just concentrate on getting yourself better."

"That's what the doctors keep telling me." His eyes welled up. "Whatever I did or didn't do, they didn't have to do what they did to Lotty. That was ...beyond anything."

"Try not to think about that, Alex. Everything will sort itself out. I'll find Shaun, somehow. Together we'll smooth everything over."

Alex's breathing slowed and the tears receded. "He spends a lot of time in The Englishman's Bar in Colmenar. You know it?" Chaise nodded. "If not, he has a flat, down in Torre del Mar. The address is in my coat." He pointed towards a jacket hanging behind the door. "Address book."

"Okay, I'll find him. The next time I see you, everything will be as it was. Normal." Chaise smiled, hoping that his lies weren't too transparent.

"But it's gangsters we're talking about, isn't it? They're hardly likely to roll over, accept our apologies." Alex clamped his eyes tight shut as the colour rose over his cheeks. "They're looking for it, and they're not going to stop. Bloody Shaun, with his pathetic ideas! I knew this would happen, I tried to tell him but—"

Without warning, his face creased up like a gargoyle, his body stiffened. Everything went wild from that moment as the bank of instruments exploded into life, lights flashing, alarms blurting. Alex lay rigid, his face like a screaming skull. Leaping to his feet, Chaise dashed to the door to shout for assistance when a tiny voice mumbled behind him, "I'm okay."

Chaise snapped his head around to see Alex forcing a smile.

Before Chaise could say anything, the door flew open and the surgeon, two nurses close behind, rushed in. Soon everyone was working like maniacs around Alex's body whilst Chaise pressed himself against the wall and looked on.

Amidst the hive of activity, the surgeon rounded on Chaise. "You have to leave now, Mr Chaise."

Without arguing, Chaise reeled into the corridor. Try not to excite him, the doctor had said, and Chaise had done exactly that. He should have spared Alex the details, kept everything light.

He checked the room through the door window. They were working less frenetically now, Alex growing calmer. Chaise took his chance, slipped back inside, and took the address book from Alex's coat pocket just as the surgeon looked up, his face contorting with barely controlled rage.

Chaise returned to the corridor to see a tall woman, dark-haired woman standing at the reception desk. She looked up as Chaise approached. From behind her, a small, blonde-haired girl studied him with big, expectant eyes.

"You must be Diane," said Chaise. He shot a smile towards the girl. "And you must be Amy."

"And who are you?" Diane asked sharply.

"A friend. Ryan Chaise."

Nothing flickered across her face. "And Alex? How is he?"

"He's okay, given the circumstances."

"Circumstances? You mean his stupidity. Is he in there, where they all went racing in?"

"I think he was taken ill."

"Ill? Another attack, for God's sake?" She shook her head. "It's attention-seeking, or an attempt to make me stay. You're a friend? Then you should know all about his histrionics."

Chaise flinched at the harshness of her voice, the condemnation in the words taking him by surprise. "Er... I'm not sure if that's the case. He's experiencing some pain. I think they're just making sure he's comfortable."

"Bloody typical of him this is. He knows we're about to leave, so he pulls this."

"I don't think he—"

"No, well you wouldn't, being a friend. How do you know him? I've never met you before."

"I'm an estate agent. I was following up a call to my office about selling your house when we met. Seems like a lifetime ago now ..." Chaise thought about how much had happened in such a short space of time, how everyone's life had turned completely upside down in a matter of, what was it? Hours?

"I blame all of this on Shaun. Bloody low life that he is. Waste of space." She gathered herself, taking Amy by the hand. The little girl hadn't said a word, all the while her eyes boring into Chaise. "Well, as long as he isn't in danger, we'll go. You'll tell Alex we called, but obviously..."

Yes, obviously. "I will, don't worry."

"I'm not worried, Mr Chaise. I've lived with him for nearly fifteen years. I know exactly what he thinks, how he works. That's why I'm leaving. I've had enough." She went to go.

Resisting her mother's tug, the little girl pulled back, her eyes wet with tears as she spoke. "Promise me my daddy is going to be all right."

Stunned, Chaise reeled as if punched in his solar plexus. Clearing his throat, he nodded, his voice nothing more than a croak, "Yes, he's going to be fine, Amy."

"I want you to promise."

Chaise looked across to Diane, whose eyes had narrowed, face darkened. "I promise."

Diane took a tighter hold of Amy's hand and marched her towards the hospital entrance. Chaise thought he heard Amy's voice floating back to him, "I like him, he's much nicer than the other doctor."

The normality of Alex's world suddenly hit him, Amy's voice so tiny, so innocent, so full of everything that life should be. Not a cruel life, filled with threats and hate, not the life Chaise had tried so hard to leave behind. Alex had all of that. But normality could be shaken, even shattered, turning into something alien, full of danger. Chaise had made Amy a promise that Alex would be all right. Now, he made himself another promise. He would restore it all, bring it all back to how it was. The normality.

He let out his breath in a long stream. That wouldn't be easy. What he was thinking might mean making things a lot worse before they got better.

Chaise was more than prepared to do just that.

TWENTY-NINE

With no luck at The Englishman's Bar, Chaise decided to go to Shaun's apartment, but not before he gathered his thoughts. After saying farewell to the owner, he went outside and considered sending Linny a text to let her know what was happening. She'd said she was going away but gave no hint as to when. It could be now, and he imagined her busily packing a couple of holdalls, throwing them into the back of her car before speeding off ... to Alicante? She must have cleared it all with her employers so perhaps this was something she'd planned for a while, deciding enough was enough? He had no idea of knowing, but one thing he was certain of – the car sitting on the other side of the square was the same vehicle he'd spotted in his rear-view mirror as he'd driven away from the hospital. Without glancing over, he got into his own car and set off for Shaun's apartment. Things, he realised, were coming to a head.

It was an uneventful drive down to the coast. Torre del Mar hadn't quite hit the summer hiatus yet, so he found a parking space without much trouble. So did his tail, which swung in opposite. Chaise stepped out into the warm afternoon and walked the few paces to Shaun's apartment block.

The flat was on the third floor, so Chaise took the lift. No one had followed him in so as the lift slowly ascended, he closed his eyes, letting the tension ease from his limbs.

The door hissed open and he stepped out into the empty hallway. He waited. There was only one entrance, the stairwell. He listened. When nothing stirred, he moved to Shaun's front door.

He rapped lightly on the door, waited, then tried again. He pressed his ear against the woodwork and closed his eyes, listening intently. There was a strange sound emanating from within, but he couldn't tell what it was. The faint drone of machinery, or an electrical device perhaps. As he stepped back, the lift door opened and he turned, his heart missing a beat.

A powerfully built woman emerged, struggling with several heavy-looking shopping bags. She cursed as one became caught between the closing door. Chaise quickly crossed over to her and helped tug the bag free. Muttering her gratitude, she swore at the closing lift door.

Chaise smiled. "Hard work, shopping," he said.

She looked at him, grunting again.

"You must know Señor Shaun?" She frowned before giving a sharp shake of her head. "The Englishman?"

Her eyes widened with sudden understanding. "Ah, him. I have not seen him for days." She gathered her bags. "Try Miguel, he will tell you better than me."

Miguel? Who the hell was Miguel? She must have noted the perplexed look on his face and sighed. "The janitor," she explained. "First floor, apartment three." He grinned his thanks and, as she disappeared inside her apartment, he raised his arm and called the lift.

It opened almost at once. A tall man dressed in a fawn suit, his hair slicked back in traditional Spanish style. But this man was not Spanish. He was the driver that had tailed Chaise from the hospital. His face froze in abject horror, clearly not expecting to find Chaise standing there right in front of him. Recovering, he took a step and Chaise struck. Three hard fingers directly into the little hollow below the man's Adam's apple. Croaking, hands clawing at his throat, the man fell back against the wall and slid down to the ground. Chaise deftly took the gun from the man's shoulder holster. Chaise called the lift again and bundled the man inside. Without another glance, Chaise pressed the button for the first floor.

There was a service cupboard on the first floor and Chaise put the man in there. He'd be fine after a good rest, perhaps a sore throat, but nothing more. He pressed the door closed and pulled his shirt out over his pants, to hide the Glock automatic that was now in his waistband.

He listened outside apartment number three. The sound of a television or radio came barking from within and Chaise pounded the door with his fist. The rattle of a chain soon followed and a small, squat man, presumably Miquel, poked his head out. The mandatory cigarette drooped from the corner of his mouth forcing him to screw up his eyes against the smoke as he croaked, "Que?"

"I need to speak to Shaun," said Chaise. "The lady in number thirty-two, she said you might know where he is."

"Well, I don't."

Miguel went to close the door, but he wasn't quick enough, and Chaise put his foot in the jamb. Before Miguel could offer up a few choice swear words, Chaise already had the fifty-euro note presented between finger and thumb. He smiled. "It's really important I take a look inside his apartment."

Nodding Miguel took the money and grunted, "I'll just get the key."

THIRTY

Michael hated this kind of work. He felt it was beneath him to go running around after busybodies who should know better than to involve themselves in business that didn't concern them. He'd much rather be at the beach, sunning himself, eying up some of the boys. There had been one boy, only a few weeks ago, lovely looking lad. Only short, but well put together. He'd come and sat down next to Michael, not knowing who Michael was. Perhaps it was for the best because later after he'd taken him for a ride and screwed him in the back seat, he'd snapped his neck and dumped him amongst the tall grass. But that was how Michael worked sometimes. Every now and again he simply needed to purge himself, rid himself of the excess adrenalin. Well, that's what he liked to say to himself, to stop the nightmares. This poor kid had come across Michael in the aftermath of what had happened to Shaun. That had been messy. Damned messy. Shaun was a big man, took a lot to put him down.

Put down he was, however, and Michael had got everything from him before he'd slit his throat. The blood had spurted over his cuffs. God, how he hated that. No amount of laundering ever got the stains out, so Michael burned the shirt and that made him angry. It had cost a lot and when he'd gone to the beach to try and get some rays, this bloody kid with the big cock had come and sat next to him. Some days, nothing ever goes right.

He rapped his fingers on the dash and looked out across the street. Lawrence had been gone too long. He was only supposed to check where the other guy was going, not try anything stupid. Michael didn't want any aggravation at this time of day. Just a simple job, quick and easy. He should have stayed at home.

Five more minutes. He looked at his watch. Five more minutes and then he'd go and see.

He put his head back and closed his eyes. Bloody mundane, boring jobs. How he hated them.

It stank. Miguel baulked, turning away as soon as he'd pushed the door open, a hand clamped over nose and mouth. Chaise knew the smell far too well. He pressed another fifty into Miguel's hand, winked, and eased him back outside.

He to the window and stopped. He was going to open it, let some fresh in and the stale stench of rotting flesh escape, but then he thought better of it. Fingerprints, they had to be kept to a minimum. Domingo would have a field day, placing him in this place. But then, Miguel and the lady in thirty-two would do that anyway. "Fuck it," he hissed and pushed the window open. He put his head out and took in great gulps of thick, hot, afternoon air. It felt almost as good as a glass of ice-cold beer.

The place was a mess. Someone had literally taken it apart. Furniture upended, ornaments, CDs, books, magazines all strewn over the floor. Blood too. A trail of it, as if a body had been dragged into the other room.

Chaise followed the trail to the tiny kitchen. Here, whoever it was who had destroyed Shaun's world, as well as his life, had played the last, perverted card. Whether it had been an attempt to prevent decomposition, or simply some awful joke, Chaise didn't know. It hadn't worked.

The noise, what he thought was machinery, wasn't. A blanket of flies, a writhing mass of them, clambering over one another, spread out all over the door of the refrigerator in the corner. And over something else as well.

Shaun had been stuffed inside. Badly. He had been a big man and, despite their best efforts, the killers hadn't quite managed to shove in the whole body and the door could not shut properly. Consequently, the contents had gone off – milk, cheese, vegetables, the whole stinking lot. Shaun too. It had to be him. The flies made clear identification difficult, even if Chaise had known the man by sight.

He'd seen similar things before, the grotesque attitude of bodies frozen in death, bulging eyes, arms reaching out in supplication, but this was infinitely worse. A deliberate act, designed to terrorize the onlooker, bring not only the gall into their throat but also the fear into their belly. What Chaise saw sickened him, the man's bloated corpse, maggots and flies writhing over the face, the stink biting the back of his throat.

He was about to swing away when something caught his eye amongst the bubbling black mass. He craned his neck to look closer. Dangling from around the dead man's neck, a label, handwriting scrawled over it: Sell-by date expired.

The anger brewed up inside. These were animals he was dealing with. Worse than animals, monsters. That little shit at the swimming pool hadn't learned his lesson.

A sudden knock at the door caused Chaise to suck in a sharp breath, despite the foul smell. He went across and peered through the tiny spyhole. It was Miguel and he looked sick. Chaise opened the door.

"What the fuck is going on?" he demanded.

Chaise frowned. "What do you mean?"

Miguel nodded down the hallway and Chaise took a step to

see what the man meant. The service cupboard hung open and a man lay on the floor, half in, half out of the tiny space. He'd tried hard to get out, but right now, his face a ghastly shade of yellow, he didn't look very well at all. "I think he is dead," said Miguel.

Chaise shook his head. "He'll be fine. Just throw some water over him." He eased himself past Miguel saying, "Trust me, he'll be fine." He thrust the last of his money into the janitor's hand. "Give me ten minutes before you ring the police."

From the expression of dread on the man's face, it was clear it would take far longer than ten minutes before Miguel found the strength to get his limbs working once more.

The man standing in the entrance to the apartment block was big, athletic-looking, and when he saw Chaise his face froze. Keeping his eyes set straight ahead, Chaise pushed past and stepped out into the daylight. He took a deep breath and decided to give the tall man a dismissive look because he wanted to rile him, get some reaction. There was none. Although Chaise did not recognize him, there could be no doubt that this man had something to do with Shaun's death. Chaise debated whether or not he should break the man's neck there and then, but it was late afternoon and plenty of people were in the street. Forcing himself to relax, Chaise lifted his sheet briefly to reveal the Glock, grinned, put a finger to his right eyebrow in a mock salute, and strode over to his car without another glance. The day would come.

Michael seethed. That was Lawrence's gun in that bastard's waistband, he just knew it. What the hell had happened, where was Lawrence, and who the hell was that guy? Shaun had mentioned nothing about a third partner. Michael knew if there was such a partner he'd tell, given he'd broken every one of Shaun's fingers. When attention was turned to his balls, Shaun bleated like a sheep but not a single word about anyone else. Nevertheless, here he was, giving that bloody salute. Well, the bastard was heading for an early grave, that much was certain. Michael would find out who the stranger was, and he'd do so from the one person who had such information.

Alex.

THIRTY-ONE

"If you didn't already know, my name is Gomez."

Alex smiled at the tall man leaning over him. Dressed in a white coat, a stethoscope dangled from around his neck, he was the epitome of a hospital doctor, as was his bedside manner. Alex appreciated this and, since coming round from his attack, he had received nothing but efficient, caring attention from everyone he'd met. "I didn't but it's nice to know with whom you are dealing."

Doctor Gomez frowned and stood straight. "Is that correct?"

"Is what correct, doctor?"

"That statement? That word, *whom*? My English is ..." he smiled, somewhat self-consciously, "*good*, or so I like to think but I am not so arrogant to assume it is perfect."

Alex laughed. "I'm trying to be as grammatically correct as I can, doctor, and I do believe that is the correct usage. With whom. Sounds weird I know but it is how you're supposed to say it, I think – or should I say, how *one* is supposed to say it."

"A minefield." Doctor Gomez stepped back to allow a group of nurses to shuffle about and take notes whilst adjusting readings, dials, tubes, and whatever else required attention. Gomez looked at his watch. "I can go home now, Mr Piers, now that your little attack is over. Well, I say *little* but the truth is, Mr Piers, that any sort of complication with the heart is serious. You must try your very best not to over-excite yourself. Rest, Mr Piers, is the key to a speedy recovery."

"I understand. Thanks for your help."

"I think maybe it was your friend who overexcited you in the first place?"

"No. It wasn't him. He's a good man, please don't think anything less of him."

Gomez smiled. "Good. For now, I will leave you in the excellent hands of our nurses. I shall visit you again, Mr Piers. Tomorrow. Then, with any luck, you too will be able to go home."

Alex raised his hand and the doctor drifted out. The nurses fussed around for a couple more minutes before they also went away, leaving Alex alone in his room. He was well propped up with an abundance of pillows behind his head, magazines and novels on his bedside table, fruit juice, apples. What more could anyone want? He closed his eyes, tried to shut it all out. What more could anyone want …

Gradually his mind grew less fuddled.

He'd promised to play 'bogeyman' with Amy, he remembered that much. A few days ago now, before all of this, they were chasing each other around the swimming pool and Alex had slipped, cut his knee. They'd laughed, Amy too young to realize that it could have been more serious. When Alex had tried to straighten the pain hit him and he realized the cut was deep. More than a plaster would be needed to staunch the blood, so he placed two across the wound. The next day, with his knee swollen and puffy, he'd managed to hobble into the kitchen where Amy waited to play 'bogeyman'. This usually consisted of Alex jutting his bottom teeth out over his lip and making suitable "Quasimodo" noises as he lunged at her with outstretched arms. She would squeal and run as he relentlessly tracked her down and corner her before throwing her on the bed and blowing raspberries across her tummy. She loved that game, and Alex loved it too. But his knee hurt like hell as if crushed by an elephant. The idea of playing "bogeyman" would have to wait.

It was the last thing he'd said to her. 'I promise, we'll play it tomorrow'.

"Tomorrow" was the day he'd dropped off Ricky Treach. And now seemingly a hundred "tomorrows" had flickered by, like scenes from an old-time movie, staccato, difficult to fit together smoothly. All he did know was that his world had been turned upside down. Diane was taking Amy away and that game of "bogeyman" would have to wait. For how long, he had no way of knowing. A year, a hundred ... a lifetime either way. Sighing, he opened his eyes and gasped.

An athletic-looking man stood at the foot of the bed. Tall, well-groomed, square-shouldered, and angular. Swimmer perhaps. He smiled as he spoke, his voice sang with a lilting Irish brogue. "Hello there, Alex. Sorry to trouble you whilst you're not feeling so well. I'll only keep you a small second."

Still smiling, he sat down on the bed next to Alex. Propped up by the pillows, Alex had no opportunity to shift position or move away. He didn't know how long he'd slept, be it two minutes or two hours but right now, he was wide awake, a new, cold fear creeping across his shoulders. Here he was alone in a small room with an Irishman who stank of Paco Rabanne and looked too good to be true with that clean-shaven chin and those manicured hands. It was as if he'd prepared himself for an interview, or a screen-test.

Alex cleared his throat and did his best not to sound too

concerned. Because he was concerned, concerned and afraid. "I don't think I know you."

"No. That hardly matters though. What does matter is the answer you give me to my next question. Then, I'll be gone. Out of your life for good." He checked around quickly, then returned to Alex, patted his hand. "You're shaking, Alex. Don't shake. It's not good ... for your heart."

Inside Alex was falling apart, not simply shaking. This was not good – another attack would finish him for good. Concentrating on controlling his breathing, he did his best to calm himself and lessen the effects this man was having on him. Danger oozed from the man's every pore. "What do you want?"

"I want to know where you've put the drugs."

Alex gaped. All at once, the walls came pressing in around him, trapping him inside that small, airless room, with no hope of escape. Beyond the door, nothing moved, the whole hospital unearthly quiet. As his heart came up into his throat, Alex struggled to breathe, the tightness becoming more noticeable right across his chest. Talking now was impossible.

The man laid a large, dry hand on Alex's bare arm and patted it gently. "You mustn't fret," he said, his sing-song voice empty of threat, more the concerned friend, the mindful servant. "I just want you to tell me where the drugs are, that's all. I'll pay you, of course. A good price. After all, Mr Piers, we're not gangsters."

Alex relaxed, but only a little. The man seemed so genuine, so kind, almost like the good doctor Gomez himself. And yet, there was something. A fire in those green eyes, an intensity of thought, something in the way his large hand rested on Alex's arm, heavy yet menacing. The threat of something massive simmering under the surface. Alex gathered his senses. "I need to speak to my friend Shaun."

"Don't be worrying about him, he's fine."

"You've spoken to him? When? Is he all right?"

Another gentle pat. "As I said, he's fine. He gave me what

dope he had, but it wasn't very much. He told me you had the rest." Alex felt the fingers of the man's hand tighten their grip slightly. "So… where is the stuff?"

The grip grew progressively stronger but the smile, the smile remained.

THIRTY-TWO

A t this time of year, the heat intensifies, its presence
pressing down like a ton weight, making sudden
movements uncomfortable, causing sweat to break out in a rush
with every extra step. It is constant, both day and night with no
let-up. It drains you of energy, makes you irritable, brings
violent headaches. Chaise's headache began as soon as he'd
struggled into his car and driven out of Torre towards his home.
The higher he climbed, the worse the headache grew. This
always happened to him with the on-set of high-summer. As
soon as he parked near his front door he was running into the
house, desperate for a glass of water and a couple of pills.

Then he spotted Linny's letter and everything else faded into
insignificance.

Propped up against the toaster in the kitchen, he knew
instinctively it contained bad news.

She'd gone. But not to where he had feared, to her mother's.
Nearer, to a friend's house. She'd informed him, with chilling
simplicity, 'I'm at Rachel's. Please meet me there.'

She had not sent a text, almost as if she didn't wish to speak
to him. Clutching the note, he went back to his car and took the

drive down into the village, headache forgotten, replaced by a new, creeping dread, a realisation that something bad had happened.

She ran to him as he arrived. He caught her in his arms, and she remained like that, pressing her face into his neck. She trembled in his arms and he felt the heat pulsing from her body. She'd been crying. "What's going on?"

She looked back to the house. Rachel stood in the doorway, face drawn and worried. Linny took Chaise by the hand and led him inside. Rachel prepared them long, cool drinks whilst they sat in the lounge.

"They came this morning when you were out. Three of them."

"What do you mean, *they* came this morning? Who did, the police? Who?"

She sat forward, head down, hands pressed together. She didn't seem to have the strength to lift her head and look him in the eye. Perhaps she didn't want to, he thought.

Rachel came in and silently settled the drinks of the glass-topped coffee table, then went out again. Chaise ignored the glass, leaving it untouched. "Linny?"

She began to cry, tiny sobs at first, hyphenating her words as she struggled to explain, "They said ... I was very lovely. That you should be very happy to have someone so ... beautiful as a girlfriend. But how would you feel if I wasn't so lovely anymore ..." She took up her glass, drank, hands shaking. He went to move to her, but she brought up her palm to stop him. "They said that you must love me very much to trust me to go out to work every day, at the hospital, tending to the sick ... that together we were good for one another. But what if something happened ..." She pulled in her breath which gurgled in her throat. She put the drink down, pressed her hands against her face. "Oh Christ, Ryan … they were so … so fucking awful. They just kept on looking at me, telling me how lovely I was, what a wonderful home we had, but how would we manage on nothing, nothing at all. You in the hospital, me … Jesus … me with no face."

He sat and tried to listen, but the words were blurring now, of no real consequence. The meaning behind them, the threat, caused him to seethe inside. His hands shook but not from fear or dread. The monsters had come to his home, walked into his life. Monsters he believed were gone, buried. Like his past, a past he'd thought he'd left behind. Had left him.

This, threatening Linny, threatening him, their life, this was in another league now.

She turned to him, her eyes red-rimmed, cheeks strewn with tears. She did not attempt to wipe them away as she stared blankly. "Whatever it is you've done to upset them, they are fucking upset, Ryan. They want to meet you."

"Meet me?"

Linny nodded and pulled a piece of paper from the pocket of her jeans. She passed it over to him. "They want this resolved, I guess, whatever *this* is. They told me to give you that, then stay at home. Not say a word to anyone."

"But you came here." Ryan held the paper, reading the typed message.

"I know." She picked up her glass again and drained it. "I couldn't stay in that house on my own. Rachel doesn't know anything. If you can take me back home …"

He frowned. "Linny …" He reached over to take her in his arms. She crumpled, all of her emotions pouring out.

He held her for a long time.

. . .

On the journey back, she sat huddled-up, like an admonished schoolgirl, frightened to say a word in case her parents rounded on her, shouting their outrage.

Chaise, however, did not shout. Seething inside, he remained externally calm, in control. "These men," he said. "Three of them? Two big guys, and a smaller one who spoke with a Liverpool accent?"

She immediately sat up. "How did you ... oh shit, you've met them before!"

He glanced across to her, saw those accusing eyes, the flash of anger. "It's not ... Linny, I'm not deliberately keeping things from you."

"You could have fooled me!" Bringing her knees up to her chest, she turned away and pressed her face against the window. "Jesus Ryan ... I wished to God I was anywhere else but here right now."

"I ..." He struggled with what to say, or how much. He'd already lied, hadn't disclosed anything, but if she knew, would she ever trust him again? "Okay, I have met them. It was at the pool, in Benamargosa. We had words."

"The little one had a bruise," she said, without turning around. "One side of his face all purple and swollen. You did that. Don't deny it."

"I won't because it's true. Linny, I—"

"I don't want to know, Ryan. Just drive the fucking car."

THIRTY-THREE

The indigestion was becoming worse, a burning fire lodged somewhere inside. Every time he swallowed, it seared down into his stomach. He'd tried drinking milk, but after two large glassfuls, he was bloated. Miriam, his housemaid, had brought him ant-acid tablets. Wolfing them down, he lay back on the sun lounger and waited for them to get to work.

The news from Estepona arrived earlier. A car full of brutish Lithuanians had forced their way into one of his clubs, beaten up the doormen, threatened the manager and then proceeded to bust the place up. In full view of witnesses. The place was packed. Word had got out. Arthur Morgan had lost his touch, gone soft in his old age. The rotten fruit was about to fall off the tree. Time for a new gardener perhaps.

And now, Jimmy McNulty.

Together with his thugs, he'd come in, faces sullen, ashamed. Especially Jimmy, sporting a large red welt down one side of his face. Arthur didn't need to ask. Instead, he poured himself a large Scotch and drank it down without offering anything to the others.

"Just tell me," he said, already expecting the worse.

It was one of the others, Ken Leech, who spoke. Ken, a big man, used to pummelling his victims into a pulp and enjoying every second of it, spoke in subdued tones, struggling with what he had to say. "He was like a pro, Mr Morgan. Like nobody I'd ever seen."

"I told you to be careful." Arthur looked across his swimming pool, a second whisky in his hand.

"No one does that to Jimmy," continued Leech, shuffling from one foot to the next. "But he was so quick."

"He caught me by surprise. It won't happen again."

Arthur swung round, shaking with rage, spit spewing out from his mouth as he erupted. "Fucking grow up, Jimmy! *Caught you by surprise?* I told you, I fucking told you to watch him. And now it's happening, just like I said it would … all of it. Fucking Lithuanians have smashed up the club in Estepona, so, what do I do now, eh? Just sit back and twiddle my thumbs." He snapped his fingers, pointing directly towards Leech. "Get over to his girlfriend. Talk to her, make her understand. I want this stuff back. Arrange a meeting, anything. I want the stuff back now. Not tomorrow, not next week, now!" Fuming, Morgan drained his glass. "Jimmy, you can go along too."

Leech nodded before slinking off, the second heavy trailing behind. As McNulty went to follow, Arthur's voice brought him up short. "Jimmy. A word."

"I'm sorry about all of this, Mr Morgan."

"Save it. I don't want to hear excuses; I just want results. This bloke, there's something wrong about him. I want you to talk to our contacts in the consulate in Malaga. I want everything on this guy, you understand. Everything." He took in a huge breath. "This time, get it right."

McNulty turned and walked away, his head down.

Arthur stretched out on the sunbed, going over the conversation in his head for the umpteenth time. Ryan Chaise. Just a man, one single man, an estate agent. No one special.

Living the ex-pat dream with his girlfriend in a lovely little villa stuck on a hilltop overlooking the valley. What was so bloody special about that? What was so bloody special about him?

Massaging his stomach, desperate to relieve the pain building up, release the gas, Arthur pressed the flat of his hand down hard and groaned. When all this was over, he'd treat himself to a nice holiday. Somewhere quiet, relaxing.

His mobile shrilled into life and he groaned again when he saw who the caller was. His indigestion suddenly became worse.

Chaise's mobile went off just as he pulled into the driveway. It was Alex and he sounded in a terrible state. "Please, just get here as soon as you can."

He showed it to Linny, who made a face and got out of the car. "What was the point in saying you'll be with me if at the drop of a hat you rush off to be with your new friend?"

Getting out himself, he leaned across the car roof. "It's not like that and you know it."

"Do I? Ever since you got yourself involved in all of this, whatever it is, you've changed. Harder. Unfeeling."

"That's nonsense. Alex is sick, he just needs—"

"What about what I need? If those men come back …" She stood head back, eyes closed. Dressed in crop-top and tight jeans, she looked youthful, almost like a teenage girl and Chaise felt the yearning developing in his loins, those honey-coloured limbs so enticing.

"Why don't you come with me. It shouldn't take long."

She sighed. "No." She fished out the front door key from her pocket. "I'm going to bed. You do what you need to do, and when you come back and find me lying there, with my throat slit, I hope you feel at least a tiny pang of guilt."

"Jesus, Linny, don't be so …" He let his words remain unfinished as she strode across the gravel towards the house. He watched her, debating whether or not to follow. He needed to honour his words to be with her, comfort her. Damn this whole bloody mess, and damn Alex most of all for not taking the stuff to the authorities right from the very beginning. Heat rising, he got into the car and drove off.

He found Alex sitting on the edge of his bed, trousers on, shirt gaping open. "I've had a visitor," he said without turning to Chaise.

Chaise stopped. They were working fast. "What did they say?"

Alex shook his head, fumbling with the buttons on his shirt. "There was just the one. Big guy, Irish."

Chaise took a moment before sitting down beside Alex. This was suddenly becoming more complicated than he thought.

"They want to do a deal. They ..." Alex rubbed his face as if trying to wash away the filth or the mess that clung to every part of his skin. "Shit! They've got Diane and Amy."

The words froze on Chaise's lips. So, they'd done it, something he'd always expected. They'd begun to put pressure on the families. First Linny, now Alex's wife and child. Racking up the fear, as slime always do. He squeezed his hands into fists. "All right," he said, gritting his teeth. "You can come back to mine and we'll work out what to do next."

"Ryan, I want this to end."

"Don't you think I do? I'm sick of this, all of it. We'll meet with them, end it once and for all. Then we can begin to get our lives back to normal."

"Meet with them? You mean to say they've contacted you too?"

Chaise noted the fear in Alex's voice. "Yes, they went to my house, spoke with Linny." He spoke slowly, watching the colour draining from Alex's face, which wasn't good. "Alex, I want you to try and leave everything to me, okay? I don't want you to stress over all this."

"Stress? Jesus God, don't you think I'm more than bloody stressed?" Shaking his head, he muttered, "How did they know where you live, Ryan?"

Knowing the news might bring on another attack, Chaise gently squeezed Alex's arm. "I want you to take it easy, but there's no easy way to say this. I went to see Shaun." He paused. Next to him, Alex tensed as if preparing for the worst. "They killed him."

Without a word, Alex stood up, went to the door, pulled down his jacket and slipped it on. His shirt remained unbuttoned, but Alex wasn't concerned about that. Alex turned, his face a perfect, white mask of barely controlled rage.

Chaise waited, his eyes fixed on his new friend, this man who had brought chaos into his life. He should have felt anger towards him, but all he felt was pity. Alex had lost everything, almost his life. Wife and child held captive, his best friend dead.

The air crackled with tension and Chaise, half-expecting another attack, braced himself to press the emergency button next to the bed. Instead, Alex remained calm and spoke with a voice low, full of dread. "Ryan … you're missing something."

"What do you mean?"

"I mean about Shaun." He shook his head, staring into space. "Shaun didn't know anything about you. So how could he tell them where you live?"

THIRTY-FOUR

The suspicion had been growing in Chaise's mind for some considerable time and now it was confirmed. What Alex told him brought everything into clear focus.

There were two gangs, each one prepared to go to any lengths to find the dope. Chaise didn't understand why. The haul, if it could be classed as such, was a mere bundle, so there had to be something more to all of this. What Ricky inadvertently left behind in Alex's car was part of a much larger shipment and the gangsters suspected that Alex, Shaun, and perhaps even Chaise himself had the rest. He shuddered at the thought.

After Alex signed the form at the desk, they left the hospital and crossed the car park. The evening air was thick, uncomfortable with swarms of mosquitoes buzzing around them.

Almost as soon as he opened the car door, Chaise's mobile went off. He checked the name and cursed. Alex raised an eyebrow. Chaise waved him towards the car, turned and answered the call.

"Señor Chaise." Domingo's voice sounded annoyingly calm. Chaise doubted it would remain so once what had happened at the apartment block in Torre unfolded. "Where were you? I tried your house, spoke to your lovely partner. She seemed a little tense."

"I'm at the hospital. Visiting."

A long pause followed. Chaise could almost hear the cogs turning in Domingo's mind. "I see. What it is, I have a slight problem, Señor Chaise. Nothing that can't be, how you say, overcome."

Chaise waited. This game that Domingo liked to play was tedious in the extreme.

"Are you still there, Señor Chaise?"

"Yes." Chaise blew out a loud breath. "What is it you want exactly, Domingo?"

"Ah, you are always so impatient, Señor Chaise. Perhaps you have appointments to keep?"

Chaise knew he must remain calm, careful not raise any suspicions. "It's late. I just want to go home."

"Yes, yes of course. I won't keep you. I have had an interesting conversation. With my superiors. More accurately, everyone's superiors."

"I don't understand ... who are you talking about?"

"Spanish secret service, Señor. The CNI. Not as well-known as your country's MI6, I suspect."

For all the wrong reasons, mused Ryan. The Centro Nacional de Inteligencia had been linked with several high-profile attempts to undermine British support amongst the locals in Gibraltar and open sores between the British and the Spanish governments. "I've heard of them."

"Yes. I thought you might have." Another pause before Domingo continued, changing the tone of his voice from thick oil to hard steel, "They have told me to leave you alone, Señor

Chaise. Leave you alone. Those were the words they used. Why do you think they might wish that, do you know?"

"Haven't a clue."

"Really?"

"Why would I?"

"Indeed, so to confirm things, for myself you understand, I telephoned your Mr Phelps. You remember him, I am sure. The man who came down from—"

"Yes, I know who you mean, Domingo. Just get to the damned point."

"I'm already there, Señor. I don't like being told what to do, certainly not by faceless officials in Madrid. Phelps, he confirmed what they said. I must leave you alone. Must. Again, that was the word used. What I want to know is, what makes you so damned bloody important?"

"If you want my advice, Domingo, I would do exactly what they say."

Domingo snorted. "Yes. I thought you might say that. The problem is, Señor, I'm not going to."

Chaise raised his eyes. "Well, that's your decision."

"Indeed, it is."

The phone went dead. Chaise stood for a moment before slipping the phone into his pocket. He slapped his neck where a mosquito had decided to land and returned to the car. He got in beside Alex.

"Anything wrong?"

Alex's face was that of a lost boy, out of his depth, frightened, confused. All he wants, thought Chaise, is a way out, an end to all of this shit. The problem is, the end isn't going to be nice and neat. It's going to be bloody and brutal and people are going to die. Chaise forced a smile, the best reassuring smile he could manage. "No, everything is just fine."

. . .

They drove back to Chaise's house in silence. Chaise revealed nothing of the conversation with Domingo, but inside he unpicked it, pleased his old bosses back in London had applied pressure. Domingo's response, however, irked him. The man was unpredictable, a loose cannon. Once information about Shaun's death and Chaise's subsequent altercation with the men who had trailed him came out, Domingo wouldn't hesitate to bring him in for questioning. What might then follow would almost certainly be outside the law. Domingo was going to make this personal.

"There's something I've been meaning to ask you," said Alex, staring into the blackness ahead.

His words cut through Chaise's thoughts, bringing him back to the present. "Nothing too complicated, I hope."

"Maybe it is. I don't know you very well so this may sound, oh, I don't know, strange? I just wanted to know how you remain so damned cool all the time. Nothing seems to faze you or causes you stress." He gave a tiny chuckle. "Thought you might be able to pass on some tips."

"You feeling okay?"

"Fine, apart from when I think about Shaun. How did he … die?"

There was a tremble in Alex's voice that Chaise did not like. "I think it would be best if you tried to put that to the back of your mind, at least for the time being."

"I'm all right, I promise. They gave me some beta-blockers. At least, I think that's what they are. Look more like horse-pills!" He laughed and patted his pocket. "A load of other things too. I've got about half a dozen pills they've ordered me to take each morning."

"It'll be okay, Alex, as long as you remain calm."

"I know, but things have been getting on top of me. Too much happening too quick. I've had scares before, but nothing like this."

"With your heart?" Alex nodded. "You don't appear like the usual candidate for a coronary."

"Well, that's something I suppose. I don't look like a candidate, even though I am one." He gave a short laugh. For a time, he gazed out of the window into the night before saying, "So, how do you do it? Stay so detached?"

"It didn't come naturally. I had training. Lots of training."

Alex sat up straight. "Training? What does that mean, exactly?"

"What else can it mean? I was trained, Alex. Years ago. You didn't think I'd always been an estate agent?"

"I did actually."

"We all have a life, Alex, a life that goes through changes."

"So, you did something else before? Something, I don't know, unusual, that required training, training to keep you calm?"

"That and a lot else besides."

"I see. Who trained you?"

"The army. Well, sort of army. Navy as well. I was what you might call cross-services."

"Cross-services

"There's not much I can say, to be honest. What I will say is the stuff we're going through right now is very similar to what I've experienced before. Let's just leave it at that."

"My God. You mean …"

Chaise raised a hand from the steering wheel. "Let's just leave it for now."

"Okay."

The car bumped over a speed ramp and a large villa loomed from the blanket of the night. A single light burned over the door, casting a yellow circle across the driveway, illuminating another car parked there and a man, arms folded, leaning nonchalantly against it. In the half-shadow, the bulging biceps poking out of his rolled-up shirt sleeves seemed impossibly large. He exuded strength and danger, even from this distance.

"Who's that?" asked Alex.

"Not a friend." Chaise pulled his car in next to the other one and switched off the engine. He looked at Alex before getting out. "But someone who could prove very useful."

THIRTY-FIVE

Slumped on a bar stool, Jimmy McNulty stared into the dregs of his drink. The barman hovered close by, wiping the countertop whilst humming a soulless tune. Without looking up, Jimmy growled, "Can you stop that, please."

The barman did so without comment, turning away to polish the optics in silence.

Jimmy clunked his glass on the counter. Immediately, the barman drew another beer from the pump, laid it down and took away the empty glass. Jimmy took a long drink, dark thoughts swirling around inside his head. Nothing mattered to him anymore except the memory of what had happened. He replayed it over and over in his mind, hoping that somehow, he could change the outcome. But every time he knew it would always come out the same. He'd been bettered and nothing hurt more than that.

Could he have done something, he mused. Something to change the outcome. It had happened with no forewarning and which such ferociously that Jimmy doubted he could have reacted any differently. Arthur's vague warning hadn't given any indication of just how formidable Ryan Chaise was. In their next meeting, Jimmy would be ready. He'd hit first, then we'd all see how the bastard fared. Jimmy stared at his drink. Dreams of the future might make him feel slightly better, but nightmares from his past, what Chaise had done, that would always send him down the spiralling tunnel of blackness.

The door opened with a crash, causing the heat to blast in. The barman breathed a sigh. "It's Ken Leech," he said and poured a beer.

Jimmy sighed. He barely looked as Leech sat next to him. "What do you want?"

Leech took the proffered beer. "That's not a very nice welcome, Jimmy."

"I asked you what you want."

Leech took his time, slurping at his drink. "I've been looking for you everywhere."

"So now you've found me." He finished his beer and indicated for another "Now you can go."

"Not so hasty, Jim. Arthur wants—"

"Arthur always fucking wants something."

Leech shifted in his stool. "He wants to know why you haven't done anything since he spoke to you earlier."

"How does he know I haven't?"

"What?" Leech looked around the deserted bar. A sad, seedy little place frequented by sad, seedy locals. On this evening no one ventured out. Mid-week. Pay cheques depleted. "You mean you have?"

Jimmy chuckled. "No, but I might have for all you know."

"I know quite a lot, as it happens."

"What do you mean by that?"

"That someone has been to the hospital, to speak to our friend Alex. Tony clocked some big guy talking to him.

Jimmy's stomach tensed. "Not that Chaise bastard?"

"No, that Chaise bastard isn't big. Just punches big." He chuckled, drank his beer.

Jimmy held his breath, struggling to prevent his anger from spilling over. Leech always did fancy himself, thinking he was above Jimmy in most things. Jimmy's success came from the fact that, due to his size, almost everyone underestimated him. Leech, on the other hand, was massive. A real bear of a man. Perhaps he believed Chaise had shown Jimmy up to be something of a fake. Well, if Leech believed that, he was in for a very rude awakening. Slowly Jimmy released his breath. "He didn't punch me." Unconsciously, he rubbed the swelling on the side of his face. No, the bastard hadn't punched him. He'd chopped him, edge-of-hand, harder and more precisely than any man had ever done. He remembered that night at Tiffany's, how the bouncer there had chopped a big guy across the side of the head, how the big guy had gone down like a sack of spuds. Jimmy didn't think it was possible. Now he knew it was. "So, who was it?"

"Dunno. Tony tried to follow him but lost him in the traffic. Typical." Leech finished his beer and shook his head as the barman approached to serve a second. "Arthur wants us to go and give Alex another visit, find out who the guy was and what he wanted."

"What, at the hospital?"

"No. When Tony got back, Alex had gone. He's discharged himself."

"Why would he do that?"

Leech shrugged. "Who knows? But I think it's got to have something to do with his visitor."

Jimmy rolled his beer glass between his palms. "That turd took my gun."

"Who did? Alex?"

"No, you dumb bastard – Chaise. I want it back, then I'm going to flay him alive."

"Flay? What's that?"

Jimmy shook his head, looked at the beer dregs then drank

them down. He made a face. "Jesus, this is shit beer. It's times like this I wish I was back home." He stood up, threw a screwed up five-euro note on to the counter and buttoned up his jacket. "First, I want to talk to Tony. Get a description of this 'big guy' who went visiting, then we'll go and see Alex."

"And what about your gun and that Chaise bloke?"

Jimmy forced a smile. It was difficult, but the chance to exact revenge made him feel slightly easier. Depression was not something he was used to. It was rare for him to feel so low, so morose. Of course, it was also rare for anyone to have bettered him the way Ryan Chaise had. Recompense would be sweet. "Oh, don't worry about that Ken. When we meet up again, I'll be taking more than my gun from Mr Chaise. I'm looking forward to it."

THIRTY-SIX

The clinking of glasses of another sort made it seem almost normal. Chaise listened as Linny busied herself in the kitchen. He couldn't believe the events of the last few days, nor how those yet to come might change everyone's lives forever. Nothing would ever be the same again.

Chaise glanced over to where Major Embleton stood, one arm propped on the mantelpiece, gazing into space.

"So, what's the plan, Major?"

Embleton didn't look up. "This whole thing is a total mess, Chaise. You should never have become embroiled in it. And you," he levelled his gaze at Alex, who sat hunched up on the sofa, "what an absolute bloody idiot you've been."

Alex gaped. "Exactly who the hell are you to talk to me like that?"

"Calm yourself, Mr Piers," smiled Embleton, "don't get yourself too worked up, what with your dodgy ticker and all."

"Pack that in, Major." Chaise turned to Alex, whose face had coloured alarmingly. "Major Embleton works for the British government, Alex. He's what could be termed a friend, although perhaps not one that you would want to have, given the choice."

"Which none of us has," put in Embleton.

Chaise smiled. "Precisely. So, apart from the barbed insults, Major Embleton, what have you got in mind?"

"This meeting was arranged with your lovely girlfriend, where exactly will it take place?"

Chaise unfolded the piece of paper Linny had given him. "Underground car park, Totalán."

"Never heard of it."

"Don't worry," Chaise put the paper away, "I have. Midnight it says."

Embleton checked his wristwatch. "Just under an hour. If we get there first, perhaps we can get ourselves in a better position. I very much doubt they have any idea about me."

Chaise nodded, decision made. "Okay. We'll have to leave sharpish. It takes about forty minutes to get there from here. I'll go and tell Linny."

Alex watched Chaise pad into the kitchen and sat back, letting the air come into his lungs slowly. He must keep calm. He'd listened to Embleton's barbed remarks, almost lost control. Who the hell did he think he was? Alex wasn't used to being spoken to in that manner, but he had to let it go, turn his mind to other things.

The meeting.

The Irishman had mentioned the meeting, but it had nothing to do with underground car parks. The question now remained, who had given the information to Chaise's girlfriend? Could there be two meetings, two messengers from rival gangs? And here everyone was, right in the middle of them. Alex recalled the Irishman, what he'd said, the way he'd said it and a buzz ran through his scrotum, the fear returning. Whoever these people were the time had come to end everything, hand over the drugs, take whatever money was offered and draw a line through the whole business. Go back to the U.K., forget Shaun, keep close to Amy, try and salvage something from the cesspit his life had become.

For this to go off smoothly, Chaise and the so-called Major could not be involved. Alex needed to come up with some way to get clear of them. How to do that, he had no idea. Time was running out, and he had to think of something very good, very soon.

Chaise came up behind Linny and slid his arms around her waist. She flinched, pulled away, turned, and scowled. "Don't think you can just push all of this under the carpet," she said, voice low but laced with anger.

"I take it that means you're still going?"

"As soon as this nonsense with Alex is over."

"It will be soon."

"Alex can stay here. Any more excitement would probably kill him."

Chaise opened up the refrigerator and brought out a carton of orange juice. As he poured himself a glass, he said, "I don't want you to go." His eyes came up and held hers. He didn't know what else to say, never having had the emotional depth or attachment to reveal his true feelings. But this was different. Linny was everything to him, his life, his reason for being. They'd met each other by chance, at a launch party for a planned residential complex up in Mollina. Something sparked between them and three years later they still sparked. Now, this. He hadn't purposely kept things from her, his only desire to shield her and protect her. In so doing, he'd made her suspicious, shown something of himself that he would have preferred to have kept hidden. A darker side. An older side.

"I think it's for the best," she said, her voice detached. She'd begun to build the wall. His attempts to break through by small shows of affection wouldn't succeed. He knew it, sighed, bit his lip, and drained the glass of juice. He went back into the room.

Embleton looked up as Chaise returned, Linny close behind, carrying a tray with the juice. She settled it down on the coffee table and stepped over to the window.

Reaching under his shirt, Ryan tugged the Glock automatic he had taken from the man who had followed him to Shaun's. Embleton frowned. Ignoring him, Chaise stepped over to Alex. "You know how to use one of these?"

Alex shook his head. "What do you have in mind, Ryan? Me as a back-up?"

"No, you as staying at home, here with Linny."

"Eh?"

"You're not going to the meeting, Alex. You're staying here. It's too dangerous. The Major and I will sort everything out, have no worries."

Alex's face took on a distinctly scarlet tinge. "You're kidding, right?" He stood up, a limp hand taking the gun. He weighed it in his hand.

"It's for the best," Chaise continued. "If things start getting hairy, it might, you know …"

"Bring on another attack," said Embleton, finishing off Chaise's awkward-sounding sentence.

Alex slowly drew back the gun's sliding mechanism, engaging the first round. Chaise looked up and saw it. The change. But he was too late, and so too was Embleton, half-standing from the sofa.

Linny yelped as Alex crossed the room in a blur and took her around the throat. Spinning her around, he put one hand across her mouth and pressed the gun's muzzle against her temple with the other. He was grinning, but Chaise could see that the upturning of the mouth had nothing to do with pleasure, more the maniacal snarl of someone close to the edge.

"I take it that means you know how to use that thing?"

Alex strengthened his grip on Linny as she struggled and mumbled something beneath the clamp of Alex's hand around her mouth. "Enough to know that I will do what I have to do." He pressed the muzzle hard into the girl's head. She squirmed but went quiet. "I'm going to the meeting, alone."

A tiny trickle of sweat meandered down Chaise's left cheek. The knot in his stomach tightened, but he needed to maintain an air of cold calm if Alex wasn't to break and let that damned gun could go off. "All right, Alex. Whatever you say." Embleton gawped at him. Chaise raised his arm slightly and the Major sat back down. "You do what you need to do, but please, leave Linny here."

"Can't do that, my friend. She's my guarantee against either of you supermen trying anything silly. I'm going to take her car, drive to the meet, and if you try and follow, I swear to God I'll put a hole in her. It might be in the arm, it might be in the leg, but I can tell you now, it'll hurt."

Chaise nodded. "Okay, Alex." Another rivulet of sweat joined the first. The Major remained tense, a coiled spring, jaw hard, eyes bulging. Chaise saw it and raised his arm a fraction higher, warning Embleton to back off. "We won't follow. Just take it easy."

Still holding Linny, Alex edged towards the door. Chaise remained still, making the occasional glance towards Embleton, willing him to do the same.

They followed Alex outside. Opening the passenger door, he, at last, released his hold on Linny. She gasped, almost fell. Alex motioned her to get in behind the wheel before looking at the others standing in the porch, the light picking them out like actors on a stage. "Go back inside and close the door."

Chaise complied and leaned against the hallway wall, studying Embleton's contorted face. "What the hell are you playing at?" fumed the Major.

"I didn't exactly have much choice, did I?"

"We could have rushed him."

"What, and take the risk of him blowing Linny's face apart? No thanks." From the other side of the door, they heard Linny's sports car roaring into life. Chaise ran a hand across his brow. The palm was soaked with sweat.

"So, what do we do now?"

Chaise sighed. "We'll take my hire car, try and head him off but without him noticing."

"That's one hell of a risk, Chaise. If he spots that we're following him …" He pursed his lips, shook his head. "I thought from what you said that the girl meant something to you."

"What exactly are you saying?"

As Chaise prepared himself to bounce Embleton down the hallway on his backside, there came a tentative knock at the front door. Chaise sucked in a breath and glared at his new 'partner'. Embleton had a knack of winding him up more than anyone he'd ever met – including his handlers over in London.

Another knock, more insistent this time. Chaise swung around and pulled the door open and there stood Linny in the porch, bedraggled, tearful but safe. In her fist, looking overly heavy, was the handgun Alex had used to force her outside.

For a moment they both stood there, transfixed until she reeled forward, Chaise catching her. The wave of relief was overwhelming and suddenly lightheaded he fell with her to the floor. For a long time, he held onto her, not having the strength to think, let alone move whilst Embleton deftly picked up the gun, stepped back without saying a word, and faded away into the distance.

THIRTY-SEVEN

"W here did you get this?" asked Embleton as he handed the gun to Chaise.

"From the little weasel at the swimming pool." Chaise checked the gun's magazine then snapped it back into place. He glanced across to Linny who sat on the sofa, eyes blank and red-rimmed, a distant look on her face.

Embleton checked his watch. "I reckon he's got a good fifteen minutes on us."

"Bang goes our idea of getting there early."

"Unless we leave now – and drive fast."

Chaise grunted. None of this was panning out the way he wanted and that made him nervous. He got down on his haunches and took one of Linny's hands in his own. He peered into her face. "I have to go. I'll phone you every half hour, make sure you're okay."

Her face didn't register anything when she replied, "Don't worry about me, Ryan. Just get this sorted."

"Are you sure you'll be okay?"

Her face came up, eyes as lifeless as black coals. Nothing

there, just a dull acceptance of fate. "Do you think he would have shot me?"

"I don't know. He's desperate. Desperate people are capable of anything."

"But … to shoot me?"

Chaise shrugged, placed a hand on her knee. "Lock the doors, turn off the lights. We'll be as quick as we can."

"Ryan." She reached out and grabbed his arm. He felt his whole stomach lurch. "You take care. Whatever happens, whatever has happened, I still love you."

The affirmation that their relationship was as strong as ever meant everything to him right then. "Everything that's happened is an opportunity for me to look deep inside myself, re-evaluate what matters. And it's us that matters, the love we have for each other." He stood up, the strength returning to his limbs, a new fire lit inside. "I'm going to finish this, Linny. And I'll never lie to you again."

She smiled, let him go.

As the two men crossed to the waiting car, Chaise heard the bolts snapping home. All she needed to do was wait. Wait until it was over.

Jimmy McNulty sat in his car, barely able to make out the surface of the nearby lake but that didn't matter. With the window wound down, the gentle lapping of water against the tiny beach came to him and calmed him. Not usually the type to dwell on thoughts of mortality, of what lay beyond this life, the dark place developing in Jimmy's head pushed him towards asking the age-old question: what was it all for?

They'd gone to see Ryan Chaise's girlfriend, spoken to her, given her the message. Now all they had to do was go there, to the underground car park, confront Chaise and end it. Something, however, had surfaced inside Jimmy, bundled up amongst the depression, the self-doubt – barely controlled rage. The news from the radio sparked it. A body, found in an apartment block down in Torre del Mar. Murdered. The grim details of the discovery, the wailing voice of the janitor as he described the scene. The appeal for witnesses, anyone who had seen three men, one very tall and well built, another man, tight-cropped hair, athletic looking. The third, hardly a mention, except that he had been taken away to hospital. Police in a flap, no motive as far as anyone could tell. Then the name of the man, Shaun Glacken.

"A low-life," Ken said, leaning back in the driver's seat, rolling up a cigarette with meticulous care. "Does a little bit of dealing along the coast, nothing special."

"I think the guy, the 'athletic-looking' one, I think it's Chaise." Jimmy chewed at the inside of his cheek.

"You're obsessed," Ken said and got out of the car to stroll down to the water's edge and smoke his cigarette.

Jimmy knew he was obsessed, but that didn't make him any less troubled. If the visitor to Shaun Glacken had been Ryan Chaise, it was clear things had become far more complicated than he had previously assumed. Chaise. Who the hell was he, how did he get to be so damned good with his fists? That wasn't usual. Sure, a man could be tough, well-trained even. Jimmy had seen them many times. But this guy, he had something special. A willingness. Not many had that. A willingness to destroy their opponent. Mercilessly.

Ken got back in, exhaling loudly as he slumped into his seat. Jimmy ignored the stench of tobacco clinging to the man's clothes, and declared his intentions, "We're going to see Piers at his house."

Ken didn't answer, put his head back, closed his eyes and waited.

"He won't be expecting it, so he'll be off-balance. I'll put the frighteners on him, get him to spill everything."

"Everything? About the drugs or Chaise?"

"I don't want to take any chances."

"Any chances over what? Chaise is bugging you, Jimmy. Why? Because he gave you a smack? You need to get over it, it's clouding your judgement."

"Chaise is not just some normal grunt and he's the key to this. Piers will know where he is. And the stuff."

"We need to go easy, Jimmy. The police and the newspapers are all over everything. First that girl, the body found down in Torre … We take it easy, nice and quiet like."

"Don't worry. We'll pick up Piers at his gaff and after some gentle persuasion, he'll lead us to the stuff *and* Chaise."

"Whatever you say, Jimmy. This is your show."

"That's right, it's my show. So, we'll give it a few hours, then we'll bring on the finale."

Not so very far away someone was thinking similar thoughts. Michael Brannigan lay on top of his bed, wondering who the man was that he'd passed outside Shaun's apartment block. He knew he should have asked Alex, but he was mindful of poor Alex still recovering from a heart attack. Any more stress could easily kill him. When Michael had mentioned that Alex's entire world would come tumbling down before his eyes, he'd noted the green smudge appearing along the man's jawline and thought that the time had come. He'd backtracked, forced a smile, tapped Alex gently on the knee. 'Not to worry, everything would be fine,' he'd told him. 'We'll meet up at your house, discuss the whole ghastly business, then I'll be on my way with the drugs and you can go back to your life. Oh, and one other thing, you can tell me where I can get some more.'

The greenness hadn't dissipated so Michael made a brisk retreat.

He hoped Alex hadn't died. He hoped that after their next

meeting, the whole tedious affair would be brought to an end, then he could relax. Kill Alex and relax.

That guy whom he had met at Shaun's, that troubled him. Something about him, the look in his eyes. Michael had seen that look before. The look of a man who knew how to handle himself and handle himself extremely well.

He turned over and tried to get some sleep. No matter what he did, the face of that man kept looming up in his mind.

Alex parked the sports car in a dip behind a clump of olive trees, turned the engine off, and waited. He wanted to get his bearings, think things through. He also wanted to be close to the house before the big Irishman came, surprise him, run him over if need be. Then he could get away, drive across to Portugal, make a deal with someone, somewhere. He closed his eyes. Soon, all his worries would be at an end.

Or perhaps, chillingly, this night would conjure up a whole lot more.

THIRTY-EIGHT

L eaving Linny behind, the two men drove across country and headed towards the motorway to their arranged liaison. Chaise knew there was only one direction for Alex to take but in the sports car, once he hit the main roads, he would easily make the underground car park well before anyone else.

Next to Chaise, Embleton slept.

The volume of traffic was light and soon Chaise was turning into the entrance of the shopping mall. Embleton stirred, sat up, and checked his gun. "You've got yours?"

Chaise nodded. "Let's hope we don't have to use them. Two Brits discharging guns in a confined space is not something the Spanish would take too kindly. Or," he shot a glance to his partner, "or shooting a gun anywhere. They've just about had enough of British and Irish gangsters using the *Costas* like their own private Dodge City."

"I thought the Spanish were chilled out with all that *mañana, mañana* stuff?"

"Don't you believe it. They may leave things to the last minute, but their law enforcement agencies are effective, and they won't hesitate to throw foreigners into jail. So, just take care and hold your fire until we can identify the target."

"I'm not a novice, Chaise. I've done this sort of thing before. Many times."

"I'm counting on it."

The car park was in darkness and seemingly deserted. Turning the headlights off, Chaise rolled the car to a stop. Without a word, Embleton slipped out into the night. Chaise waited and watched until the darkness swallowed his partner up.

Chaise got out and waited, senses alert. He'd been here many times before, to shop. This, however, this was different. He pressed the car door shut, pulled out his gun, and slowly moved farther into the vast gaping cavern of the car park.

Keeping himself close to the wall, he pondered over what might be lurking in the inky depths. Three men, armed with submachine guns, perhaps or a sniper aiming through infra-red sights, already picking him out? Criminals were so well equipped nowadays, anything was possible. It was the security forces that had to rely on sub-standard equipment nowadays as budgets were constantly squeezed. The well-oiled drug barons, with their links to the smooth trafficking of arms, along with everything else, had no such monetary constraints. This plague of the modern world made it an incredibly dangerous place.

He got down on his haunches and tried to adjust his eyesight to the blackness. Way over on the far side glowed a smudge of dull red. An emergency exit sign, nothing more. Chaise checked his watch and, realising it wasn't illuminated, cursed silently. They could be early, of course, if Alex had chosen to take some sort of detour, but there couldn't be much in it. Doing his best to ignore the growing feeling something bad was about to happen, Chaise settled himself against the wall and allowed his head to drop onto his chest. Just a few moments rest before they arrived, that's all he needed. Calm the nerves, prepare himself.

Something metallic and loud clattered across the ground on the far side, shattering the silence, Chaise, instantly alert, rolled over to his right and positioned himself behind a pillar, gun trained forward.

He waited, straining to listen.

A voice, nothing more than a muffled hiss, came out of the darkness. "Ryan?"

Something – someone – moved close by. Chaise whirled around, gun coming up.

"It's me, damn it!"

Embleton crept out of the dark, face like a white mask, his breathing amplified and tinny sounding in that voluminous space. Chaise didn't like it. "Anything?"

"There's no one here. Not a soul."

"You've checked the whole perimeter?"

Chaise picked up on the barely controlled annoyance in the man's voice when he spoke, "I've checked everywhere. We're all alone." He stepped slightly closer. "Are you sure you had the right instructions?"

Ignoring him, Chaise sighed and stood up. "Perhaps we should wait, just a few more minutes."

"It's almost half-past three. Nobody's coming. I think Alex may have given us the runaround. We need a rethink."

Chaise grunted. A rethink indeed.

The return journey was more sedate. They came off the motorway at Velez Malaga and took the back roads to Benamargosa. By the time they returned to Chaise's house, the sun was well up, birds were singing, and it promised to be another spectacular day.

Chaise made them both coffee and they sat in silence as they drank.

Putting his coffee cup down on the table, Embleton put his

head back and closed his eyes. Chaise watched him, finished his drink, and went off to the bedroom.

Linny was deep in sleep. Chaise lay down next to her, fully clothed, put his hands behind his head and stared up at the ceiling. He'd give it an hour, then go over to Alex's house. That was the only answer now. Somehow, Alex must have changed the rendezvous place. He'd made that decision long before anyone left in that useless, time-wasting pursuit. Perhaps he'd made some agreement with that weasel, a deal, deciding it would be best if he kept everything to himself and

———

Chaise sat bolt upright, wide awake.

Of course. How could he have been so stupid, for so long? Given all that had happened, all those encounters with various thugs, Shaun, the swimming pool, the visit to the hospital.

Chaise strode into the lounge, shook Embleton roughly by the shoulder and watched as the man roused himself, groaning, rubbing red-rimmed eyes, gazing around disorientated. "Alex didn't go to the meeting."

Embleton rubbed his eyes. "What?"

"Alex. He didn't go."

"I know that, you idiot! I was there, remember!"

"No." Chaise sat down. "He didn't go to the meeting at the car park because he'd made a deal to be somewhere else."

"Eh? What are you talking about? Why would he do that? There's no way he could handle it on his own, he'd—"

"Listen. He's made a deal, but not with the people who made the deal with me." Chaise could see Embleton's confusion, but he ploughed on regardless, "There are others. The guy who went to see Alex in the hospital was not the same guy who confronted me at the swimming pool. Not even on the same team. They're rival gangs. I don't know the details for certain but what we have here is the beginning of a gang war, I'm sure of that much. One of the gangs is the original owners of the stuff, the others have got wind of it and want it."

"Hold on." Embleton sat up. "Even if what you say is true, why are they so concerned? A war? Over a kilo and a half of drugs. That's madness."

"I've thought of that. On the face of it, what you say is true. It's just not worth the hassle. But what if one group, the original owners who have been ripped off by Ricky, what if they are seriously pissed off about that. If you can steal from a big-time gangster outfit, that says a lot about you as a thief, but it says an awful lot less about the outfit. They want retribution, simple as that."

"All right, but that doesn't explain why another gang – if there is another one – would want to get involved. It's not worth it, not for such a paltry amount."

"I reckon they want control of the supplies. That's got to be it. They've had a sample, like it, think it's worth the risk. They see Alex, or me even, as the lynchpin, the go-between. They think we know something."

"And when they discover that neither of you does?"

Chaise shrugged and stood up. "They'll kill us. Or at least try to. In the meantime, Alex is in real danger, from both gangs. He's gone into this deal thinking he can negotiate, but he's naive if he believes any of them will do so. Either one of them will get what they can from him – either the drugs or the suppliers – then they'll kill him and dump his body in the Med. Or bury him in the foundations of a newly built apartment block … either way, Alex is not long for this earth."

"But I thought you said that he told you they had his wife, his daughter?"

"I know." Chaise bit his lip and raced back into the bedroom. Linny was already sitting up, hair dishevelled, bleary eyes, the ghost of a smile on her full lips. "Hello," she moaned, voice thick and heavy with sleep.

"Listen," Chaise slumped down beside her. "I need you to phone Alex's wife. You know her, yeah?"

"Only slightly. I haven't got her number. Why? What's happening now?"

Chaise didn't have time to give her all the details, explain his growing anxiety. "Linny. I need you to ring round your friends, get in touch with this woman—"

"Diane. Her name's Diane."

"Okay. I think she's in danger. Alex wasn't at the meeting place." He saw her eyes widen. "I don't know where he is, or what's happening. But he mentioned they had his wife"

"They? You mean the same ones who came here?"

"I need to know if what he said is true."

She nodded, swept the hair back from her face. "I'll get to it."

Chaise returned to the lounge, but Embleton was not there. He quickly crossed to the window, the dreadful thought that the SAS Major had decided to go it alone, take the car and race down to the coast on some futile attempt to find Alex developing in his mind. But the car was still there. Pressing his head against the cool of the glass, Chaise released a long sigh.

"Are you all right?"

Chaise whirled around to see Embleton standing in front of him, adjusting his trousers.

"I thought you'd gone."

Embleton arched a single eyebrow. "Hardly. I don't know one piece of this parched, baked land from the next." He smiled as he finished tightening his trouser belt. "Call of nature, that's all. Your girlfriend is safe with me."

Chaise stared for a few moments before he ran a hand through his close-cropped hair. "I'm not worried about that."

"What then?"

"I'm getting too old for all this Cowboy and Indian bullshit."

"You're out of practice, that's all."

"You think?"

"Well, we'll soon see, won't we? Something tells me that the climax is fast approaching. You're going to need your wits about you when we go up against this lot – or lots, if what you say is true."

"We could always let them shoot it out between them."

"Yes, we could. But you won't let that happen. For some reason, known only to you, you feel obligated to this Alex character, and you're not going to let anything happen to him. If you can prevent it, you will."

"So where does that leave you?"

"Where it always has – right here. My orders are simple: keep you out of trouble. I don't think I could stop you from doing what you feel you have to, so I'm just going to have to do the next best thing. Watch your back."

Linny came in, gave the merest of nods towards Embleton, and brushed up against Chaise's arm.

"I've spoken to her."

Chaise gasped. "Oh my God – brilliant! What did she say?"

"She was pissed off, what do you think! It's not even seven o'clock." Linny sat down on the sofa, crossed her legs. "Anyway, she's fine. Knows nothing about any heavies, drug deals or any of it. She's leaving for the UK later on this afternoon, taking Amy with her. She says Alex knows all about it and thinks this is some sort of ruse by him to stop her from leaving."

Chaise shook his head. "I don't buy it. The visits to the hospital were real, the receptionist told me."

"Whatever, Alex is not with Diane. She's at a hotel, staying there because she felt sure Alex would try and find her. She says he's lost it, freaked out, doesn't know what he's doing."

"Where the hell is he?"

"At his house, so she reckons."

Chaise reached over and gently squeezed her bare knee. "Thanks, Linny. We'll go and check, but you, you stay here. Lock all the doors and windows and stay close to the phone."

She nodded, looked across to Embleton who was busy checking his automatic pistol for the umpteenth time. "Looks like you're fully prepared for any eventuality." She shook her head. "Who are you, another government operative?"

"Major Embleton, Special Air Service, now working for M.I.6."

Linny turned her astonished face towards Chaise. "I was only joking, but he's serious right?"

Chaise smiled. "Deadly serious."

"Not too deadly I hope."

Embleton breezed past her, "More than you can possibly imagine," and he was gone.

Chaise bent down, kissed her mouth. "It'll be all right."

"Jesus, Ryan. Tell me this will be the end of all this cops and robbers shit."

"It is, Linny. As soon as I find Alex, it's over." He kissed her again, then went out, closing the door quietly behind him.

"Nice girl," said Embleton as Chaise went around to the driver's side of the car.

"When this is over, Embleton," said Chaise, opening the door, "I want you to fuck off back to wherever it is you came from."

"Gladly, old man. Gladly."

Chaise got in and when Embleton sat down beside him, Chaise gunned the car and drove it out of the driveway at speed.

THIRTY-NINE

The burning pain in his neck penetrated deep into the ligaments. Cramped up, with his head twisted to one side, Alex had slept through the night in the sports car, and now the muscles across his upper body had frozen and he felt like shit. Clambering out into the sharp, clear morning air, he stretched and winced as a new stab of pain struck his shoulders. At least his heart still pumped. He pulled out the tablets, flipped open the lid and helped himself to one.

Taking his time, he climbed the grassy bank edging the road and looked out across the lonely, rolling fields and was just able to make out the roof of his villa. The plan he'd formulated remained the same. No heroics, just cold, hard action. Get to the house before that Irishman arrived, make the deal, then get the hell away. Once he was safely in Portugal, he'd contact Diane, get his personal life sorted, see Amy again, put all of this behind him.

He was certain no one had passed by whilst he slept but now, in the distance, he heard it. The throaty growl of an approaching vehicle. Moving quickly, he scrambled down the incline and returned to where the sports car sat, hidden from view. He crouched beside the far side of the bonnet, craning his neck, watching.

He didn't have to wait long. As the car cruised past, Alex caught sight of two men in the front together with a much larger big guy in the back seat. Cursing, he ripped open his car's door and got in. If he moved fast enough, he could still make the villa before they did. The road followed a wide, sweeping path up to the villa, but if he took an alternative route across the fields, he could arrive much sooner.

As he drove, the developing hopelessness of the situation took hold. All of this was way beyond his experience. Drug dealers, gangsters, the whole bloody lot. He'd always lived a quiet life, a life startlingly normal. To be thrust into this violent, unknown world of intimidation was something totally alien to him. Sure, he'd had it all sorted in his head, rehearsed the speech, roleplayed the scenes. Just like a film. And, just like a film, it all seemed so easy to believe. Sat in the comfort of a cinema seat, detached from the reality, one can so easily slip into fantasy with little effort. The hard, stark truth, however, was that his limitations of courage and expertise were serious handicaps. He should have kept his mouth shut, agreed to anything the Irishman had said, revealed the whereabouts of the drugs, stashed away in their hiding place. He could have stayed in his hospital bed, closed his mind to it all, believing everything was a terrible nightmare. Apart from Shaun, of course. No nightmare that. Terrible and real.

The car bucked over a rise, slithering through the broken ground. It was already hot and sweat rolled down Alex's forehead and dripped into his eyes, stinging them. A trembling hand wiped the perspiration away. He looked at it. What the hell was he doing, playing macho-man? He'd been nothing but an idiot from the very start of this. And now, it had all caught up with him and there simply wasn't anywhere for him to go. Except here, and now.

He erupted onto the main road, the villa standing silent before him, the honey-coloured hue of the walls reflecting the early morning sun. For a moment, he considered how beautiful it looked, how desirable. There would be no trouble selling it, surely. He'd make a tidy profit, help him begin that new life he dreamed of. When added to the money the Irishman gave him, he'd be laughing all the way to the bank. If the Irishman gave him anything, of course. He could renege on any deal; he was a gangster after all. Perhaps there would be no offer of payment, merely threats. What to do then. He was hardly in any position to make demands. He had to try. He'd come this far; *Shaun* had come this far. He wasn't about to give up this chance, this opportunity to make something of himself. The money from the house wasn't enough. A hundred thousand would be a good addition and a good deal if the going rate for such a quantity of drugs was to be believed. A hundred thousand would be a bargain!

He drove across the open driveway, skirted round the back. He'd still try to see his plan through. The Irishman seemed to be a reasonable fellow. Quite charming in many ways. Nothing like the usual gangster type, if the Hollywood films were anything to go by, which is what Alex based it all on. Al Capone, Frank Nitty, John Dillinger. The Irishman, he was different. Nice suit, well-groomed, affluent, and pleasant. More of a businessman than a thug.

Alex parked the car and ran across to the door, eased the key into the lock and went inside. He stood and listened. The house was silent. All he had to do was wait. The track along which that other vehicle had driven led directly to the villa and nowhere else. The Irishman and his cronies would be here at any moment.

He crossed the room, meaning to go into the lounge and wait. As he did so, the car pulled up outside. He heard the doors opening, slamming shut, the tread of approaching feet crunching across the gravel. As if in a dream, he went to the front door and opened it. No point in postponing the inevitable. Perhaps the Irishman would respond graciously to his openness? Who knows? He stood and waited, eyes closed, breathing even. There was no pain in his chest, for which he was grateful. It was all going to be fine. All he had to do was keep breathing, nice and steadily, keep his mind clear, and before he knew it, they'd be gone, together with the drugs, and he would be thousands of Euros richer.

Simple.

He opened his eyes.

There were three of them. He'd expected that. What he hadn't expected was the absence of the big Irishman, the man who had arranged the meeting in the first place. Instead, two very large men in black suits and a much shorter one staring and smiling. Broad, open smile. Friendly you might say.

For a second, Alex's surprise gave way to a feeling of elation. This wasn't going to be very bad at all. These were not gangsters at all, probably salespeople, here to do some business concerning the house, sent by Diane possibly.

However, the more he studied them a dread feeling developed deep inside and Alex knew he'd got it wrong. The cheery smile from the smaller one hid something, something sinister and dangerous. But even as he struggled to bring some understanding to what this all meant, something smashed against the side of his head. He floundered backwards, the ceiling rolling over him, lights flashing across his eyes, and Alex realized what a dreadful mistake he'd made. From far away a man was shouting, but he didn't care anymore. The blackness was wrapping itself around him and he surrendered to its embrace.

FORTY

Opening the French-window wide, she stepped out onto the balcony, turned her face towards the sun, sighing, said, "It's so gorgeous here. Even now, it's just so warm."

Moving behind her, he slipped his arms around her waist and marvelled at how aroused he felt. So far as he could remember, he had not felt any longing for his wife for months. He loved her, of course he did, but their life had become 'comfortable'. They were a team, everything moving along in the same old, unchanging, mechanical way. They rarely cuddled now, let alone kissed. Physical closeness was not something that tended to encroach upon their lives. But now, as the sunlight bathed them both in its seductive glow, his hardness pressed against the small of her back and he wanted her more than he had for so very long.

She turned in his arms, deliberately leaning into him, feeling his erection, and smiling. "I wish we could buy somewhere close by, just a little place. Then we could spend every summer here." She tilted her head, waiting for his reply. She gasped as his hands clawed away at her thin nightdress, pulling it from her.

Thrilled to be naked, exposed as she was, she ran her hands through his hair. "God, you're frisky!"

His mouth found hers and he took her to the bedroom and threw her onto the bed. He stood there and released himself from his shorts, desperate to plunge inside her, satisfy his lust.

She lay back and didn't resist.

Michael rolled over onto his back and rubbed his eyes. It had been a difficult night, frustrating and tiring and as the morning dawned, the thick, muggy air didn't hold the promise of anything much better to come. He'd laid here, amongst the tough, dry grass, watching the villa through his binoculars and spotted Alex emerging from the low-lying trees. Michael studied him carefully and caught him dipping amongst the gorse as a large vehicle sped past. Now, after taking a short cut, Alex was inside the villa and shortly afterwards the big car pulled up in the driveway. Michael did not recognise any of the three men getting out at first, but he was interested to note the short baseball bat in the hands of one of them. The largest of the three scanned the horizon. He appeared tense and was perhaps looking for any unwanted visitors. The third, a much smaller guy, approached the front door, motioning for the others to follow. With a start, a knot instantly tightened in his stomach as Michael recognized the smaller of the three. Jimmy McNulty. What the bloody hell was he doing here? This was not how Michael thought things would play out. With McNulty's involvement, whatever that involvement was, the whole situation had become entirely different. And dangerous. For a moment, he contemplated phoning Nigel, but it was too early for Nigel to have surfaced yet. For now, he was on his own.

Putting down the binoculars, Michael pulled out the Sig Sauer, checked its action and fitted the silencer. Keeping low, he moved stealthily across the undulating hillside towards Alex's villa.

The light hurt his eyes. Confused, he wondered why they hurt. Blinking, he tried to turn his face away, but the harsh, fluorescent light continued to scorch deep into his retina. As he twisted his body around, steel fingers gripped his cheeks, squeezed them tight, and straightened his face up. Alex moaned. His head pounded, the temple area pulsing frantically. He'd been hit with something, but what the hell was it?

A face, chiselled out of granite, thrust close into his. "Morning, Alex."

He recognised the accent. Northern. Merseyside. He tried to focus in on the eyes, but the man was too close. Close enough to smell breath laced with coffee and taste the tang of expensive cologne.

The man stepped back, a smile spreading. "How are you feeling?"

Alex strained to bring his head up and gasped at what he saw.

He was naked. Totally. They'd laid him out on the kitchen table, tied down his arms and his legs, just as they had done to Lotty, the bastards. Alex struggled against the ropes binding his wrists and ankles, which merely caused them to cut ever deeper into his already raw and painful flesh. Useless. They'd trussed him up well.

"You killed my dog, you shit." It was all Alex could say, all he could think about at that moment.

The small man – because Alex could see now that he was small compared to the other two, much bigger men standing behind him – frowned. "Your dog?" He shook his head, looked at the others who also shrugged. They had their jackets off, sleeves rolled up over bulging biceps. The small man stared at Alex. "Don't know anything about your dog, mate. Sorry."

"Liar."

The small man moved fast, faster than Alex could believe possible. A bunched fist smashed against the side of his face, causing him to cry out as the pain exploded across his cheek. Salty tears burst from his eyes and he tried to wriggle free but those steel fingers seized him once more. Again, the small man's face pressed close.

"Don't ever call me that, you little shit!"

"Steady, Jimmy."

The man loosened his grip and Alex almost swooned as the relief washed over him.

The one the other had called "Jimmy" stepped back, flexing his neck. One of his large companions put a hand on his shoulder. "We don't want him dead before we find out where it is."

"Yeah," said Jimmy, breath snorting through his nose. "All right." He tugged himself free of the man's hand and smiled at Alex. "Sorry, mate. I get a bit, you know, upset when people call me names." He grinned, patted Alex's cheek. "Say you're sorry and we can get to business."

Struggling to keep his increasing panic at bay, Alex tried to think. Clearly, this man was a lunatic so he decided it best not to antagonize further. Clearing his throat, he muttered, "Sorry."

Jimmy smiled, clamping his hands together and wringing them in a fine Uriah Heap impression. "There's a good boy. Now, let's get to it shall we…"

Alex didn't know what was to happen but had a terrible feeling that whatever it was pain would have a huge part to play.

Wearing his cheap, practical summer canvas shoes, Michael moved across the gravel driveway without making a sound. He made it to the open door, the Sig Sauer in both hands, squatted down and prepared himself. The low murmur of several voices came from somewhere within. They wouldn't be expecting him. His trump card. When he played his hand, it would have to be decisive. And massive.

"You think he's made a deal?"

"Almost certainly," Chaise said, taking the car into the village of Riogordo. "He's probably finalizing it right now, as we speak."

"So, what can we do?"

"I don't know. For all I know, we're already too late."

Embleton grunted as he stared straight ahead. "I'll be glad to get home."

"You said that with feeling."

"I mean it. This place, it's like something out of … well, I don't know what it's like. A mix of virtually medieval practices and modern tokenism. Almost as if they know they should be in the twenty-first century, but don't actually want to be."

As if to emphasize his point, an aged man came into the village square astride a decrepit mule, a second trailing behind. Both animals were laden down with canvas bags. Embleton chuckled, "See what I mean." Then he exhaled as a brown tide of bleating, clanking goats appeared, busied along by a leather-skinned herdsman, who occasionally tickled a more obstinate animal with a long, thin stick. The bells around collars clanged rhythmically. "This isn't happening."

"Yes, it is," said Chaise, pulling on the handbrake. "And all we can do is wait for them to pass."

. . .

Jimmy patted Alex's exposed belly and clicked his tongue. "You need to lose some weight, lad. No wonder you've got a dodgy ticker."

"Fuck off."

Jimmy straightened his index finger and plunged it into Alex's navel. "Don't be nasty." He pressed down hard. Alex squirmed beneath him and Jimmy laughed, seeming to enjoy Alex's discomfort. "This is not pain," continued Jimmy, "not yet, not true, deep hurt. Just a little tickler. Nothing more. It'll get worse if you don't listen to some advice."

"I don't need advice from the likes of you," said Alex, biting down on his bottom lip as that damned finger continued to press down.

"What you need to do, is take up a gentle hobby. Like golf. Swimming. Swimming is good, keeps you fit. You can do as much or as little as you like."

"What are you, some kind of personal trainer?"

Jimmy smiled. "I like that. I like a man with wit." He turned and nodded as one of his two companions came into the room. "Did you find anything, Ken?"

"Miguel found these," Ken held up a pair of hair straighteners.

"Well," Jimmy withdrew his finger and clapped his hands together, "they just might do. Plug 'em in for me, will you." He looked down at Alex and traced his index finger from the top of the navel to the hollow of his breastbone. Alex's eyes bulged. "Now, you listen carefully, Alex. You have something we want, and you are going to tell us where it is. I haven't got time for any more games, so I'm going to say this to you once. Listen carefully, yeah." He grinned, leaned forward. "Where is the dope?"

. . .

217

From his vantage point outside the front door, Michael could clearly hear the voices, the words. Jimmy McNulty's Scouse twang reminiscent of his birthplace back in Ireland. He remembered how his mother and Aunty Martha used to take the ferry across from Dublin to Liverpool and visit the shops in the city centre. Owen Owen, Lewis's, Blacklers. Christmas was always the best time; they'd return with packages and parcels, the thrill of it all, the excitement, still very clear in his memory. He sighed at the memory, wishing he was back there now, with his mother. Both her and Aunty Martha were dead now. No more trips to Liverpool. No more trips anywhere.

Someone screamed.

Michael braced himself. The time for action had come.

FORTY-ONE

The office stank of stale sweat and cigarette smoke. Domingo wasn't usually in this early, but the call had been insistent and his boss, Enrique Hernandez, did not usually take kindly to being kept waiting.

Hernandez was close to retirement age but still carried himself well. An amateur boxer in his youth, his torso still bristled with heavy muscles, and he sneered as Domingo came through the door, breathing hard. "Jesus, you look like you've run a marathon!"

"You said it was urgent." Domingo crossed to the water dispenser and poured himself a cup. He drank it down quickly. "It's damned hot."

"You need to lose some weight, my friend." Hernandez sat down in Domingo's chair and propped his chin up with his hands. "The results have come through about the fire."

"Is that what this is about?"

"Partly." Hernandez let his eyes roam over the chaos that was Domingo's desk. "Look at the state of this crap. Don't you ever tidy up? And it fucking stinks in here."

"Just get to the point, will you. I'm busy."

"Looks like it." Scowling, Hernandez leaned back in the chair. "Let me just go through things for you, just so I know we're all on the same track." He began to tick off each incident with his fingers as he spoke. "First, we have a drug dealer who beats up a local woman. Then, the same dealer is shot dead by a local estate agent. Accident ... maybe. The drugs are nowhere to be found. Then, a local petty criminal is found dead in his apartment, together with the janitor of the block. Professional ... perhaps. No witnesses, no evidence to lead us to the killer." Hernandez shook his head and continued. "Now things begin to get really bizarre. The girl, who was beaten up by the drug dealer Treach, is burned to death in her house. Foul play ... almost definitely." He came forward again, his eyes black as pitch. "Forensics have come back. Gasoline. Drenched all over the garage, the kitchen, the hallway. It was deliberate, and that poor girl was murdered. Not by our drug dealer, because he is dead. And not by your chief suspect ..." He reached inside his pocket and brought out a thin, black-covered notebook which he quickly flicked through. "Yes. Here he is. Ryan Chaise. The same man who killed Ricky Treach." He slapped it shut. "The problem is, we didn't find any of his fingerprints at the girl's house. But we did find fingerprints, Domingo. Do you know whose they are?"

"Enlighten me."

A smile. More of a beam. "Jimmy McNulty's."

Domingo felt his legs go weak. He reached out for the hard-backed chair close by and dragged it over. He slumped into it.

"This is a fucking mess, Domingo." Hernandez closed his eyes for a moment. "What the fuck is McNulty doing leaving fingerprints everywhere."

"Perhaps he thought they would never be found. In the fire I mean."

"Well, if he thought that, he's a bigger fool than I ever gave him credit for." He looked over to the window, a thick smear of grime making it impossible to see through. "You know of the call from Madrid. That we are to leave Chaise alone?"

"I know of it, yes."

"It's not an order we can ignore. It is from the very top."

"If that is the way it is, what do we do?"

Hernandez turned his face towards Domingo, the eyes narrowing into slits. "We don't do anything, my dear friend. It's down to you, Domingo. This McNulty business has brought everything out into the open and that was the last thing we needed."

"Can't you suppress the report?"

"Impossible. Francisco Ruiz is in charge and, as you know, as the chief forensic scientist of the Malaga region, he is unscrupulously honest."

Domingo groaned. "He has a history of denouncing any colleagues who so much as breathes corruption in his direction."

"Precisely."

"So, what happens now?"

"You've already asked that, Domingo. I don't want anything to do with it. This has already gone too far." Hernandez stood up, pulled his jacket together and shot his cuffs. "You are an arse, Domingo. You seriously thought you could keep all of this low key, sort it out nice and quietly?"

"I could have done but McNulty's a loose cannon."

"Well, you know what one does to them ... you spike them."

"Easier said than done. McNulty's dangerous."

Before Hernandez could offer a suitable retort, the door burst open and a breathless uniformed Guardia stood there, eyes wide with alarm.

"What the hell is it?"

"We found a body. Well, a local farmer has found it. Shot, through the head, point-blank range."

It was Hernandez's turn to groan. "Tell me it was an accident, a shotgun blast or something."

"I'm afraid not, sir. It looks like a professional hit."

Domingo waved the man away and stood up, exhaling loudly. "I'll get on it."

"You better. I bet that McNulty killed this man. Find out who the victim was, then get this sorted. Because if you don't," he came round the desk and placed a large, gnarled hand on Domingo's shoulder, "we'll both be swinging, my old friend."

FORTY-TWO

I nching quietly down the hallway, Michael paused to check the lounge. Another cry forced him to freeze. Bringing up the heavy automatic in his hands, he waited, senses alert. After some seconds, he continued along the hall with measured care until at last, he stood outside the open door at the end of the hallway. Flattening himself against the adjacent wall, he took a breath and chanced a quick look inside.

Standing with his back towards him was a man the size of a truck. He was stooping over and, as Michael craned to see, a naked foot dangled over the edge of a table. Someone lay there, and Michael was certain this was the person who had screamed.

He saw the man's foot convulse. Another, smaller person came into view and almost instantly a cry followed, much louder than before, more a pig-like squeal, high-pitched and prolonged.

Michael had heard enough.

He'd seen many things in his life and had been responsible for much suffering. Men had died before his eyes, blood-spattered, screams of mercy ringing in his ears. He'd closed himself to it. Business was like that. His business, the one he'd chosen. One didn't, *couldn't* run a leisure business without being hard. Michael Brannigan was hard. He had to be and the things he'd done, none of it reached him or changed him. But even he recoiled with revulsion when he saw the act playing out in front of him.

The man stretched out on the tabletop lay naked. Legs parted, tightly bound arms stretched above his head, the muscles strained as if he were on medieval torturer's rack.

But medieval people didn't use electrical instruments.

The small guy held a pair of hair straighteners. He had just finished applying them to one of the man's fingers. Michael could see where the bright red flesh had burned off. He noted that most of the naked man's other fingers were glistening red also. This was not the end of it, as Michael now witnessed. The big one lifted the man's shrivelled penis and the small guy brought the straighteners around to allow the victim a good view.

"You're a tough guy, Alex, I'll give you that. But I doubt even you could hold out after what I'm going to do next."

"Jesus Christ, please, please don't do this!"

"Just tell me where the stuff is," said the short one, his accent distinctly northern. He was grinning as he slowly lowered the two arms of the straighteners next to the man's penis and positioned the organ between the arms. "This is going to hurt, Alex. So, why don't you just tell me?"

Michael squeezed his eyes shut and waited for the inevitable screech.

Jimmy McNulty enjoyed his work, always taking great pride in his professional approach. Detached, unfeeling, it made no difference to him whether or not Alex revealed the whereabouts of the drugs either now, or in an hour. It wasn't inflicting pain that pleased him, it was the knowledge that, in the end, he would succeed. Alex had held out so far as the straighteners burned toes, then fingers. He'd resisted it all and Jimmy was impressed. Burning his prick, however, now that was in a different division. Jimmy doubted if he would even have to close the arms of the straighteners before Alex told him what he needed to know. But if nothing was forthcoming then so be it. Alex would scream the place down, before giving up the location of the drugs. If he didn't, then the curling tongs would follow, and Jimmy knew exactly where they were going.

He leaned forward. Alex more than likely didn't believe that Jimmy would be capable of frazzling his prick to a cinder. Well, if he thought that, he was an idiot. Alex must have already realized that Jimmy would do anything required, even if, ultimately, that meant Alex would die. Jimmy would prefer for that not to happen, but if it proved necessary, then after Alex's death they would tear the place apart. A thankless task, and one that might prove useless if the drugs were not in the house. Hence the torture. Quick and expedient.

"Just tell me, Alex. Then, you can relax, have a nice bath, see to the burns. We will be out of your life forever."

"You promise?"

"Of course. Now, come on, be sensible and tell me where you've put the drugs."

"Please promise me you'll stop hurting me."

"You have my word, Alex. Just tell me."

"Behind the toilet cistern."

"Good lad." Jimmy smiled. "If you're telling me porkies, Alex, I'll come back and I'll hurt you bad, so bad you'll think what I've done already was like a smack on the wrists."

"Oh, God."

Jimmy, convinced that Alex had not lied, felt a little disappointed that he wouldn't be able to singe the pathetic little man's prick to a cinder. He studied it in Ken's big fist and decided he didn't like disappointments.

Alex must have noticed the changed look in Jimmy's face. He

screamed, struggling wildly against the cords binding him, "No, no, you promised, you bastard!"

"I lied," said Jimmy and leaned closer, closing the arms, watching with rising excitement how Alex responded.

Lost in the delicious thrill of it all he barely noticed a movement out the corner of his eye. A shape, in the doorway. A shape that shouldn't have been there. As he turned his head to get a clearer view, his bowels loosened as he saw the gun.

Jimmy wished he had one of his hands free. At least then he could have brought out his own gun. At least then, he might have stood something of a chance.

———

Alex had never known such agony. His eyes had boiled in his head as the straighteners were applied to each finger, the stench of sizzling flesh filling his nostrils, followed swiftly by the searing pain. It lanced like knives burrowing into his skin, deep down into the very ligaments, the bones. Now, however, an even worse fate beckoned. Alex writhed in a desperate bid to escape, using what little strength remained to try to rip himself free from the ropes that bound him. His fingers were screaming from the aftermath of previous assaults, but this latest was like no other. The big man had so delicately rolled back the foreskin, exposing that most sensitive area completely until now, those cursed straighteners pressed tight, the heat excruciating. Unceasing, the pain lodged into his brain like some new addition to his nervous system. He prayed, bawled, pleaded for it to end, but it continued relentlessly. The stinging, sour taste of vomit rose into his throat, but he didn't care about that. He could no longer focus on anything, all of his world enmeshed with blinding, increasing anguish. He longed for death, for it all to end, but was there any way to end the nightmare his life had become?

"Oh, Christ!"

All he had to do was tell them.

"All right! Please...Please, I promise, I haven't lied. Please, just stop, please, stop!"

The instrument of torture, his wife's hair straighteners, set at their highest temperature, finally pulled away from his abused member. He half-expected that face, that hateful, contemptuous face, to come into view. It didn't. The pain, like any burn, lingered. A constant.

Despite the red mist covering his eyes, he became aware of movement. Raising his head, he tried to make out something but was only conscious of the hand leaving his penis and the massive wave of relief washing over him as the pain receded. Then, he heard it. A single word, laced with an Irish brogue.

"Stop."

Alex collapsed back onto the table, unable to suffer the fiery vestiges of what the straighteners had inflicted any longer. He opened his mouth and screamed.

"Stop."

Michael couldn't help his outcry. He'd seen enough. More than enough. The little one, the one he now recognised as Jimmy McNulty, had frozen, mouth open. Disbelieving or not, it was obvious he was struck dumb. But Michael was taking no chances. He lifted his gun and fired just as Alex screamed.

The first bullet hit the man with his back to him in the head, propelling him forward as if hit by a wrecking ball. Another large goon, unable to react quick enough, merely gaped as Michael's next two bullets hit him in the temple and the cheekbone, the head exploding as if it had been ignited from within, a great geyser of blood and brains and bits of bone flying out in a wide arc.

The straighteners fell from Jimmy's fingers as he seemed to have at last gained control of his functions. He tore at his waist for the gun there, but it was too little, too late. Michael shot him in the throat. Staggering backwards, squawking, Jimmy's hands pressed against the dreadful wound in a pathetic attempt to stem the flow of blood. Michael took his time and eased off two more rounds. The bullets perforated Jimmy's heart, smashing him against the worktop beside the cooker. As he slid sideways, he knocked over a collection of carefully stacked cooking pots, which clattered noisily to the kitchen floor to join Jimmy in a bubbling mess of thick, almost black coloured blood. He lay, quite still. Eyes wide open. Sightless.

Letting out a long sigh, Michael quickly checked the others before crossing to the table. The colour of Alex's skin was ghastly, and Michael didn't like the look of that. He leaned close and said. "I'm going to get the drugs, then I'll be back."

Alex's mouth worked open and closed, but no sound came out.

No sound from his mouth. But a sound from outside. A car, pulling up into the driveway. Michael cursed, patted Alex's face, then took the exit through the back door without another look.

FORTY-THREE

"I don't like this."

Chaise put the car into neutral and sat there, staring. Embleton worked the automatic he pulled from inside his coat and sighed. "I'll go take a look."

Before the man could move, Chaise gripped him by the arm. "Watch it."

Embleton flashed a smile. "Is that you being concerned about me, Commander Chaise?"

Ignoring the sarcasm, Chaise shook his head and let Embleton go. He watched the SAS Major running over to the open front door of the villa, brought out his gun and got out.

It was deathly quiet. Chaise ran his hand across the bonnet of the massive, black four-by-four standing a few feet away. It felt warm. Throat becoming dry, Chaise went into a crouch and scurried over to the other side of the front door to Embleton, pressed himself up against the wall and waited.

The silence continued for a moment. Then a barely audible sound reached him from within the house. A low moan, like a wounded animal. Guttural and deep.

In a blink, Embleton dipped into the hallway and waited.

Chaise whispered, "I'll slip around the back to cut off any escape route."

"Escape route? Escape for whom? Escape from what? You cover my back." He edged further inside. Almost immediately his voice cried out, "*Chaise!*"

All caution gone, Chaise ran down the hallway and turned into the kitchen.

He stopped in the doorway, blood running cold at the scene before him.

Three lifeless, twisted bodies lay crumpled on the floor, wax faced, the blood from the bullet holes not yet dry. Embleton busied himself with untying the naked, dishevelled man on the tabletop, and turned ashen faced towards Chaise. "It's Alex. He's alive, but only just. Fucking animals."

Chaise, as if in a trance, barely registered the scene. He'd seen things like this, in the arid wastes of the Middle East, but here, in this domestic normality, it all seemed so much more terrible, alien, almost perverse. Such extremes of violence didn't belong here. It shouldn't happen. But it had.

Embleton soaked a towel through with water from the nearby sink and returned to mop Alex's forehead. "Who the hell has done this?"

Chaise waited until Embleton had finished then helped Alex sit up. He spotted the red-raw fingers and sucked in air. His eyes found the hair straighteners, discarded, lying next to the man propped up against the oven. A red light blinked on the handle of the implement, telling everyone that the power supply was still connected. Chaise tore it from the mains socket, then gazed into the man's dead eyes. The same man at the swimming pool. "The person who did this was very good." He reached out a finger, touched the wound in the man's forehead. "And it's happened very recently."

"An argument perhaps? Over the drugs." Embleton had his

arm around Alex, holding him close. "We should find some clothes for him."

Chaise grunted, went through the hallway and up the stairs. In the bedroom, he found a towelling robe and brought it back to the kitchen. Embleton took it and placed it around Alex's shoulders.

"I thought there were two gangs," said Chaise, "and this proves it. This was no argument. This is one gang wiping out the other."

"Well, whatever it is, we need to this poor bugger to a hospital. He's in shock and needs care."

"No hospital." Chaise held Embleton's questioning glare. "If Domingo gets wind of this…"

"It's your call, Commander. I'll make some phone calls, get all of this tidied up."

"You can do that?" Chaise was genuinely surprised.

"I can do lots of things." Embleton sighed. "For now, I'll just get this poor sod a brandy."

"Good idea. We'll then take him back to my place."

Embleton squeezed past the inert bodies and began to search through the various cupboards until he found a bottle of spirits. He filled a glass with a generous measure. "We need to find the drugs," he said, supporting Alex's head as he tipped the glass to his mouth. No sooner had the alcohol touched Alex's lips than he went into a bout of violent spluttering. "Take it easy," said Embleton, holding him. The second sip brought no reaction.

Chaise sat down on a nearby stool and gazed at the dead man from the swimming pool. "I wonder who the bloody hell he was."

The dead man's mobile phone suddenly trilled into life, causing Chaise to jump.

Embleton chuckled. "Well, whoever he was, someone wants to speak with him."

. . .

Standing beside his pool in his best Bermuda shorts and scarlet-coloured beach robe, Arthur Morgan closed his mobile phone shut with an exasperated snap and sighed loudly. It wasn't like Jimmy to fail to report in and the thought that something might have gone wrong gnawed away at him. This whole bloody business was turning in to a monumental cock-up. He flexed and rolled his shoulders, trying to relax, but he failed. "Pedro!"

Within a couple of seconds, a well-oiled young man plodded out from the sprawling villa, well-muscled torso bare, bronzed, and gleaming. "Yes, jefe?"

"I can't get in touch with Jimmy. I don't like it."

"Perhaps his phone is not working? Or he cannot get a signal."

"Perhaps. I want you to drive over there, find out how things are, then get back as quick as you can." Pedro nodded and, without another word, went away.

Arthur watched his retreating back and wished he could spend a relaxing day exploring the delights of Pedro's body, but he needed to know what was happening. The phone call he had received not moments before left him in no doubt that his customer had come to the end of his patience. Things had to be brought to a head today.

Linny swore loudly as she watched the two of them bringing Alex's limp, abused body into the house, all strength gone from his body, feet trailing across the terracotta tiles.

"Get him into bed," she said, running towards the kitchen. "I'll fetch some water."

Alex's body was a dead weight. The struggle of getting him into the car was eclipsed only by the effort of getting him out again when they arrived. Embleton remained behind for a few moments to make the necessary phone calls before following in

Linny's sports car. Now, he helped Chaise to lower Alex gently onto the bed.

Mopping his brow, Embleton stared at the sweat on his palm. "To think you live in this heat for pleasure." He pulled a face. "I hope he's worth it."

Linny breezed in with a glass of water. "So do I."

"My people will clear his house and find the drugs. Once we have all that sorted, perhaps we can all go back to living a normal life."

"I've been thinking about that," said Chaise quietly. "I want you to phone 'your people' again."

Embleton checked Alex's forehead. "Feverish. Not good." He straightened up. "What do you have in mind?"

"A plan, that's all. A plan that might bring all of this to an end."

Pedro drove past the entrance to the big villa. He spotted Ken's big four-by-four parked in the driveway but he didn't recognize the featureless van next to it. Several men dressed in white overalls, like painters, buzzed around and Pedro accelerated away before anyone noticed him.

At the top of the hill, he stopped and sat for a moment, gripping the wheel with both hands. Tendrils of fear spread across his gut. Something had gone wrong, he felt sure. Those white-clad men, who could they be? They looked vaguely like police forensic investigators, but investigating what? He toyed with the idea of phoning Jimmy but discounted that thought almost at once and decided to contact Arthur instead. "Mister Morgan? I am here, but there are other people here also."

Arthur Morgan's voice cracked like chipped glass, "What the hell do you mean, 'other people'?"

"I don't know, Señor. There are maybe three or four of them

and they seem to be investigating Ken's car. I cannot see Jimmy."

"Get the hell back here, Pedro. *Now.*"

"Si, Señor." Pedro had rarely been party to any of Arthur Morgan's schemes. Most of the time he spent chauffeuring the great man to this or that place. It was always down to Jimmy or Ken to sort out any difficulties. But now, it looked as if Jimmy and Ken were in some sort of difficulty themselves and that frightened Pedro. He knew what his two colleagues were capable of, had seen them in action many times. Not men to be crossed, under any circumstances. And yet, now … What could have happened? Best not concern himself too much with any details, best to simply return to Señor Morgan, he would know what had to be done. Convincing himself of the sense of this, he forced himself to relax. He would slip the car into neutral and allow the vehicle to roll back down the hill in a whisper. Best not to take any unnecessary chances at being heard.

He glanced into the rear-view mirror and swallowed down a squawk. He caught sight of two white-clad men placing a body bag inside the van. None of this augured well. But then he spotted a man with a gun and knew he had to get out of there without delay.

Unfortunately for Pedro, he wasn't quite quick enough.

FORTY-FOUR

I n the dank darkness of the club, it was easy to believe that
this could be anywhere in the world, perhaps even
somewhere romantic. Anywhere but the Costa del Sol, where
the sun burned your very eyes out. Or so Nigel believed,
convincing himself more and more that he had to get away, find
somewhere cooler. Life was a constant battle to keep himself dry
as the sweat leaked from every pore. He'd tried every make of
antiperspirant available, but nothing seemed to work. Propped
up against his bar, a sodden serviette pressed against his eyes
and the electric fan giving him no relief, he prayed for the heat
to subside.

It never did.

Michael came through the door, a blast of heat like
something from a thermo-nuclear oven accompanying him.
Nigel squawked, turned away, and pressed the tissue harder
against his eyes.

"What the hell has happened to the air-con?"

"Bust."

"You are joking?"

Nigel gave him a look. "Do you honestly think I'd joke about something that important?"   .

Ignoring his partner, Michael went around the bar and fixed himself a Jameson's. He threw it back in one, slammed the glass down hard on the counter and grinned at his friend. "Business is, as they say, taken care of."

Nigel frowned, the heat momentarily forgotten. "What does that mean?"

"It means Morgan's henchmen are no more." Michael turned around again, put the glass under the optics and poured himself a second whiskey. "They were with that Piers guy. I couldn't hang around ... visitors arrived."

"Hang on, back up a bit. What the hell happened?"

"They're dead, Nigel. That's what's happened. I went round to Piers's place, found them torturing him, the poor bastard. Jesus, do you know they were squishing his little fella between the blades of some curling tongs or some such thing."

Nigel felt his mouth grow dry. "They were doing *what*?"

Michael swilled the remnants of his whiskey around the glass. "I shot the bastards." He drained the glass. "They were Morgan's 'big' boys, but I use the term loosely as Jimmy McNulty was one of 'em."

"Shit ... you killed Jimmy McNulty?"

"You're impressed, Nigel, I can tell."

"But ..." Nigel groped forward and picked up Michael's glass. "Fix me one of these," he said and waited as Michael did so. He took the proffered glass in a shaking hand and downed the fiery liquid in one, enjoying the burning sensation as it trickled down his throat. "This means," he continued, voice hoarse with the effects of the drink, "that the entire situation has changed. We could be looking at a shift in our fortunes here, Michael. The chance to elevate ourselves."

"Indeed, my one, true friend. But first, we will have to go

and pay dear old Arthur Morgan a visit. Enlighten him about one or two points."

"I couldn't agree more." Nigel stood up from the barstool and flexed his arms. "It's so fucking hot, Michael. I'm going to change my shirt – for the fifth time this morning."

Michael chuckled, poured himself another hefty measure and raised the glass. "By the end of today, Nigel, you will be able to afford the finest air-conditioning system money can buy."

"By the end of today, we'll be able to buy the fucking world!"

At that same moment, Arthur Morgan stood beside the villa swimming pooled and gripped his mobile phone so tightly his fingers hurt. The voice on the other end sounded angrier than ever. Not that Arthur could blame him. The whole stinking edifice was crumbling, and Arthur didn't have a clue what to do.

"This is a mess," said the voice. "You can't get hold of any of them?"

"No. Not Jimmy, Ken, or Pedro. Their phones are dead."

A prolonged silence followed. "Or they are dead."

The thought had occurred to Arthur, but hearing it voiced by another struck him like a bullet. He collapsed into his sun lounger, putting his head in one hand, eyes closed. "Jesus. What the fuck can we do ...?"

"I'm coming over."

Arthur felt his chest tighten. His eyes bulged as he stared across his swimming pool. "Do you think that's wise? What if someone sees you?"

"Any ideas about caution and secrecy have little relevance now, don't you think?" The man's increasingly ragged breathing proved he was finding it difficult to control himself. "Fuck that and fuck *you*, Arthur! Just don't go anywhere or do anything stupid until I get there. Give me half an hour."

The phone went dead, and Arthur let it slip from his fingers.

He pressed both hands over his face, wondering if, by the end of the day, the situation might improve. The more he considered this the more unlikely it seemed.

He dropped his hands as Thomas, his servant, appeared unbidden, carrying a long, tall glass of gin and tonic. Arthur smiled his thanks, then waved to Thomas to sit. A short, balding man the bad side of sixty, Thomas frowned but did as he was bid. "You're always here when needed, Thomas. It's like you have a sixth sense." He took a sip of the gin and smacked his lips. "Delicious, as usual. Thomas, can I ask you something?"

Sitting on the second sun lounger, Thomas's frown grew deeper. "Is there a problem, sir?"

Arthur had always liked Thomas's thick Scottish brogue, such a welcome change from the nauseating twang of the Cockneys who seemed to proliferate his organization far too much. "It's a simple question, Thomas. Do you think I'm a good person?"

Clearly perplexed, Thomas adjusted his position on the lounger and spoke in calm, measured tones. "I like to think so, Mr Morgan. You've always been very fair."

"So why do you think everything has gone so wrong?" Carefully putting his drink down, Arthur went over to the edge of the pool. He had his back to the servant, but he knew that the man's discomfort was growing, fearful even that this was some sort of test. A test he had to pass. "I'm looking for honesty, Thomas, because things have gone a little awry lately. I have a feeling I'm being punished."

"Punished? I don't understand, sir. Punished by who?"

"God, perhaps." Arthur chuckled. "I'm not a religious man, Thomas, nor am I particularly kind in my dealings with others. Perhaps that's why it's all coming home to roost, as they say. I was expelled at fourteen for punching a teacher." He turned his head, winked. "A female teacher, I hasten to add." He turned again to the pool, studying its crystal depths. "I didn't have much education after that. I made my own way. Studied, read the right books, learned what I had to about business, all of that. Somewhere along the way, I made enemies. Friends too, of course, but those enemies ..." He shook his head. "Too many really. I had to tidy things up more than once, and I think it's all catching up with me."

He sensed Thomas standing up behind him and he turned and looked at the manservant, who was smiling somewhat self-consciously. "Someone at the door, sir."

Arthur hadn't heard anything, lost as he was with his own spoken thoughts. "It'll most likely be Jimmy, hopefully with some good news at long last." He motioned for Thomas to go and went to his drink. He drained it and sat down on the edge of the sun lounger. The return of that miserable package of high-quality dope could herald a new start, a chance to put the house in order. Never again would he allow himself to be manipulated in this way. He'd make this point with his irate caller when he arrived, let him know that it was he, Arthur Morgan who called the shots and made the decisions.

He glanced up to greet his visitor with a friendly smile.

For one, sickening moment, he felt he was dreaming. But not fond memories of his simple life back in Salford long since gone, but a nightmare. Bowels loosening, he stumbled backwards, groping for the sun lounger.

He recognized his visitors in an instant. And in that instant came total terror.

"Hello, Arthur."

For the moment, Arthur Morgan wasn't listening, all of his thoughts now concentrated on the terrible realization that everything he had ever known was about to come tumbling down, and there was absolutely nothing he could do about it.

The man Arthur knew only as Nigel smiled and leaned forward, hands clasped together in a strange, seemingly apologetic attitude. Arthur gave him a fleeting glance because all of his attention was centred on the second, much taller visitor who held a very black, very big looking gun.

"We need to talk to you about the product, Arthur," said Nigel.

"We'd like to have some more of it," said the man with the gun. "I never got the chance to ask Jimmy. So perhaps you'd enlighten us."

Arthur had to force the words out from a throat dry and constricted. "Jimmy? Where is he?"

The gunman shrugged. "I shot him, Arthur. Along with his mates."

"So, you see," continued Nigel, "there's no one left, only you. Tell us where it is."

"Tell us," the other said, smiling sweetly as he pressed the gun against Arthur's forehead, "everything."

FORTY-FIVE

Linny came out of the bedroom, drying her hands on a small towel. She looked at the two men on the couch. "He needs hospital care," she said.

"That's exactly what I said," Embleton pitched in before Chaise had the chance. "However, your boyfriend took the more cautious route and brought him here."

"That was kind of him."

Wincing at her sarcasm, Chaise spread out his hands, "Could you not talk about me as if I'm not here, please." He stood up. "I'm sure Alex will be fine. If we take him to the hospital, police will get involved – again. I'd rather we just kept out them of it. For now."

"For now?" Linny threw the towel towards the other chair with some force. "We're already up to our necks in shit, Ryan. Have you forgotten all about those thugs that came round here?"

Chaise gave Embleton a look before he turned to her once again. "I don't think you'll be hearing from them again."

She frowned. "I think you should tell me exactly what's been going on."

"I can't tell you exactly … it's too horrible."

"Ryan," she measured him with a hard stare. "I want to know everything."

Embleton cleared his throat and went to stand up. "I'll go and get myself a drink."

"No," said Chaise, "you stay right where you are. I might need you to add a detail or two." Turning to Linny, he took a deep breath and told her what she wanted to know.

Keeping the car at cruising speed, they pulled into the verge just before the bridge and took in the view. The great sweep of the lake, with its mirrored, silver surface, reflected the surrounding mountains, a tranquil, idyllic scene, not like Spain at all. A far cry from crowded beaches and busy bars, Lake Vinuela was a part of Malaga tourists rarely saw. A missed opportunity for so many.

"It's so beautiful."

He nodded, pressing her hand gently in his own. "I've made an appointment with an estate agent."

"When did you do that?"

"After what you said … I went along to see what's on offer. Apparently, they have a lovely villa for sale, at a bargain price. The owners want a quick sale."

Her face lit up, "You think there's a chance?"

"More than a chance," he smiled back. "I've made an appointment for a viewing."

They got out and crossed the road, arms around one another, the old magic returning with each step. A slight breeze played across the surface of the water, sending ripples radiating outwards. Over to the left a pair of ducks, mated for life, serenely slipped by. "They're so lucky the people living here," she said, "to have all this to themselves." She let her head fall on his shoulder and closed her eyes.

"I'm hoping our luck will change too. If this villa ticks all the boxes, then this area could be the hub of a new life together." The thought made her go all warm inside and she turned in his arms and kissed him.

Domingo waited, the only sound the ticking of the engine as it cooled. He'd parked up on the road, just a few hundred meters from the sloping driveway that led to Arthur's sprawling mansion, with its commanding view of the lake. Domingo had always been envious of this place, its opulence, its stench of luxury. This was part of the reason why he had made this play, to undermine Arthur's business. The weak point, of course, had been Ricky. Always something of an unknown quantity, it had been Hernandez who had voiced the most concern. He'd been proven right, as he invariably was, and this made Domingo even more infuriated. When Ricky had decided to go alone, take the drugs for himself, it shouldn't have come as a surprise. What had been surprising, and totally unexpected, was Ryan Chaise's involvement.

Ryan Chaise. Domingo squeezed the steering wheel until the knuckles beneath the skin showed white. Damn him, and damn those interfering bastards in Madrid. It was another layer of difficulty that he didn't need and had repeatedly failed to resolve. Madrid made their stance abundantly clear. Chaise was off-limits and he, a mere provisional police captain, did not need to know the reasons. Well, so be it, he'd need to swallow down his shame, his impotence. At least Arthur was a problem that could be solved quickly and immediately. He'd spoken to him earlier and everything seemed fine.

Or was it. Unease played around across the nape of his neck. As long as Chaise was on the scene, nothing could ever run smooth. His interfering, arrogance and seeming invulnerability irritated Domingo beyond words. He needed to sort the situation out fast before any more meddling officials from Madrid came along and poked their unwelcome noses in. He pulled out his gun, checked it was fully loaded, and got out. It was unbearably hot, however, the walk along the driveway would calm him. Hopefully.

Almost immediately, as he went through the open double gates, he realised nothing about this visit was going to be simple. Sprawled in the doorway was the crumpled body of the man Domingo recognised as Arthur's manservant.

FORTY-SIX

Embleton slowly replaced the telephone, considered it for a long time and turned. "Let me get this straight," he said, taking a good mouthful of the gin Linny had poured him. He stopped and watched her mesmerised as she ran a cloth over the worktop. She drifted back into the other room. "You're a lucky man," he said, voice distant.

Chaise frowned. "Is that what you wanted to get straight?"

"Eh?" Embleton shot him a quizzical look. Then realization dawned. "Ah, no ... sorry! No, I mean this business with Alex Piers."

"What about it?"

"Your plan. The idea that you can lure the thugs back by leaving the drugs out for them, like a sort of bait."

"Something like that."

"And you just expect them to come waltzing in, without a care in the world ..." He shook his head. "They wouldn't be that stupid."

"They haven't been particularly bright up until now, why should they suddenly change?"

"They certainly showed their lack of imagination over at Alex's."

"What does that mean?"

"It means, our men have found the drugs. Whilst they were busy tidying away all the mess, they found the bag taped to the back of the lavatory cistern."

Squeezing the bridge of his nose, Chaise shook his head. "Jesus, couldn't he have thought of a less likely place?"

"Obviously not. I think his only redeeming act was to put it in the en-suite bathroom, not the main one."

"They tortured him, but were interrupted before they found anything." Embleton nodded and for a moment both men fell silent, remembering the dreadful scene of Alex pegged out like a piece of prime beef. Except, Alex hadn't been so prime, Chaise reminded himself. "For my plan to work, I need the drugs put back where they were found." He held up his hand. "Get onto your men, tell them to return the package. And do it quickly."

Grunting, Embleton picked up the phone again.

"That Scouser, the one shot dead," said Chaise, "do you know anything about him?"

"A little. He was an enforcer working for a small-time crook called Arthur Morgan. His name was Jimmy McNulty. A nasty little shit by all accounts."

"I know, I met him remember?"

"Ah yes, your little tête-à-tête at the swimming pool. Didn't go too well for him by all accounts."

"Not exactly."

"You're too modest." Embleton finished his gin before continuing. "Morgan runs a few clubs, sex bars and brothels along the coast. Nothing too fancy. We've used him once or twice."

"You've used him ..." Chaise blew out his cheeks. "Christ, is there nothing you people won't do."

"We just needed a little help. Usual stuff. Gibraltar. The

Spanish are kicking up their annual fuss, claiming it as their own. They sent a little patrol boat along the Straits, just inside territorial waters ... Arthur very kindly rammed it with one of his pleasure yachts." He smiled. "We covered the cost of repairs."

"You are joking?" Chaise could see by Embleton's straight face that joking had little to do with anything the man had said. "Bloody hell ... so in one fell swoop, you cause the Spanish maximum headaches whilst averting an international incident ... clever."

Embleton shrugged. "It's not my role to get too involved, so I don't know all of the details. I'm only seconded to the SIS, don't forget. I'm not a regular church-goer."

Chaise took Embleton's empty glass and placed it, along with his own, on the worktop Linny had cleaned so scrupulously. He quickly wiped a cloth over it. "We need to somehow get a message to this Arthur Morgan once the drugs are put back and lure him to Alex's. He must wonder where his goons are so it shouldn't be too difficult."

"For all we know, the ones who got rid of those goons are paying Morgan a visit whilst we speak."

"Unless of course, he had them killed."

"His own men?"

"Why not. He could have made a back-handed deal with this other outfit, cutting his losses whilst protecting his back."

"The old double-double cross trick?" Embleton sucked at his teeth, thinking. "Nah, I don't buy it. Someone else is muscling in, wanting to know where the supply centre is. If the dope is as high quality as you say ..."

"That was Domingo's assessment, not mine."

"Ah yes, our diminutive policeman friend. We have yet to see the best of him I fear ... or the worst."

Chaise pushed himself away from the worktop and turned around. "What will you do when all of this is over?"

"Me? Don't know. Whatever I'm told. Unlike you, I have not got the luxury of retirement."

"It's no luxury, believe you me."

"I'm beginning to believe you." He smiled. "Still, can't say it hasn't been interesting. I shall probably return to the regiment, prepare myself for the next adventure." He chuckled. "Always something to do in our game, eh?"

"I suppose so."

"Back to my original concerns. We are to return to Alex's and lay the trap, is that it?"

"Yes, but we have to wait for Alex to recover enough for him to help us. He's the hook that will lure them to the villa."

"How long is that going to be?"

"Who can say. It's a waiting game, Major, and we are all in the hands of nature to take its course."

Embleton settled himself back in the sofa and closed his eyes. Studying him closely, Chaise knew that by the bunched muscles in the man's jaw and the deep frown on his face that Major Embleton had more than just Alex Piers and the problems of drugs on his mind.

FORTY-SEVEN

Michael Brannigan repositioned the overlarge sunglasses he wore, crossed his legs, and leaned back in the canvas sun chair. He smiled broadly, a smile brim-full of self-confidence thanks, no doubt, to the gun in his lap, a gun he'd used only moments before.

Arthur also sat, his demeanour anything but relaxed, however. Inside, he boiled with anger. How had this happened, where were his men, his team, his insurance against such an invasion of his inner sanctum, his home? The other man, the one who had introduced himself as Nigel, was the one doing most of the talking, and his oily, self-important delivery made Arthur cringe and seethe.

"What we have here, Mr Morgan," Nigel droned on, pacing backwards and forwards, "is an impasse. We don't know where the drugs are, and we want them."

"*You want them?*" Morgan felt himself close to exploding and struggled to keep his voice calm. For the moment, these men held all the cards and he needed to bide his time, keep them friendly, prevent them from unleashing the same violence they had demonstrated when they shot poor Thomas. Alone, Arthur would be unable to do very much to defend himself. He forced a conciliatory tone as he continued, "It's only a tiny amount, nothing for us to fall out about."

"Indeed." Nigel came and sat opposite Arthur on the other sun lounger. Michael sat a little off to the side, the gun always close. "Your associates were none too successful in discovering where the drugs are. Michael had to act quite quickly before they killed … what was his name?"

"Alex," said Michael.

"Yes. Alex. He has the drugs stashed somewhere, but Michael was interrupted in his endeavours."

"Interrupted? What does that mean?"

"A group of official-looking gentlemen in white suits," said Michael. "I made a quick getaway before I could search the house properly."

"Police? Jesus, if the police have got wind of this then we're all—"

"I doubt it was the police," said Michael.

Nigel leaned forward. "So, Mr Morgan, perhaps you could help us and tell us where the drugs might be."

"How am I supposed to help you—my men will know where they are, and I haven't heard from them yet."

"No." Michael gave a small chuckle. "And you won't be either."

Arthur bristled, turned to this annoyingly overconfident thug, and narrowed his eyes. "Why's that?"

"I told you, but no doubt the shock has numbed your senses. I killed them."

A cold slab of fear settled inside the very core of his being. A moan trickled from the corner of his quivering mouth. "All of them?" Michael nodded. "Jimmy? You killed Jimmy?"

"The little shit? Yes, I shot him three times. He won't be torturing anyone else ever again."

Collapsing back in the sun lounger, Arthur covered his eyes

with his forearm and wondered what he was going to do to prevent himself from becoming the next victim on the list.

No doubt about it, the heat of the day was now almost unbearable. The sweat settled around the rim of Domingo's collar as his gaze settled on the corpse at his feet. Flies were already gathering. In this atmosphere, the victim would soon become overly ripe. He ran the back of his hand across his forehead, wondering if his nerve would hold. He'd killed before, but that was years ago, and he'd suffered in the aftermath, consumed with guilt and so many sleepless nights. The way the bullet had hit the man, crushing him, deflating him like a balloon. Just one bullet. That was all it took. A life ended. A miserable life, but a life, nevertheless. This situation, however, this was on a different level. He knew Thomas. A gentle, quiet man, always so polite, so helpful. Why kill him this way. Professional. Single bullet in the forehead. Poor Thomas, who would never harm a fly, except perhaps those buzzing around him right now.

Domingo rubbed his chin. The time for hesitation had passed. He not only had to save Arthur but secure the drugs and get Hernandez off his back. As the lilting Irish brogue of the killers trickled down from the pool area, he checked his gun one more time, closed his eyes, made the sign of the cross, and entered the house.

Nigel studied Arthur with all the patience of a priest.

"Trust me, my son, open up your heart. Confess and the Lord will forgive."

Arthur's face came up, consumed with confusion. "Eh? What's that you're saying?"

"That's what Father Donaghue used to say," said Nigel,

"every bloody month, the same tired words, spoken as if he'd read them from a speech. St Claire's Church, Limerick. Tiny, a little unfriendly, but the place me mother would drag me to every week. Now, here we all are, a thousand years later, and all I want Arthur is for you to do the same. To open up your heart, tell it all."

Michael blew out a loud breath. "Where are the fucking drugs, Arthur?"

Everyone fell into silence.

Arthur waited, not daring to think about what might happen next. He looked at Michael standing there, one hand tucked under his armpit, the other holding the gun. If he was decisive enough, Arthur could rush him, bowl him over, grab the gun, turn around and … Fanciful thoughts he dismissed in an instant. It would never happen. Arthur was past his prime now, relying on the shits he employed to do the tough-guy routine. Not that they would be doing much of that now, of course.

"Don't be thinking of doing anything foolish," said Michael, as if reading Arthur's thoughts. "Without your boys, you're nothing but an overblown puffball. You think you're so bloody tough, Jesus, I've seen tougher guys on the late-night Gay TV Channel!"

"I reckon you'd know all about that," snarled Arthur through gritted teeth. "First time I saw you I knew you were a bloody poofter."

He saw the change in the Irishman's face, knew he was about to react. Unfortunately for him, the fates acted before he could do anything.

Arthur saw him first and rolled off the lounger as Domingo burst from the rear of the house, his squat body covering the short distance to the patio with surprising speed. The gun, an extension of his outstretched arm, barked loudly.

Nigel received the first bullet in the side of his neck, projecting him sideways. He clamped a hand over the wound as the blood pumped out like an overfilled coffee pot on the hob. Squawking with either fear or confusion, Michael turned in time to receive the next round high up on the left shoulder, the sheer force of it hurling him backwards. He hit the surface of the swimming pool with a loud, flat splash, blood spreading across the water.

Arthur thrust trembling hands aloft and watched the little detective cross to the edge of the pool. Michael floated on his back, eyes wide open, jacket billowing outwards like wings. An angel. Angel of death.

The explosion came from somewhere to the right and Arthur saw Domingo staggering backwards like a drunkard, clutching at his side. His knees buckled and he fell, the gun clattering from numbed fingers.

Nigel came into view, a hand pressed against his neck to stem the flow of blood. Stupid of Domingo, thought Arthur, not to have made sure of Nigel. Stupid.

Arthur took a moment to sum the situation up. Michael dead. Domingo wounded in the side. Right side. Probably the bullet had passed through his lung. Bad. Very bad. Probably kill him in the end. For the time being, Nigel looked worse, the bullet having hit the carotid artery. He'd be dead shortly, but he had time if he could remain conscious, to turn the gun on Arthur, fire again. Make it a full set. Bastard. Like hell, he would. Arthur picked up Domingo's gun, aimed, fired, and kept on firing until it was empty, and Nigel's chest resembled a bloody pin cushion, his body a mangled mess, draped lifelessly across the sun lounger.

Arthur sank onto the sun lounger and stared.

It was over.

FORTY-EIGHT

"You need a doctor."

Arthur had taken him into the kitchen, sat him down, poured out a brandy. Domingo sat, face as white as a sheet, cupping the glass in both hands, sipping at it whilst Arthur packed the wound with thick wads of lint dressing. The policeman had yelped like a wounded animal as Arthur took off jacket and shirt. Now, breathing weak and shallow, it seemed the worst of the pain had passed.

"You know where the drugs are?" asked Domingo weakly.

"Christ, is that all you're fucking interested in?"

"It's all anyone is interested in. They've caused more trouble than …" He gritted his teeth a stab of pain burning through him. He took another mouthful of brandy.

Arthur went to the sink and ran his hands under cold water. "I should never have used that fucking Ricky. Stupid bloody twat that he was." Drying his hands on a tea-towel, he leaned back against the sink. "Once we find the drugs, it's over. I don't want anything more to do with you or that bloody Hernandez. I wish to God I'd never gone into partnership with the pair of you."

"We've worked well for you Arthur." Domingo's smile

looked like that of a wild animal. "All the times your places could have been raided ... and weren't."

"Yeah, well, there's no need to worry about any of that now. I'm retiring. All of this ..." He waved his arm around, "it's not worth it. I'll have to pay people to tidy all of this up, recruit new men ... replace Jimmy. That's not going to be easy."

"When it came down to it, he wasn't as good as you believed. That Irish monkey, he did for him. Did for them all."

"Yeah. And you did for him. I've got to say, I'm impressed."

Domingo sneered, looked down at the padding at his side, the way the red flower bloomed across it as he spoke. "I didn't do so well, either."

"Well, like I said – you need to get to a doctor. Get that bullet out."

Domingo nodded. "I know someone so don't worry. First the drugs though. We go and get them."

Arthur closed his eyes, bit his lip. "All right." He glared at the policeman. "Then we go our separate ways. Deal?"

"Deal."

The woman behind the counter efficiently arranged the details of the various villas that seemed to fit their requirements. Looking over them, Jim Owen squeezed his wife's hand. She responded, rested her head on his shoulder, smiled. "Can we go and see them today?"

"I'll try and get in touch with one of our agents." The receptionist punched out the number on the phone. "I know that this one is vacant," she tapped one particularly spectacular home, "so you could drive up there on your own if you like, have a look around outside. The area is stunning. I'll give you a map and then—oh, Ryan! You're in! Thank goodness. Listen, I have a couple here who would love to take a look at Mr Piers's place. Do you think you could help?"

. . .

Chaise gently replaced the receiver and made a face at Embleton. "Seems like fate has caught up with us. I have to go to Alex's. Show an interested couple around."

The SAS Major was already half out of his chair, "You've got to be out of your fucking mind!"

"I think it's best to maintain some degree of normality. You said your people had cleaned everything."

"Even so, for all we know those Irish nutcases could be up there right now."

Shrugging, Chaise checked the Glock and stuffed it into his waistband. "I have to go. You stay here, look after Linny. I'll be back as soon as I can." He scratched his head, not fully convinced of his thought processes. "If they are there it'll be best if I arrived first."

"I'm coming with you."

"No." Chaise held up his hand. "I want you to stay here. If anything happens, anything at all, I'll ring you. But I won't do any hero stuff. If it's all clear, I'll show them around, make out as if nothing untoward has happened, then get back."

"I think you're being foolish, Chaise. Those men are killers."

"And I think you're being too cautious, Major. Remember, I'm a killer too." He went to go through the door just as Linny came in from outside. It was late afternoon, the sun past its zenith, but the heat still intense enough to crack glass. Returning from the pool, Linny stood and dabbed at the hair plastered across her face. Chaise ran his eyes over her slim waist, long legs, the way her breasts swelled in the bikini top, and he felt the heat rise to his cheeks and the stirring begin in his loins.

"You're going out, aren't you?" She patted her face with the towel and hurled it into the sofa. "I knew you would."

"I'm doing a viewing."

"Liar."

"It's true."

"And that?" She jabbed her finger at the gun in his waist. "I've never known you take one of those to a viewing before."

"It's just a precaution."

She gave him a look. "I'm sick of this, Ryan. Sick of the worry, sick of the lies."

"I'm not lying. I promise you, I'm—"

"Save it for your bloody clients." She stomped off in the direction of the bedroom.

Embleton gave a long sigh. "You're making a pig's ear of this, Chaise."

"And you can keep your thoughts to yourself."

Embleton touched his forefinger to his temple. "Try not to be too long ... *Sir.*"

Chaise stood looking out across the valley to the tiny, insignificant village nestling amongst the foot of the rolling hills. He'd never really considered it before now, passing through it as he did on an almost daily basis, barely giving the white-washed buildings or their inhabitants a second glance. Now it took on a very different persona. From somewhere down there, violent men had entered his life, disrupting everything he'd built; a new existence, as far removed from the old one as it was possible to imagine. They had rekindled all the old bitterness, the old ways. They had forced him to bring into the light the skills that had lain dormant for years. And he hated them for it.

Lowering his head, the bitter consequences came to mind. Linny would leave him. Of that, there little doubt. He hadn't lied, he'd simply not been completely open. He thought that by not telling her, he could protect her. Instead, when everything had been revealed, she decided enough was enough.

She wasn't prepared to be kept in the dark. It was frightening in there, more frightening than the truth he should have revealed. She would leave him, and he couldn't blame her. To prevent it, the bridges he needed to build were going to be massive, but he knew he would have to do it. Linny meant more to him than anyone else alive. In the old days, relationships were difficult to forge, but Linny had changed all of that, making him realise how precious life could be. To fall in love proved a lot less frightening than standing in front of someone and blowing their brains out with a gun. And a lot more preferable.

He crossed to the sports car, got inside, and sat staring into space for a moment. His old life had returned and punched him square in the face. He doubted it had ever truly gone away. He had tried to bury it, but it was always there, simmering beneath the façade he had created. All the old skills had resurfaced. A little rusty perhaps, but still working. And he'd need them to sort out this mess. Once it was done then he could concentrate on winning Linny back.

Chaise reached down to adjust the seat. Embleton, smaller, had brought it too far forward for comfort. As his hand groped underneath for the catch, his fingers brushed against something. Something which he knew shouldn't be there.

For a moment everything went into freeze-frame. Even his mind seemed to solidify. He must have it wrong, all he needed to do was settle back, start the ignition, and set off. He had allowed himself to become entangled with emotion. His mind was a soup, nothing coherent going on. Yes, he must have got it wrong.

He knew he hadn't.

With extreme care, his fingers traced out the shape of the device strapped under the seat.

It was a bomb, the tilt fuse designed to engage with either the motion of the car or, as he now assumed, the depressing of the brake or accelerator. It could have been rigged to the door, of course, in which case conscious thought of any kind would by now be ended. He worried that the action of pulling the seat back could have started the fuse. If so, he probably had less than a few seconds to get out.

Time. No more of it left. Chaise closed his eyes, knowing that even if he managed to exit the vehicle, he would still be caught in the blast. Death would be the preferable option to the mangled mess his body would suffer. Limbs blown off, brain scrambled, fed through tubes for the rest of his life. He'd seen it too often and nothing terrified him more.

He took several easy breaths to calm himself. Glancing back to the villa, there was no sign of Linny, thank God. Or, come to that, Embleton. Embleton who had offered to accompany him to Alex's home. He didn't take much dissuading, so it was probably safe to assume it was Embleton who had rigged up the bomb. He'd know how to do it, no question. At any time through the night, he could have slipped out and taped it to the underside of the driver's seat. He was the last person to drive the car. There was no one else. Opportunity. All his. But what about the motive?

No one looked out through the window. Chaise hadn't started the car yet. He was still alive, so presumably, the bomb would ignite as soon as the ignition was turned. Embleton would be chatting with Linny, as natural as natural could be but all the while wondering why the hell Chaise hadn't started the car. Fairly soon he'd be coming out through the door to check what was going on.

That would be the point when Chaise killed him.

FORTY-NINE

B ody numb, limbs frozen almost solid, cold like a steel vice clamped around his chest, Michael grunted and groaned but managed to haul himself out of the water. He rolled over onto his back and, gasping for breath, stared at the sky. Everything ached, not least his shoulder where Domingo had shot him. He had known pain before, been around the block where that was concerned, but this was on another level. Not just pain. Total agony. He gingerly touched the spot where the bullet had hit and passed directly through. It must have glanced off his breastbone, sheered away to the left, ripped through his deltoid muscle to erupt out of his back.

Nothing but mere details. What mattered was that he was still alive. Racked with pain, muscles stiff and unresponsive, his one overriding thought was to escape. But not until he had redressed the situation. Plans had gone wrong before, but never so badly nor completely as this.

Michael turned his head to see Nigel's corpse and suddenly his pain retreated. The death of his partner, his friend was something far, far worse. They'd grown up together, shared the good times and the bad. Neither of them had deliberately set out to journey along a path of crime, but it had proved lucrative, exciting, fun. Together they had carved out a niche, struggled and fought. Won. But now Nigel was dead.

Not one usually given over to shows of emotion, seeing his friend lying there, lifeless eyes staring into nothing, the black blood congealed across Nigel's throat, Michael Brannigan broke down and cried, probably for the first time since he was in nappies.

Sitting with his head pressed against the cool of the window, Domingo wandered in and out of consciousness, pain jarring him awake every time he slipped into blissful sleep. Next to him, Arthur drove the car cautiously along the winding road towards Alex's villa. Arthur rarely drove, one of his men usually taking up the task. Now they were dead, Arthur had no choice.

He had made some quick, haphazard calculations, estimating Domingo would be dead from blood loss within a couple of hours if he didn't get him patched up. The policeman's death might, of course, be the best outcome. Arthur hated him. Always lurking in the shadows, a scavenger waiting for any pickings, the recent drug's deal the last straw. Arthur blamed himself for not doing something about the situation long ago.

It had been a scorcher the day Domingo had visited him. Shirtsleeves rolled up, jacket over his shoulder, sweat rings bloomed dark blue under his armpits. He stank of garlic and alcohol, a liquid lunch no doubt, paid for by some poor sap. Arthur had been in his office down in Mijas, air-con turned to full. He looked up as Toby, the head bouncer, opened the door, looked guilty and sighed deeply as the fat policeman squeezed past.

"You look busy, Arthur."

"I am." Arthur nodded to Toby, who went out, closing the

door softly behind him. "What can I do for you, Inspector. Or is it Captain, I never can remember."

"I answer to both." Domingo fell into a chair, stretched out his legs and kicked off his Italian shoes. He wriggled his toes. "I am thinking that today we should do some business, Señor Morgan."

"Really?" Arthur shuffled receipts from one of the local breweries. Prices were hitting the roof. Admission charges may have to go up to keep pace.

"I have learned something that might interest you. Something that I believe could help us both."

Intrigued, despite himself, Arthur propped his chin on his hands. "I'm all ears."

"We intercepted a fishing boat in the Straits last night. It was making its way down the coast, probably from North Africa." He spread out his hands. "These things happen all the time, of course. But this particular boat, it had some interesting cargo. Crack cocaine. Finest quality."

Arthur raised his eyes to the ceiling and leaned back in his chair. "I'm not into drugs, Domingo. Not as a business."

"Then you are a fool. This club business, bars, brothels, it is old, dead. You will never make the sort of money you used to back in the Nineties. Booze is too expensive now. People prefer to drink at home, invite their friends around, smoke, watch a nice Blue-Ray in front of their HD widescreen."

"They'll always want to socialize. Drink, dance. My business isn't quite dead yet. Drugs hold no interest for me. Try further down the coast if you want to make any deals."

"Who with, Arthur? Those Lithuanians you had killed?" Domingo sat forward, the grin spreading. "I am willing to help you with this, Arthur. Take a sample, see what you think. A kilo and a half. That's not so very much. You hold it, pass it around your friends. Soon everyone will be wanting more. There will be no risk because I will distribute it."

"You?"

"Why not? It's perfect. Look, I'm the bad side of fifty, I want to guarantee a nice, comfortable retirement. This stuff is class 'A', the very best. We can shift all of it very quickly and make a fortune. This could be the beginning of something big, Arthur."

"So why don't you do it all yourself if it's so good?"

"I need the contacts only you can provide, Arthur. You have clubs and bars all along the coast. The opportunities are enormous. And," he winked, slowly, "I'll protect you. No raids, no awkward questions. Free distribution, unimpeded. All I ask is a cut. A large cut, yes, but only a cut. What do you think?"

Arthur did think. He thought about it for a long time, spoke to some of his more trusted lieutenants. One of them was a young thug called Ricky Treach. It was his job to take the stuff from Mijas and distribute samples to those interested. A simple messenger job and Ricky decided to get greedy, take the main chance and run off with the drugs. Over a quarter of a million, all for himself.

"Bastard."

Next to him in the car, Domingo grunted, stirred, and sat up. "What? What did you say?"

"Nothing. I was talking to myself." Arthur glanced over to the policeman. He was so pale, his pallor a ghastly lime green colour. "You look bloody awful."

"I feel it." He grimaced a mad grin in a skull-like face. "But I'm not going to die, Arthur. Not yet." He patted the gun stuffed in his waistband. "Let's not get any ideas, eh?"

Arthur concentrated on the road. "I just want this over and done with. Find the drugs and end it. I'm sick to bloody death of it all. My business has been turned upside down, all of my best people killed ..." He rubbed his face with his free hand. "I should never have agreed to any of it."

"Just drive the fucking car, Arthur and stop beating yourself up. What's done is done." He winced, clutched his side. "Damn that fucking Irishman."

"Yeah, well you did for him and the other one too. I have to tidy all that little lot up when I get back, thanks to you."

"Arthur, you are one ungrateful bastard. If it hadn't been for me, they would have strung you up like a pig! Now just drive and shut the fuck up."

Sound advice admitted Arthur to himself. Just drive, drop the little shit off, then get the hell away. He still had some men down at Mijas. Damage limitation, that was what was required now. Leave Domingo to his own greasy life, let business take care of itself. Soon, within a day or so, everything would be back to normal. Everything.

———

Frank Leonard Ferguson stood in the arrival lounge, suitcase by his side, and for the umpteenth time glanced at his Rolex. Where the hell was she? Sarah was never late. He took out his mobile. He had already tried her at least three times, now he changed tack and contacted one of her friends, a girl called Lorraine. Frank sighed loudly in relief when she answered. Within the space of two minutes, Frank Ferguson's life came tumbling down around him as Lorraine told him the news. Sarah was dead, the villa burned to the ground. It all had something to do with drugs and some madman who had attacked her. When Frank finally closed his phone shut, his legs had lost all of their strength. He found a seat and sat staring into the distance for a long time. After that, he went to the bar outside the arrival lounge and swallowed down two brandies in quick succession. He made another phone call. It was time to put things right.

FIFTY

Phelps came from behind his desk, mobile phone pressed hard against his ear. He listened to the voice coming through and winced. Anger always made him wince, especially when he was the target.

"This is going to be acutely embarrassing if he lives," said the voice.

"It's going to be extremely dangerous if he lives."

"I sincerely hope that there will be no chance of that. What you have to do, Mr Phelps is to ensure your measures prove successful."

Phelps closed his eyes. "To be frank, all of that is out of my hands."

"I believe our friend knows what he is doing?"

"As far as I am aware. He came very highly recommended."

"Then we have nothing to worry about, do we."

"I suppose not."

A pause. A long intake of breath. "Sometimes, Mr Phelps, I get the distinct impression that you are not completely on board with all of this."

How the hell can I be? You're asking me to sanction the

murder of a British citizen, and you expect me to be comfortable about it? "I'm perfectly at ease with everything, I assure you."

"Well, let us hope so. I want the report within the hour that everything has been concluded satisfactorily. Goodbye, Mr Phelps."

The mobile went dead. Phelps slowly closed the lid and dropped the phone into his pocket. He ran a hand over his face. Dear God, if this didn't go well, then the whole lot could explode. "Jesus," he said aloud, startling himself at his choice of word. Explode. He wondered if he should drive down there, see it first-hand.

Just then the door opened. Sandra, his secretary put her head in and smiled. "Mr Phelps. A Señor Hernandez is waiting to see you. He says it is quite urgent. I tried paging you, but you haven't answered."

Phelps looked at her, stunned. She'd been paging him? He'd been so immersed in his thoughts he had successfully cocooned himself from the outside world. He wished to God he could wrap himself up inside that cocoon again, this time forever. "Send him in," he said and sat down behind his desk just as the very large police chief came in. Phelps took one look at the policeman's face and knew it was going to be bad news.

Driving along the twisting road, they came down into the village of Riogordo. Slowing down, they crossed the bridge and spotted the signs for the square where they stopped. Owen asked someone who looked British if they knew the way to Benamargosa. Fortunately, the man spoke English well and his directions were clear. They drove on, heading up to the hill to the turn-off. "I wish we had more time to savour all of these lovely little villages," said his wife.

Owen smiled as he kept his eye on a road full of potholes,

awkward bends, steep inclines. "If we buy somewhere, we will have all the time in the world."

"What are the chances of us finding the perfect place in the first house we see?"

"Who knows?" He grinned. "We might just hit it lucky."

"We've certainly hit lucky with the weather so far, and ..." Her sentence finished with a squawk as she clamped her hand to her mouth. "Oh my God!"

In that fraction, Owen saw him and hit the brakes hard. A tall, well-built man, staggering across the road, his entire left side covered in blood, face like a ghost, wide, startled eyes.

The rental car slewed to a halt and the couple sat, hardly daring to believe what they saw. Owen reacted first, clambering out of the car. He ran over to the blood-soaked man and squatted down next to him.

Owen felt his stomach pitch over. Not because of the blood, not because the man looked close to death, but because of the gun in his hand. And the smile, followed by the lilting Irish brogue, "I'll be asking you to give me a lift."

Linny came down the stairs holding a bulging holdall. She frowned as she saw Embleton, standing by the window, the telephone against his ear. He replaced the handset on its cradle and turned to her. A glance at the holdall, then he brought out the gun.

For a moment she didn't believe it. Was the gun for her, or was he just checking it? It was pointed in her direction, but still, none of it registered. This man was with Ryan. They were working together, trying to get this ridiculous drug business sorted. Why would he now be pointing a gun directly at her? It didn't make any sense, but there was no denying it. None of it.

"You can't leave," he said.

Linny blinked at him, tilted her head. "Come again?"

"I said you can't leave. You know too much."

"What the hell are you talking about?"

"You're a feisty bitch, I'll give you that. That's why he likes you, probably. Your lover – Ryan Chaise. At least, that's the name he goes by now. He wasn't always Ryan Chaise, you know. Or perhaps you didn't." He smiled, enjoying it.

She let the holdall slip from her grasp, heard it hit the floor with a dull thud. It didn't matter, nothing mattered. Not now, not with this horrible man standing there with that gun. Her stomach yawned empty and the strength went out of her legs. She dropped into the nearby chair and gawped at him. "Who the hell are you?"

"I work for British Intelligence. There is a man, his name is … Well, it doesn't matter what his name is. He's my boss, your lover's too. Your lover, Ryan Chaise, inadvertently got himself mixed up in something which he shouldn't. The whole thing is a bloody mess. It's my job to sort it all out."

He spoke the words, but they were nothing more than sounds. A meaningless string of consonants and vowels jumbled together into guttural utterances. She stopped listening and stared at the floor, licking her lips, wondering when this would all stop. When he'd spoken those few simple words, that Ryan Chaise was 'at least the name he goes by now', she'd stopped listening. It all closed down. Overload. Crash.

Embleton got down on his haunches, close to her now, the gun held loosely in his hand. His hand came forward, touched her knee. She was wearing shorts, her legs bare, deeply burnished by the sun. A fine, golden down covered her thighs, so fine that from a distance it couldn't be seen. Ryan had said that up close like this, that fine down sparkled. Embleton must have seen it too. His fingers were running over her skin. She didn't flinch. She was stunned by the revelation that Ryan was using a false name.

"Commander Richard Parry, Special Boat Squadron," came

Embleton's voice from afar. "That's who he *really* is. The thing is," said Embleton as he moved his hand lightly up and down, stroking her soft skin, "he has jeopardized our entire operation. The man we're interested in, his wife becomes involved with that idiot Ricky Treach. Chaise kills Ricky Treach. Unwittingly involves some local gangsters, who come along and kill the wife, poor Sarah, then burn her house down. Our man will no doubt seek revenge, and that will just blow everything out of the water. So, my job ..." He made himself more comfortable, put the gun on the floor, freeing both hands to caress her legs. "My job is to make sure that any further damage is limited. And that, I'm afraid, means killing your boyfriend." His fingers delved underneath the hem of her shorts. He was growing bolder now, bolstered by her seeming indifference. "He's lied to you, right from the start. You're right to leave him. What you need is some honesty in your life, a bit of mutual trust and understanding." She still didn't resist, just sat there, staring into nothing. He moved closer, ran his hands under her firm buttocks, tugged at the shorts. Obediently, she lifted herself off the chair and he pulled the shorts away. He gasped. She wore a thong. Tiny and white. He felt the erection pressing against his trousers, so strong, urgent. He salivated. "God, you're gorgeous."

She blinked and she gazed into his face. "Kill him?" Her words sounded forced, her throat dry. "Why?"

Embleton rocked back on his heels and began to unbuckle his belt. His expression told her he was enjoying this. "My superiors, that's what they want. He's a loose cannon, capable of anything. He's out of control, and they want him stopped before he makes a very nasty situation even worse." He pulled his trousers away, his cock springing forward. "I'm going to fuck you; you know that don't you."

She gazed down at his impressive hardness, then slowly looked up into his face. "I don't think so," she said ever so softly.

A frown crossed his face. His erection collapsed as Chaise loomed over him, gun in hand, pointed towards Embleton's head.

"Thanks for the information," said Chaise.

Embleton craned his neck to see Chaise smiling. The gun, so very big, took all of Embleton's attention. "Turn your head away, Linny."

Linny screamed and the gun went off.

FIFTY-ONE

Half an hour later, Linny stepped out of the shower, face like death, hands shaking. Chaise watched her from the doorway, marvelling at her body, how, even now with the trauma of what she had seen, she still managed to look sensational.

Draped in a towelling-robe, she sat on the edge of the bed, hands clasped together, elbows resting on her knees. The white robe made her like a mummy, thought Chaise. An Egyptian goddess.

"I have to go," said Chaise gently. "You'll be okay?"

She gave a sharp, scoffing laugh. "What the fucking hell do you think?"

"I think," he said, drawing in a breath, "that we need to talk when all of this is over."

She turned her face to his, her eyes red-rimmed, tears still threatening to come once again. "I never want to talk to you again."

"You don't mean that."

"Don't tell me what I don't mean, Ryan. Or should that be

Richard?" She squeezed her eyes shut for a moment. "You've just murdered a man, in our living room for Christ's sake."

"He would have murdered you. As well as me."

She looked away. "Everything is so black and white with you, so fucking clinical!"

"I don't know why that so upsets you."

Linny shook her head. "I don't know you at all, do I? All of this, it's reawakened the fucking animal you've always been ..."

"I'm not an animal."

"No. No, you're worse. You're a machine. No feelings, no conscience. Nothing. You pick up your gun, you kill people. If there is no gun, then it's your hands ... Jesus, but you are one fucking good actor! All this time, I thought you were just a normal guy. Just shows you what an idiot I've been. You couldn't even find the courage to tell me your real name."

He made to step forward, but her hand came up, stopping him in his tracks. She stood up, went to the dresser, dragged a brush through her still dripping hair. "I won't be here when you come back."

"Linny ..." For a second he thought he could make the effort, but the second passed and he turned, went out of the room, walked down the hallway to the front door, barely pausing to see Embleton, or what was left of him, lying there. That would be a hell of a job. Clearing all that up, the man's brains everywhere. In this heat, it would soon turn ripe and begin to smell. That would never do. He pulled out his phone, dialled a number.

"Phelps," came the reply.

Chaise allowed himself a smile. "You're not going to like this," he said.

Michael Brannigan sat in the back, the gun on his lap, as the prospective property buyers drove towards Alex's villa. Michael knew what he was doing. The man at the doorway to

Arthur's place had told him before Michael shot him. Alex had the drugs in his home. Jimmy McNulty had been sent to try and find out where, but Michael had spoiled everything by bursting in and killing everyone. Michael had laughed at that before he ended the old man's life. Some hours later, the terrible events at Arthur's villa behind him, he'd flagged down the couple. Brits, on a quest to find a peaceful holiday hideaway. Well, he doubted if they'd continue their search in this area now.

"This is the house we were booked in to see," said the man as he swung the car into the drive.

"It's nice," said Michael, bending forward. He squeezed his eyes shut. "Very ... what is that phrase estate agents use? Desirable Yeah, that's it." He chuckled to himself. "I need you to go in and have a quick look around."

"Me?" The man turned in his seat. "I can't. I haven't got the key."

"Not sure you'll be needing a key. The back will be open."

"You're not serious."

Michael nodded, patted the gun. "Very. I want you to make sure there's no one around. And find me something to drink. Brandy or whisky, it doesn't matter which." His fingers closed around the gun. "I'll stay here and keep your lovely wife company."

Not so far away, Arthur Morgan turned his car into the road that led up to Alex's villa. He glanced over to Domingo, who was hunched against the passenger door, head lolling sideways, fast asleep. Arthur knew that before long he'd be dead. All he needed to do was keep driving around in circles until the little detective died from blood loss.

He moved the car into a lay-by and switched the engine off. Domingo hardly stirred. Taking the opportunity, Arthur pulled out his mobile and dialled the number of one of his nightclubs down in Estepona. It was answered on the second ring.

"Would that be you, Arthur?"

For a moment, Arthur felt that his chest was being crushed by a massive tonne weight. The voice that answered was one he knew only too well. He tried to force a reply but managed only a constricted squeak.

"I'm glad you phoned," continued the voice. "I've been trawling through all these numbers … you're a difficult man to track down."

"I …" Arthur coughed. God, he wished he had a drink. "When did you get in?"

"A couple of hours ago, and since then I've been doing a lot of talking, Arthur." The voice stopped, took a breath. When it returned, the assuredness was a little frayed, the tone shaky, self-control beginning to slide. "You killed her, you bastard. My wife. And I'm going to take every fucking thing you have and burn it. Just like you did to my house."

"Wait! I can—"

"I don't want to hear anything from you, Arthur. Except for the scream just before I slit your throat."

The phone went dead. Arthur sat trembling, sweat dripping down his face, not daring to believe what had just happened. Frank was back. How could it have come to this, over a poxy bag of crack-cocaine? It couldn't be real; it all must be some terrible dream.

"Arthur."

He snapped his head around and saw Domingo. He gasped. The man was ashen, face smeared with perspiration, lips blue, eyes livid. The gun in his hand looked impossibly heavy. "It's over," said Arthur, voice low. "We're all dead. Frank has come back."

Domingo gave a single chuckle. "Not over yet. Let's get up there, get this sorted."

"Sorted? Are you a fucking lunatic? You need to be in a hospital, and I need to be on a plane to Rio!"

"Well …" Domingo coughed and for a moment Arthur didn't think the little policeman would recover. Breath rattled in his chest. He groped into his pocket and brought out a crumpled handkerchief, pressed it to his mouth, took a moment. "You can do that, Arthur. After we've found the stuff."

"It might not even be up there."

"I'm sure it is. Alex Piers has the dope hidden in his villa. You're going to find it for me, then you can take me down to the hospital in Velez."

"You're nuts."

Domingo nodded, pressing the handkerchief hard against his mouth as another bout of coughing racked his body. "You could be right. Now drive, Arthur. Before it is too late, eh?"

Chaise sat outside, staring at the pool. He could hear Linny moving around inside. He knew that soon she would be gone, out of his life, and that he would watch her and wouldn't feel a thing. His world had unravelled around him, all of the careful planning, his relentless drive to put the past well and truly to bed. And it would have worked, all of it, if it hadn't been for Ricky Treach. A simple thing like picking up a hitch-hiker had led to his entire world collapsing. If he had a faith, a belief system, he would try and see some meaning amongst the mess. But any sort of faith had long since gone, buried in the acrid dirt of the Middle East, in the blood of his closest friends spilt for a cause that most people at home didn't fully understand. He had grown hard, detached, unfeeling. Uncaring. Linny had been a lifeline, a signpost for a new and better way, and he had let her down. He let everyone down. He always did.

He should run inside the house, beg her not to go, that together they could find a new life, continue to discover the sheer joy of being as one. He should do that, but he knew he wouldn't. The words would not come, the walls he had built up were too thick. Thicker than he had realized.

The sound of a car drawing up outside roused him from his thoughts. As the doors slammed shut, Chaise was already making his way outside, putting the gun in the back of his waistband. He could feel the dull metal against the small of his back and it reassured him. A true friend. One that would always be there.

Phelps stood in the driveway, squinting towards the sky, looking uncomfortable, mopping his brow. Chaise doubted the man would ever get used to the heat. Already his shirt was soaked through. He readjusted his dark glasses when he saw Chaise. Phelps motioned to the two men he'd brought with him. "Check him."

They grunted and Phelps waited.

What Phelps witnessed brought ice to his blood. He saw Chaise move, crouching low, the blows striking out before the men even realized what was happening. The second one tried to react, but elbows and palms smashed bone and shattered nerves even as he raised his fists. Then Chaise was straightening up, his eyes narrow, and he looked at Phelps, stepped over the two prostrate figures sprawled in the dirt, and pulled out the gun.

Phelps felt his stomach turn to water. He brought his hands up and backed into the car, causing him to yelp with shock. His bladder weakened and he lost control.

"Jesus, Phelps." Chaise turned away for a moment as the sound of dribbling rang across the open driveway.

Whimpering with the indignity of it all, Phelps tried to put some distance between himself and this terrible human being. His desire to run was tempered only by the thought that a bullet in the back of his brain would bring his flight, and his life, to a sudden halt. He crumpled to his knees, the wetness between his legs feeling more horrible than anything he had ever known. The shame of it brought tears to his eyes and he pulled his knees up close to his chest, wrapped his arms around them, and rocked himself from side to side.

"I want you to take Linny to the airport," Chaise was saying from somewhere far away. "First of all, arrange for some of your men to clean up what I've left inside." These last, curious words, brought Phelps back to the present with a jolt. He frowned. "Embleton," said Chaise. "He's dead."

"Oh, Jesus Christ!" Unable to comprehend the enormity of this news, Phelps wailed, dropped his head on his chest and rocked ever more violently. His world, all that he knew, was imploding. What could he do, where could he go? Embleton, *dead*? Why, what was happening?

Chaise was still speaking. "You can call your masters back in London and tell them that if anyone ever comes to bother me again, I'm coming to bother them. You understand?"

Phelps nodded but he struggled to come to terms with this information overload. He needed Chaise to understand something, to be clear. "Please, Mr Chaise, you have to believe me when I say I didn't know anything about Embleton, only that he was working for headquarters. Whatever has gone on here, I am absolutely in the dark. I'm merely a messenger, Mr Chaise, a petty bureaucrat. I promise."

"Who or what you are is of no interest to me, Phelps. If I see you again, I'll kill you." Chaise put the gun in his belt. "You can take Linny to the airport, or to her friends, or wherever she wants to go after the inside has been cleaned. I don't give a shit anymore. I'm taking your car; you can drive her sports car."

"What?"

Chaise nodded at the jeep in which Phelps had arrived. "I need to go across country. I have one last liaison to make."

From his crouched position, Phelps heard rather than saw

Linny's approach, the gravel crunching beneath her shoes. He looked up, hoping she would see his plight, perhaps offer some help.

"The sports car has no boot, Ryan," was all she said. "It's not big enough for my cases, anyway. I'll take that rental car you have."

"Yes." Chaise looked down at the stricken Phelps. "After she's gone, you can take the sports car, together with your buddies. I'll pick it up at the consulate later."

Linny's breath rattled. "Is that all you have to say?"

Chaise shrugged. "What else is there?"

Close by Phelps's associates were beginning to stir as Chaise slammed the door of the jeep shut and drove it away at speed.

Phelps struggled to stand and only then did Linny come to his aid, putting a hand under his armpit to lift him to his feet.

"He's out of control," he said, bringing out a handkerchief to dab at his face.

Linny sniffed, "You need a shower, Mr Whoever-you-are."

"Phelps. I work for the British embassy here."

"And those two."

Phelps glanced across to the two men, both of whom appeared shocked, deflated. He doubted they had ever taken such a beating. "I think their situation will be reviewed."

"Get them to help me with my bags," she said. "And drive carefully in my sports car. I don't want to see so much as a scratch when I get it back."

"I promise you nothing will happen."

FIFTY-TWO

M ichael watched the man emerging from the house at a half-run. He seemed terrified, face drawn, a frightened animal caught in the trap. Michael leaned out of the car window. "Anything?"

"Nothing. I checked every room. There's no one there."

"Good." Michael stepped outside, looked down at the shirt soaked in blood. "I need to change my shirt. I hope he's my size."

Behind him, the wife said, "You should go to a doctor."

That sounded as if the woman cared. Michael doubted it, but he welcomed the sentiment. He smiled. "Thanks for the lift. I'll be needing your car, so you'd better start walking back."

"You mean …?"

"What? That I'm not going to kill you?" Michael breathed a sigh, turned his face to the sky. "On such a beautiful day? I think there's been enough killing already." He winked at her. "Just go. I'll leave your car at the airport, so don't fret too much."

As he crossed towards the house, he didn't look back. He

listened to them running away and smiled to himself. One good deed in a fairly dreadful day.

Behind the cistern, in the downstairs toilet, that's where he found it. He hefted it in his hand, estimated its weight at just over a kilo. A tiny amount of what could be available. Nigel had wanted to find the source, to come to some agreement with Arthur Morgan and distribute the stuff all along the coast. But Michael was beyond that now. All he wanted was to return to Ireland. Forget. He had contacts in London who would give him a good price. He had contacts at the airport who would check him through. Years on the coast, providing people with virtually everything they wanted, had given him a long list of clients and associates who owed him a great deal. Besides, he had enough dirt on them to make their lives very uncomfortable.

In the bedroom, he changed his clothes. Alex's trousers did not fit, so he kept his own, found a baggy shirt to replace his blood-soaked one, which he threw into the bin. He pulled out a holdall from the bottom of the wardrobe and stuffed it with more items of clothing, together with his gun. The drugs he placed in the bottom.

Outside, the heat was unbearable. He thought of the English couple, making their way down to Riogordo, following the winding trail that offered little, if any shade. They would find it hard going. The poor guy might even have a heart attack. Things happen.

Michael got into the car and started it up. The gunshot wound hurt, but at least the bleeding had stopped. Now, he had a simple choice. Turn right for Colmenar or left for Rio. He should go right. He knew that. Pass through the village, take the route to Caserbermeja, then down the autovia to the airport. He would be there well within the hour. Book his flight, wing away to home.

The English couple played on his mind. It was so hot. Perhaps they wouldn't make it, and they were innocents after all. None of this had anything to do with them. What harm would it be to go and pick them up, take them to where they were staying, then continue to Velez and take the route to the airport from that direction? An extra half an hour on a journey that would see him turning his back on his life in Spain. Thirty minutes.

He turned left.

Domingo's constant groaning meant Arthur struggled to maintain his concentration as he negotiated the many twists and turns of the country road leading to Alex's villa. He found himself wishing the little policeman would die and give him some peace. He could then dump the body, turn the car around, and get back to Mijas. Above all else, the telephone call unsettled him. For years he had managed to keep the peace along the coast, there being enough business for everyone to share in. Lately, however, Lithuanians had tried to muscle in. Frank Fergusson put a stop to all of that. He was in a different league. Those bloody Irishmen would find that out soon enough. Fergusson was just about the most powerful villain on the Costa del Sol. Thanks to Jimmy McNulty's mistakes, Fergusson wanted revenge. He blamed Arthur, but Arthur wasn't about to take this lying down. He'd done enough of that already. If Frank couldn't be persuaded that it was all just a terrible misunderstanding, then an alternative approach would be needed. Something of his old resilience was returning. All he needed was a little time to plan everything properly. No more mistakes.

From nowhere an elderly couple half-trotting along the middle of the road sprang out ahead of him, causing Arthur to jam hard on the brakes. He swerved away from them as they skipped onto the verge, wound down his window and raised his two fingers in the time-honoured British gesture of abuse.

Beside him, Domingo stirred, raised his head. "What's going on?"

Then he screamed.

Michael saw the oncoming car sluicing across the road in front of him too late. In that terrifying moment of screeching brakes and sliding tyres, he thought he recognised the other driver and the passenger beside him. But how was that possible? How could the two men he wanted dead more than anyone else in this entire world now suddenly loom up in front of him? The fates truly were conspiring against him.

He battled with the steering wheel to try and regain control, applying the brakes with all his strength but it was useless, the forward motion relentless and he braced himself for the impact.

His car hit the other, sheared off to the right and plunged over the edge of the road. It tumbled down the steep incline at speed, smashing its way through the sparsely dotted olive trees which flashed past him. Everything cartwheeled in a terrifying blur of noise and shapes and colours as Michael was thrown around inside, out of control and out of his mind.

Arthur sat and struggled to calm himself. The oncoming car had hit his vehicle a glancing blow on the front wing and gone careening down the hillside. He thought he knew the face of the driver, but everything had happened so fast that he couldn't be sure. Quickly checking himself and Domingo, Arthur tried the door, but it wouldn't budge. The collision must have bent the chassis out of line somehow. Putting his shoulder against the door, he forced it open and stepped outside.

The couple stood at the edge looking down. The woman was trembling, the man had his arms around her.

"He's down there," said the man as Arthur stepped up to them.

Arthur followed the man's gaze. About halfway down, the mangled vehicle had tipped over onto its roof and come to rest against a large, gnarled tree. A wisp of smoke trailed from the rear and out a smashed window a white arm, laced with a spider web's pattern of blood, hung limply. "He doesn't look too well."

"Shouldn't we call an ambulance?"

Arthur looked at the man and pulled a face. "Do you think there's any point?"

"What?" The man looked incredulous. "He might still be alive, for Christ's sake! You can't just run him off the bloody road and forget about him."

"Run him off ... " Arthur threw up his hands, "He ran into me, you bloody idiot!"

"Now just a minute! If you think that—"

"Arthur."

Everyone turned at the sound of the voice. Arthur groaned when he saw Domingo leaning against the car, breathing hard. Covered with a film of sweat, Domingo's face had taken on a hideous virulent green colour. "It was him, the Irishman. Didn't you see?"

"I was concentrating on these two morons strolling in the middle of the bloody road!"

"Well, it was him." He nodded towards the boot of Arthur's car. "You don't happen to have anything in here do you?"

Arthur frowned. "Anything? What do you mean?"

"Like a rifle or something."

Arthur sensed the couple next to him stiffen. "No, Domingo, nothing like that."

The policeman grunted and wandered over to the edge of the road to gaze down to where Michael Brannigan lay trapped inside the broken car. He carefully brought out his gun, ignored the inhalations of the couple, took a bead on the car's petrol tank and let off half a dozen rounds.

The sudden ferocity of the explosion almost threw him through the air. He managed to keep his footing as the car erupted into a great blast of flame and smoke. Shielding his face from the heat, he staggered backwards. The woman was screaming, the man holding her tight against him as he pressed his mouth against her forehead. Touching, thought Arthur, knowing he would have to kill them soon.

Domingo, as nonchalant as if he'd just plucked a flower to smell before discarding it, sniffed. "The stench of that petrol will bring the curious out to see what has happened, so we need to move fast." He put his gun in his waistband. "We will go up to the house, get the drugs, then end this."

Arthur looked at his car. "We won't be going anywhere in that," he said. "The wing is crushed up against the wheel. Fortunately, the house is just at the top of the rise."

"Then I will go on alone," replied Domingo and made to walk away.

"Drugs" The man looked up from comforting his wife. "You said drugs? Is this what all of this is about?"

"Don't concern yourself too much," said Arthur. "It is no business of yours, and the least you know the better."

"You said it was me, but you're the bloody moron in all of this," continued the man, standing up, looking angry. "Jesus Christ, who the hell do you think you are? That man down there," he jabbed his finger towards the still blazing car, "that man held us at gunpoint, forced us to drive up here, to get drugs."

Arthur felt his stomach tighten. He saw Domingo react and turn his piss-hole eyes towards the man. "What did you say?" he asked, his voice breaking.

"He brought us here," continued the man. "I had to look

around, check the house. Then he went inside to retrieve the drugs."

The silence fell like a ton weight upon the two other men. It was as if time itself had stopped. Nothing moved, no sounds save for the distant crackling of the flames down below.

"Well that's bloody brilliant, isn't it," said Arthur, staring at what was left of Brannigan's car. "All this trouble, violence and death, all for what? To watch it going up in flames?"

"Our dream," said Domingo, voice small, tired, "dreams of establishing a distribution network..."

"All of that is over now, my friend. We brought together a group of disparate people whose only thought was greed. All of it for nothing." Arthur gave a wry smile and turned to see Domingo slumped on a large boulder, head on chest, tiny sobs reverberating through him.

Something else caused Arthur to look skywards. Above the sound of the blazing car and Domingo's noise came a low, deep-throated drone. Screwing up his eyes, he peered towards the horizon. There, like black, flying ants, approaching at speed, three or four helicopters.

"Shit."

Ignoring the others, Arthur broke into a steady run, head down, pounding up the slope. He had only one chance. To get away. Check that damn house, just in case. Perhaps Michael Brannigan missed something. Perhaps. Either way, he needed to hide. So, he ran, as fast as he could, not daring to take another look backwards.

FIFTY-THREE

Driving up through the village of Colmenar, Chaise also saw them. The noise of the helicopters was becoming difficult to ignore and soon every villager would be out, craning their necks to get a glimpse of this peculiar happening. He gunned the engine and covered the short distance to Alex's villa in rapid time.

He knew, almost as soon as he swung into the driveway that he was too late.

Standing in the open doorway, hands on hips, was the man he recognized as Arthur Morgan, looking pale and drawn.

Chaise got out and slowly approached him.

Arthur looked up as if seeing Chaise was the most natural thing in the world. "Ferguson send you?"

"Ferguson?"

Arthur shook his head. "It doesn't matter. Nothing matters any more. The drugs have gone, all of them. I was hoping some might still be here, but ..."

This close, Chaise could smell Arthur's sweat. The helicopters were close too, their great blades beating through the air. Chaise turned to see several black figures abseiling from the bellies of the great hovering beasts. Special forces? Who the hell had sent them?

Arthur sighed. "This is such a mess."

Chaise nodded. "Seems that way. Who took the drugs?"

"Domingo shot out the fuel tank, blew up the car. The Irishman was inside. Both he and the drugs ... poof!"

"Maybe it's for the best. A lot of people have died because of them."

Arthur took in a deep breath, nodded to an area beyond Chaise's shoulder. "Looks like the ghost is up for both of us."

Chaise was about to agree when Arthur's head erupted into a great cloud of blood and brain. Chaise dived for cover as the crack of a gunshot following a split second later reverberated through the driveway. As what was left of the gangster's body jerked backwards, Chaise rolled through the doorway. He crouched against the hallway wall and tried to gather his thoughts. Why the hell would special forces take Arthur out like that, without any warning? Unless, of course, they weren't special forces.

The beat of the helicopter blades could not disguise the roar of four-by-four engines, the slamming of doors, the screaming voices. More people were arriving. Above all of this, the swiftly diminishing sound of another motor vehicle moving away cross-country. Someone, an assassin maybe, but not special forces. A bullet meant for Arthur and nobody else.

From outside, the Spanish voices were urgent, demanding he throw out his weapon, surrender.

Here is how it ends, thought Chaise, and did as he was bid. He didn't have any other choice.

He sat across from Hernandez whose voice sounded efficient, unemotional as he spoke. "We found your girlfriend's car, a mangled, blackened shell. Inside it were two men, or what was left of them."

Outside, the weather had broken, and the rain beat down. Chaise liked the rain. It gave relief from the heat, freshened up everything and reminded him of home. Britain, towards where Linny was winging her way. "Was Phelps one of them?"

"Your friend from the Consulate?" Hernandez smiled. "I'm afraid not, Mr Chaise. Phelps took your girlfriend to the airport." He leaned back, hands settling across his stomach. "You didn't know there was a bomb rigged up in that sportscar?"

"No."

"No, how could you ... you just being a civilian."

Chaise turned away. He'd had enough now, exhaustion gnawing away at every fibre. He doubted he could keep up the act any longer. "Who killed Arthur Morgan? It wasn't your men?"

"*Udyco* do not undertake assassinations, Mr Chaise, despite what you may have heard. Our intelligence units have been studying Arthur Morgan and his associates for months. Not only have we had operatives placed in his nightclubs and other 'leisure' activities, we've also been following him everywhere he goes. We have built up a well-detailed view of this man ... and then, just as we swoop ..." He shook his head. "He made enemies, our Mr Morgan. Enemies that are more ruthless and more violent than anyone else on the coast. And I'm not talking about silly Irish amateurs or disillusioned policemen ..."

"What will happen to him, our disillusioned policeman friend?"

Hernandez shrugged. "Arrest, imprisonment, disgrace. Domingo was a fool, trying to augment his pension with some illegal drugs money, idiotic to be honest."

"Seems you had it all sewn up, except for Arthur's death."

"Yes, that was unfortunate. But Domingo is a fairly good consolation prize. Of course, the big prize, Fergusson, may take a little longer. Thanks to you." Hernandez stood up, crossed the office to a large filing cabinet and pulled it open. He produced a bottle and two glasses, filling each with a generous measure of Spanish brandy. "When they told me all of our files were being put on computer, I thought of the perfect use for my now-defunct cabinet." He raised his glass and drained it in one. "Perfecto."

Chaise took a sip. He wasn't a great lover of Spanish brandy, but at that moment he'd take anything on offer. "What happens now, Señor Hernandez?"

"You go back to doing whatever it is you do, Mr Chaise. You go about your work, live in your house, and keep well away from Mr Fergusson."

"Fergusson? You mentioned him before, as did Arthur ... just before he was shot."

"The killer was one of Fergusson's men, no doubt about it. Fergusson is tied into everything that has happened. It was his wife Ricky Treach attacked and Jimmy McNulty murdered."

"Perfectly understandable therefore that he wanted Arthur dead."

"I don't want you becoming involved in our on-going operation to bring Fergusson down."

Ryan took a sip of brandy. "No fear there, Señor Hernandez. I have no reason to. Besides, that sort of thing is all behind me now."

"I hope so." Hernandez gave Chaise a withering look. "I had to become like a slime myself, Mr Chaise, worm my way into Domingo's trust. Have you any idea how distasteful that was for me, to be so close to that stench? I hate corruption, I hate lies. So, please, don't lie to me, Mr Chaise. Because if you do, I promise you, you will not survive."

"I get the point." He placed the half-finished glass of brandy down on the desk and pushed it away. "No doubt Mr Phelps will want to talk to me."

"No doubt. But then it ends. I make myself clear?"

"Perfectly."

"No press, no telephone calls, no snooping around."

"I've told you, it's all behind me. I'm going to talk to Alex. He'll need to have the same message, and I think it's better coming from me."

Hernandez chewed his bottom lip, mulling over the sensibility of Ryan's words. "Very well. But, Mr Chaise." He came forward, brows knitting. "Keep it brief."

In his hospital room, Alex did his best to fold his few belongings. Every so often he gave a tiny gasp and slowly spread his bandaged fingers. Chaise, looking on from the corner, said, "Do you need any help with that?"

"I'm fine," he said, unable to disguise the bitterness in his voice. "Life isn't going to be quite the same from now on," Alex said, almost to himself. He took a breath, snapped the lid of his suitcase shut and set it down by the door. "What a bloody mess everything has been."

"It's all sorted out now, Alex. None of us have to worry anymore about gangsters, drugs, or anything else."

"No. All we need to concentrate on is living our lives," he turned wet eyes towards Chaise. "A life without friends or loved ones."

"It's all been shitty, Alex. I'm sorry."

"So am I. I wish to God that when that gun had gone off in your car, you had died, not Ricky Treach."

"I sometimes feel the same way." He stepped forward and struck out his hand. "Good luck, Alex."

Alex looked at the hand, turned away, picked up the suitcase and left without a word.

Chaise didn't follow for some time.

By the time Chaise stepped out into the hospital car park, the rain had stopped. The man leaning against his car was built like a heavyweight, huge arms folded across his chest. Close by were several other men. Was this another reminder from Hernandez that he would always be a part of Ryan's life or Fergusson perhaps?

"I have a message," said the man nonchalantly as Chaise came closer. "A simple message, Mr Chaise."

The man, heavily tanned, dark glasses masking his eyes, was not Spanish. He spoke perfect, refined, public school English.

"And you are …?"

"It doesn't matter who I am. I have a message from London, Mr Chaise."

"All right." Chaise glanced towards the others. This wasn't going to end in a fight, not out here in front of the whole world. "Why don't you quit the theatrics and tell me. Then you can get the fuck away from my car."

The man glared at Chaise from over the rim of the glasses. "Don't get tetchy."

"And don't you bloody push it, mate. I'm tired and I'm at the end of my tether."

A standoff. Chaise waited, breathing easily.

The man took off his sunglasses with an exaggerated sweep of the hand. "We want to know why you killed Embleton."

"Embleton betrayed everyone. You, me, all of us. He was about to rape my girlfriend when I blew his brains out. I suspect that he was going to take the drugs for himself."

The big man nodded as if was half-expecting such an explanation. "Whatever the reasons, we don't believe you can be trusted, Mr Chaise. You're dangerous, unpredictable."

"Get to the point."

"I'm already there, Mr Chaise. Here, in Spain, you're too ... how can I put it, you're too detached."

"What the hell is that supposed to mean?"

The man turned the arms of his glasses between his fingers. "You're coming home, Mr Chaise. So we can keep a closer eye on you." He smiled. "And you're coming home right now."

For a moment, Chaise didn't know what to say. He was stunned. Staggered. Going home? "But ... but I can't just pack up and leave, I ..." The man was smiling. It appeared that all of Chaise's choices had run out.

THE END

Dear reader,

We hope you enjoyed reading *Burned Up*. Please take a moment to leave a review, even if it's a short one. Your opinion is important to us.

Discover more books by Stuart G. Yates at

https://www.nextchapter.pub/authors/stuart-g-yates

Want to know when one of our books is free or discounted? Join the newsletter at

http://eepurl.com/bqqB3H

Best regards,

Stuart G. Yates and the Next Chapter Team

You might also like:
The Vienna Connection by Dick Rosano

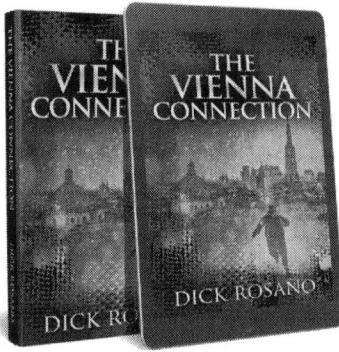

To read the first chapter for free, please head to:
https://www.nextchapter.pub/books/the-vienna-connection

Manufactured by Amazon.ca
Bolton, ON